+ Toledo-Lucas County Public Library

WITHDRAWNIMTUF

S0-BYG-456

MYSTERY

Fic
Singer, Rochelle
Samson's deal

7

BOOK!

TOLEDO-LUCAS COUNTY
PUBLIC LIBRARY

SAMSON'S DEAL

SAMSON'S DEAL

by Shelley Singer

St. Martin's Press   New York

SAMSON'S DEAL Copyright © 1983 by Shelley
Singer. All rights reserved. Printed in the
United States of America. No part of this
book may be used or reproduced in any
manner whatsoever without written
permission except in the case of brief
quotations embodied in critical articles or
reviews. For information, address St. Martin's
Press, 175 Fifth Avenue, New York, N.Y.
10010.

Library of Congress Cataloging in Publication Data

Singer, Shelley.
    Samson's deal.

    l. Title.
PS3569.I565S2   1983   813'.54   83–2901
ISBN 0-312-69849-6

First Edition
10 9 8 7 6 5 4 3 2 1

For my mother
Dorothy Singer Fenick

The author wishes to thank the
Oakland Police Department, and,
in particular, Sergeant Dave Nishihara
and Officer Curt Wengeler,
for help and information.

SAMSON'S DEAL

—1—

The directions I'd taken over the telephone helped me to find Chandler Hall without too much difficulty. The man had described the Berkeley campus building as modern, and so it was. It looked like a low-cost housing project. What he hadn't mentioned, though, was the most obvious feature: half a dozen pickets standing around outside the door in the bright October sunlight.

Three of the neatly barbered young people carried neatly lettered signs, two of which seemed to be generalized indictments of the political science department housed within. One said, DOWN WITH LEFT-WING PROPAGANDA, and the other said, TEACH THE TRUTH ABOUT LIBERAL UN-AMERICANISM. The third was more personal. It said, JOHN HARLEY IS A RED.

Harley was the man who had called me and said he needed my help. He'd refused to tell me on the phone what kind of help he needed. I hoped he didn't expect me to pad my shoulders and accompany him in and out of Chandler Hall every day, making nasty faces at a bunch of kids.

I accepted one of the leaflets they were waving at passersby, pushed open the door to the building and started up the stairs to the second floor.

The call from Harley had come a couple of hours before. It had caught me doing what I seemed to be doing a lot of lately, which was very little. I'd been lying on my lounge chair in my colorful, lush, messy, impossible-to-maintain backyard, wondering why the squirrels had planted a walnut tree six inches from my foundation, wondering why I hadn't either euthanized it or moved it when it was weed-sized, and wondering whether I was going to try transplanting the now four-foot-high tree or sell the house in five years. And wondering why the hell I was occupying my formerly keen mind with this trivial problem.

A year ago, I realized, I wouldn't have thought twice about

having nothing much to think about. At thirty-seven, I had re-
tired from the world of combat. I'd done a lot of things in my life,
and I'd had it with just about everything I'd ever done. Adding
up a small cushion of savings, a small income from a trust fund
my mother had set up for me, and a little bit of rental property, I
decided that, with a lot of economizing, I could afford to live the
life of an urban gentleman farmer.

Until I closed the savings account or got bored, or both. That
had been the plan. That was still the plan.

There was still some money in the account, but for some reason, when this Guy Harley called and said he wanted to talk to
me about a job, and that his friend Rebecca Lilly—his accent on
the word *friend* was slightly coy—had told him I sometimes handled "discreet matters," I got interested. The guy sounded like a
jerk, but maybe I was tired of walnut trees. Or maybe it was the
mention of Rebecca that did it. She might have had lousy taste in
men, but she was a bright and beautiful woman. There was a
time when I'd thought we might get something going. We'd had
a couple of dinners, talked about ourselves, and—nothing. Like I
said, she had lousy taste in men.

I didn't know what Harley meant by "discreet matters," so I
asked him. He, in turn, asked me to visit him at his office to
discuss it. Right away. I said I'd come, but I took my time. An
old policy of mine. I've learned that if money's involved, it's
never a good idea to be too accommodating. People might hire a
hungry man, but they won't think he's worth much.

So there I was.

And there, milling around on the second floor of Chandler
Hall, were half a dozen more pickets. To forestall any silly conversation, I smiled cheerfully at them and waved the leaflet I'd
gotten from their comrades out in front. They didn't smile back.
I knocked on Harley's door.

"Who is it?" The voice was high-pitched, exasperated.

"Jake Samson," I told the door.

The door opened. I slid through the eighteen-inch space with
some difficulty and the door closed again.

"Look," I began, "I'm not really too interested in bodyguard
work. I'm not very tough—"

He mumbled, "No, no, no," collapsed in a chair behind the
desk and waved vaguely at another, which I took as an invitation
to sit down. He didn't look good. It was hard to tell if he ever did.

He had what are called regular features: a straight nose, lips neither prissy nor especially sensual, gray eyes neither piglike nor protruding. He was very pale and his light brown hair, streaked sparsely with gray, hung lankly over his forehead. He looked clammy. He looked like he'd been throwing up.

I wondered briefly how Rebecca could prefer a flimsy specimen like this to me. I have been told that my mouth is wide and sexy, my green eyes piercing, my large broken nose masculine, my blond hair, my freckles, my sturdy five-foot-ten frame—but that was in another country, and alas. . . .

"What's that you've got in your hand?" he snapped at me.

I glanced down at the piece of paper the pickets downstairs had handed me. "Flyer. Something about a corps."

"Corps," he snarled. "That's what they are." He pointed at the door. I could hear them out there, walking back and forth and talking among themselves. "Campus Organization for the Return of Political Sanity. CORPS. Pompous little bastards." The sounds in the hallway changed. A new and authoritative voice had been added, and all the feet began to move away from Harley's door. Harley jumped up from his desk, strode to the door, hesitated, and opened it just enough to peek outside. He nodded once, decisively, came back and sat down again.

"Campus security," he said. "And about time, too. I called them half an hour ago. Now maybe we can get down to it."

"Right," I said enthusiastically.

"I called you about my wife, of course."

I looked blank. He stared at me.

"You didn't hear?" He was incredulous. "It was in the papers, on TV—"

I interrupted him. "I didn't."

Urban gentlemen farmers often do not read newspapers or watch TV news for weeks at a time. I never seem to miss anything. "Suppose you tell me the whole story right now." I pulled out a small pocket notebook and, pen poised, waited for him to begin.

He snapped at me again, like a testy Pomeranian. "If I knew the whole story I wouldn't be hiring you to investigate for me." He wasn't hiring me yet, but I let that pass.

"Then tell me," I said, slowly and with astounding patience, "what you do know."

A cheer rose from the gang of picketers clustered outside the building. Just about enough time, I guessed, for the advance guard from the second floor to have returned as heroes from the political science fortress.

Harley glanced at the window, sighed, frowned, and picked up a pen from atop a folder of papers on his desk. He tapped the pen on the folder as though he wished he were working on the papers. "It's incredible they'd be out there hounding me today. My wife. Margaret. She died yesterday." There was that little trick of his again, accenting the loaded word. This time, the word was *died.*

"Died?" I repeated. The demonstrators had begun a chant: "John Harley is a red."

"I'm not, you know," the man spat at me. "A communist. I'm not even a socialist. I'm closer to anarchist than anything else."

Yes, I thought. I could tell by the structure of our conversation.

I steered him back to the subject of his wife. He had gone home from his office the previous morning to find her dead, lying on the hillside below their deck. He had called the police. The police didn't seem to think the death was an accident.

"What did she die of?" I asked.

"She fell off the deck."

"Okay," I said, maintaining a professional calm. "But I mean what did the fall do to her? How did she die?"

"Oh." His voice dropped, but I heard him say, "Her neck. It was broken."

"And the police are investigating."

"Yes. It's been quite an ordeal." I wanted him to go on with his story, so I didn't mention that the situation probably hadn't been pleasant for his wife either. The CORPS people were still chanting, and even though they'd switched to insulting the political science department as a whole, Harley was having trouble ignoring them. I took a stab at looking sympathetic, and he was encouraged to go on.

"There was the first cop, and he sniffed around and asked me a lot of questions. Then he called in his superiors, first one and then two more, and they all asked me questions and wrote down everything I said. And then of course there was someone with a camera photographing everything and looking for fingerprints and I can't imagine what else."

Nothing unusual there. The beat cop had decided things

looked fishy and had gotten his district sergeant out to have a look. He in turn has made the decision to call for a homicide team and a technician. The system had not been designed to annoy Harley, but I was sure I would never convince him of that.

"So they're checking out the possibility of a killer. What do you want with me?"

"I want you to find out who did it."

I shook my head. "That's police business."

"I'll pay you ten thousand dollars."

I nodded thoughtfully and gazed around the office, giving myself a little time to catch my breath.

"Plus expenses," I said.

—2—

The question was, did I really want to do it? Maybe, after all, I wasn't sure I could.

One thing was sure. I wasn't going to get a coherent story out of Harley as long as he was being constantly distracted by an anti-Harley political demonstration. I decided to take my preinvestigation investigation a step further and check out the scene of the crime. My prospective client agreed to meet me at his house.

"Half an hour?" he asked, standing and beginning to pack the folder he'd been tapping and a couple of books into his briefcase.

I shook my head and told him I couldn't make it in less than an hour, that I had things to do. For one thing, I wanted to think. For another, I hadn't had lunch. He sighed and led the way to the door, stepping back to let me go out first. I suspected him of leaving with me because he was nervous about leaving alone. But the group outside didn't give him any trouble. They gave him, and me, an icy silence. Harley glared at them. I nodded and smiled, but they still didn't believe me. I guess it's something about my attitude.

We parted just out of earshot of the demonstrators. Harley said that since the CORPS picketing had started, he always parked on the other side of the campus and was careful that no one he recognized as belonging to CORPS ever saw him getting into his car.

"You may think that seems overcautious," he said, "but I wouldn't be surprised to find out that they're vandals as well as Visigoths." He smirked at his own turn of phrase. I said sure, I understood that, and we went off in opposite directions.

The home address Harley had given me was in Montclair, a hilly, woodsy, rustically expensive section of Oakland, accessible from Berkeley by a short freeway ride. But I'm not particularly fond of freeways. Unless I absolutely have to be efficient I prefer the streets, where you can actually see nonmechanized humans walking around. I drove south down Telegraph Avenue, east toward College Avenue, and south again, heading toward my own neighborhood in Oakland, not far from the Berkeley border and close enough to Montclair.

By the time I'd crossed over into Oakland I'd almost forgotten about lunch, I was thinking so hard. I was thinking about homicide, one of the few ugly items I'd had very little experience with. I was also thinking about cops and how funny they are about people getting in their way when they're working. That was something I knew a lot about.

Once, in Chicago, I had been a cop. A twenty-four-year-old cop suddenly swept up in the insanity of 1968. The Democratic convention. The head-smashing frenzy of the police force and the idealism, damned foolishness, and hysterical violence of the young and not-so-young who gathered there.

I'd lost my head when a young long-hair came running at me, crazed but unarmed. I'd used my nightstick on his face. I'd heard him scream and seen him bleed.

That was when I decided that somehow things had gotten out of hand and I didn't really want to do that kind of work anymore, at least not in a group. I moved to California, smoked some weed, dropped some acid, picked up odd jobs here and there, and wandered up and down the coast for a few years. I learned a little carpentry, a little plumbing, a little dealing, and, eventually, a little real estate. In between, trading on my short term as a cop, I helped out a few friends who were being hassled by outside-the-law bill collectors, discouraged a few hostile ex-husbands, and collected some debts. I didn't charge much but I took it in cash.

I got married and I got divorced. Then this city kid began drifting toward his urban roots, down from Humboldt County to Mendocino, on down through Sonoma to Marin, and finally, just three years ago, across the bay to Berkeley. I took a job with a sleazy realty company, grabbed hold of my own little lot in an acceptable section of the Oakland flatlands, and began to build up my credit with what some people like to think is the real world.

That lasted just two years. When I'd had enough of showing cardboard houses to overextended people, sweating out my commissions on nice, new, easy-to-maintain homes I didn't like and didn't want to sell, I quit. And I hadn't done much since then but work around the house—or think about it—argue with my middle-age spread and my midlife crisis, and play poker.

All right, so maybe I was getting a little bored. But maybe I could find safer ways to entertain myself. It's one thing to work around the law up in the woods where the law is county and scarce and another to walk around on the heels of city police. Not to mention tripping over their toes. Still, I told myself, with ten thousand dollars beating a tattoo in my brain, I didn't have anything planned for that day but my Tuesday night poker game. There was no reason not to hear the man out and take a look at the house where his wife had died.

Thus resolved, I stopped at a too-groovy College Avenue café. The hamburger was passable. Once I removed three-quarters of the alfalfa sprouts I was able to get my medium-to-large mouth around it. The waitress flirted with me, which was nice. She was kind of chunky, with short brown hair, pretty brown eyes, and a beautiful smile. I flirted back. The place was crowded, she was overworked and probably underpaid, and I left a thirty percent tip.

In a few minutes I had driven past the last of the antique shops, maneuvered through the frantic shopping-center intersection at Fifty-first, and was drifting peacefully along the quiet curves of Moraga behind a very old man driving at an exact and steady twenty-five miles an hour. We were both looking at the nice houses and the trees and the humans.

The old man drove straight on toward downtown Montclair, and I turned off, heading into the tall trees and narrow roads. When I got close to Harley's neighborhood, I noticed a few For Sale signs and allowed myself a moment's fantasy. Pretty area.

Harley's house on Virgo Street was a classic type for the Oakland-Berkeley hills, set back and below the level of the road, sheltered by trees and hillside. It didn't look like a particularly big house, but it's always hard to tell from the front when the view is at the back. These houses grow downhill, layer upon layer. I knew that it was bound to have at least one deck and maybe as many as three. I parked on the dirt shoulder. There were already two cars in the carport at the foot of the steep driveway, a BMW and an Audi. I found the wooden steps that led down to the house, with a redwood retaining wall holding up the hill to the right. As I made my descent, I checked my watch. Right on time. Half an hour late.

It took Harley a couple of minutes to answer the bell.

"I was just out on the deck," he said, a slight edge of sorrow to his voice. I followed him through an entry hall and a large living room. The sliding glass doors at the far end were partly open. We went outside onto the deck. The only deck, but a big one, around fifteen by twenty-five or thirty feet, furnished with a redwood table and two small benches, two lounge chairs, and a redwood rocker. On the table was the folder I'd seen him put in his briefcase. He'd been working. Everything was very neat and in its proper place. Harley sat in one lounge chair and I took the other.

'Would you like a drink?" he asked politely. He didn't look capable of getting out of the chair again, so I said no, maybe later. He sat gazing out over the railing at the wooded hillside. Eucalyptus trees, a rural feeling of privacy, a view of San Francisco that must have been spectacular at night. A warm breeze carried autumn dampness, the hint of rains to come, and the tang of the eucalyptus.

"Tell me how it was when you came home yesterday," I prodded. "Describe everything you saw." He shrugged as if to say, "I suppose I have to."

He had arrived home just before noon, parked his BMW next to his wife's Audi and walked down to the front door. He inserted his key in the deadbolt, turned the key, and found the door unlocked. Only the spring lock in the doorknob, the one that caught when the door was closed, was locked.

"Was that normal?" I wanted to know.

"Yes," Harley replied. "She was careless. I used to remind her all the time about keeping the house secure when she was in it. She never listened."

"And then?" I urged him to continue the story.

He had entered the hall, set his briefcase on the hall table, gone into the living room, and noticed that the door to the deck was open. He had walked out onto the deck and stepped to the railing. I got out of my lounge chair and went to the railing, trying to picture how things had been. I looked out and across the bay to San Francisco, The City.

Then I looked down into the garden below the deck, down to where the hill dropped away from the house.

"She was right down there," Harley said. "Margaret. Lying on her back. I could see her eyes. I knew she was dead." I nodded. It was a thirty-foot drop, but my imagination told me he would have been able to see that much. His wife, nestled crookedly on her back among the rockroses and acanthus. Lying perfectly still, her blank and foggy eyes staring up at him.

I turned back to Harley. "Okay, let's take it from the beginning. Why were you home so early?"

"I don't have any classes on Monday."

"But you went to your office anyway? Did you have an appointment?"

"No. I like to work there. On my book. My manuscript." He waved his hand toward the folder on the table. "But they wouldn't let me work. Those idiots. The ones you saw today. They were out there chanting. I couldn't concentrate. That's probably what they want. To interfere with my work. Bunch of Nazi book burners."

"But you did have classes today?" I was wondering what the hell he'd been doing at work the day after his wife's death.

"I would, normally. Someone else will be taking them for a few days." He caught my quizzical look and bridled. "I went there today because I had to get out of the house. Is that so strange?" No, I guessed it wasn't.

"What's your book about?" I asked. I didn't really care, but I've heard that writers hate that question. Harley didn't.

"Well, broadly, it's about the absurdity of political systems. None of them work, after all. Never been one I'd care to live with. You know," he said thoughtfully, "back in the sixties there was a lot of feeling that socialism could solve our problems. I never went along with that, but I could live with the kind of people who felt that way, and the things they believed in." He sighed nostalgically. "I was a teaching assistant then. Pretty involved with the antiwar movement. The students and I—well, we got along. I was one of them. But now!" he snorted. "It's like the fifties all over again. Do you remember what things were like then?" I nodded. "I certainly never thought we'd go back to that. On the campus. And at Berkeley!"

I remembered the fifties all right. And like anyone else my age with pretensions to individuality, I remembered them with distaste. But then, I had mixed feelings about the sixties, too. Harley's indignation brought to mind that old curse that says, "May you live in interesting times." Harley didn't mind living in interesting times. He just wanted them to be interesting his way.

"Yeah," I said. "It's all pretty disgusting. Now, let's take things back to when you first got home. Before you called the police. Did you notice anything unusual? In the house or on the deck?"

He shrugged, scratched his jaw, and tried to think.

"Well, not in the house. Not that I noticed. I don't know. What do you mean?"

"Just describe everything you saw when you came out here."

"Uh huh. The sliding glass doors were open. I walked through." He closed his eyes, trying to visualize. He was getting into the spirit of things now. I waited silently for him to go on. "Her coffee cup was on the table. And a bowl of apples. That was odd."

"The coffee cup?"

He waved a hand at me. "No, no, the apples. A bowl of them. They weren't out there when I left in the morning."

"So?"

He drummed his fingers on his thigh and cocked an eyebrow, Basil Rathbone fashion. "We kept fruit around the house, of course, Mr. Samson. But Margaret rarely ate any. I think that's significant."

I caught on. "Oh, like you mean she was offering fruit to a guest?" I was not too impressed. He noticed.

"Exactly."

I let him have his way. "Could be," I said, pursing my lips. "What else did you see?"

"Well, I saw her. From up here."

"That's all? You didn't go down to look at her?"

He glared at me. "I couldn't. Besides, I told you, I could tell she was dead. Her eyes. I was pretty sure."

"Anything else?" There had to be something else, or the police wouldn't be investigating a homicide.

"I didn't see anything else." He was getting snippy again.

"And the neighbors?" The closest neighboring houses were barely visible through the trees. "Did they see or hear anything?" He shook his head.

I stood up, went to the railing and looked down.

"How do you get down there?" I asked. I knew the police would have checked over that hillside pretty carefully, and even if they'd missed something, there wasn't much chance I'd find it in the wake of many official feet. But the only way to begin is to look at whatever there is to see.

Harley led me back inside the house, back through the living room, and down a flight of stairs to what used to be called a rumpus room. It didn't look like there'd ever been a rumpus in it. Very neat, with a plaid couch and fake Early American furniture. Even a spinning wheel lamp.

We hadn't hit bottom yet. We went out the door of the rumpus room and down some concrete steps past what looked like a pretty good-sized basement. When the steps ended, we were at the top of the slope. To our left was the front wall of the basement. To our left and about thirty feet above our heads was the deck.

"Where was she?" Harley thought for a moment, then sidled over under the deck, looking at the sloping ground. I followed him, walking the way I usually do.

"I guess it was right about there," he said. It? Funny way to talk about a dead woman you'd been married to. I looked where he pointed and saw a whole constellation of crushed plants, mostly acanthus. The area he'd pointed out looked only a little messier than the rest of the hillside. It wasn't hard to tell where the law had been. They'd left a trail of broken plants and gouges in the landscape. I kicked a few rocks loose myself on the way down.

I knelt on the hard-packed stony clay, dusty from the rainless California summer, and searched the crushed greenery. No blood that I could see. Without looking up, still dissecting the ground with my eyes, I asked him another question.

"About the broken neck—did you hear anything else about her? Any other injuries?" I didn't hear his answer, so I looked up at him. He was shaking his head. Terrific. For all I knew the woman had a broken neck and a bazooka wound in her back. "No other marks that you could see?" He shook his head again.

I figured I'd done my token search-the-scene act and that there wouldn't be much profit in poking around anymore. Even if I found something, I wouldn't know what I was looking at. I climbed back up and stood next to Harley under the deck.

"Well?" he said.

I ignored the challenge. "Any idea who might have wanted to kill your wife? Did she work? Any trouble with anyone at her job?"

"No. She didn't work. She didn't do anything, except of course belong to her groups."

"Groups?"

"A therapy group. And a meditation group. She said they were attempts at self-definition." He shook his head sadly, the wise man confronted with foolishness.

"That's it?"

"Well, she used to be an artist, but she hadn't done anything with it for a while."

"Was she a dabbler or was she a professional?"

"Oh, professional. Actually quite well known at one time."

"Why aren't you willing to leave it to the police?"

"Because the police deal in the obvious, and I want the real killer found before they stir up a lot of trouble."

"Trouble?"

My obtuseness exasperated him. He answered me with a series of questions. "Isn't it true that the first suspect is always the spouse? Or maybe someone the spouse is, uh, seeing on the side? If the police really get going on this, wouldn't there be all sorts of problems and publicity and maybe even arrest for the spouse or the spouse's—"

"Lover?" I finished, irritated with his indirectness. He nodded, flushing slightly.

"You should have heard the questions they asked me," he wailed. "I expected to be arrested right then and there. When did I leave the house that morning? Was she in good spirits? Were we having any marital problems? I want someone investigating this from my side. I want you to solve it before the police decide to throw me to the wolves. I don't trust them. They know my record. In the sixties—well, anyway. I can't prove I didn't kill her before I left the house. And there's someone else they might start harassing." He looked at me significantly.

"Rebecca Lilly," I said resignedly and stared out over the eucalyptus trees at the smog-tinted view of San Francisco. I didn't think the police gave a damn about Harley's politics, old or new, but they might, indeed, give a damn about his love life.

I told him I would think it over.

"I need to know now," he objected. "We have to work fast."

"I'll let you know tomorrow," I told him. There were some people I wanted to talk to that night.

—3—

Harley had assured me that he and Rebecca had been more than careful to keep their affair secret, so I thought I might have a little time to nose around before the cops started hitting too hard on either one of them. That helped. But I was going to need some kind of cover for my investigation. A private citizen wandering around trying to solve a homicide needed to have some kind of explanation for his peculiar behavior. I didn't think the Oakland police department would take Harley's ten-thousand-dollar offer as an explanation.

I had some ideas about how to deal with that problem as well as a couple of others, but I couldn't take the job until I knew for sure. Fortunately, the problem-solving involved a couple of guys I played poker with, so I could keep my one-day promise to Harley without sacrificing my weekly ritual.

Then there was Rebecca. I wanted to talk to her before I made a decision. She'd gotten me into this in the first place.

I came down out of the Oakland hills to the realities of the flatlands. As usual, my liquor store's parking lot was overful, and I had to squeeze my car into a diagonal position that practically guaranteed a dented fender. Also as usual, I took my chances, since there is no such thing as a poker game without beer and chips. I bought a newspaper, too.

When I emerged from the store, I saw that I'd been lucky. The same cars were parked on either side of me. No dents. I slid behind the wheel and glanced at the paper. A small story, at the bottom of page one. It didn't have anything in it that I didn't already know.

By the time I pulled up at my gate it was nearly four o'clock, and my tenant, Rosie Vicente, was home from work. Her pickup truck with its padlocked toolbox was sitting stolidly out in front. Rosie's a carpenter, self-employed. I hadn't seen her for a couple of days and decided to stop at her cottage to see if she'd drink a beer with me before I went on back to my house.

The usual setup for a house and cottage is big house in front, small cottage in back. Not my place. The front was fifty feet of occasional and self-reproducing vegetable garden and dirt driveway with patches of paving here and there. Beyond the garden there's a clump of bamboo coexisting with a stand of acacia trees. Behind that prolific camouflage is the cottage with its tiny yard and, to the left of that, the path going back toward my front yard and my tiny house, surrounded by other people's back yards and tall fences. Privacy and quiet.

The top of Rosie's Dutch door was open, but I knocked on the door frame anyway. Her bed was just a few feet away, and respect for each other's privacy was the best way I knew to ensure continued friendship.

She came to the door dressed in cutoffs, work boots and heavy socks, and a T-shirt decorated with the head of Gertrude Stein. Rosie is a knockout, about five foot five with curly black hair, cut short, and peacock blue eyes. She's always slightly tan from working outdoors. She's in her early thirties. We've been friends for two years, ever since she first rented the cottage. Just friends. She smiled and invited me in. Her aging standard poodle, Alice B. Toklas, also has curly black hair and also smiled and welcomed me.

I pulled two beers out of my sack, and her smile got even brighter. I followed her past her bed around the ell to her kitchen table.

"What's new, Jake?"

We sat and looked out the big casement windows into her shady, fuchsia-draped yard. I noticed a small pile of lumber under the acacia. She had mentioned that she was going to build a curved seat around its trunk.

I shrugged. "I may be getting involved in a job. If I do, I may need your help from time to time, feeding Tigris and Euphrates, that kind of thing." Tigris and Euphrates, my sister and brother cats, were very particular about being fed on time. Mutual pet-sitting in a pinch was part of the agreement Rosie and I had.

"Sure. If you're not around I'll just deal with it." She took a swig of beer and looked at me quizzically. "What kind of job? Anything interesting? Anything you might need help with?" She knew I'd been involved in some pretty disreputable chores in the past.

"Could be," I said carefully. "Sounds like you're bored."

"I am. Busy but bored. Decks, decks, and more damned decks. I haven't built anything complicated since last year. And winter's coming." If the season was particularly rainy, there'd be days at a time when she did no work at all. "And my love life? Yech. Look at that." She pointed to her desk, and I could see that her evenings had been pretty solitary lately. The desk top was piled with paperbacks—science fiction and murder mysteries: Ngaio Marsh, Dorothy Sayers, Ellery Queen, Marion Zimmer Bradley, Ursula K. LeGuin, Fritz Leiber . . .

I nodded sympathetically. I suspected she just hadn't gotten over her last lover. The relationship with Marge had ended only six months before. It hadn't been a good one, but I knew from my own experience that doesn't make the final, irrevocable loss any easier.

"Well, I don't know if I'll even take the job."

She threw me a suspicious look. "You still haven't told me what it is."

"Oh," I said casually, "someone got killed."

"Killed?" She glanced at the books on her desk. "Do you mean murdered?" Her face was a study. She was having trouble choosing between regret and excitement. Not fear. Oh, no, not Rosie. And how could I tell her I didn't want to involve her in anything that might be dangerous? She would have been righteous indignation itself. She would have accused me of being protective. Macho. She wouldn't believe that I would feel the same way about a close male friend. Not to mention a good tenant.

"Yeah, well, maybe. Or manslaughter. Or suicide, but—"

She grinned at me. "Look, Jake, it's okay. If you don't feel you need someone to help you—you know, protect you—I'll understand."

I just grinned back at her, finished my beer, and stood up to leave. "Got to make a phone call. If I decide I need a bodyguard, I'll let you know."

Tigris and Euphrates came running to meet me as I approached the house, sucking in their cheeks and trying to make their chubby sides concave, mewling the duet from "The Starving Kitty."

I fed them. They would never have allowed me to talk on the telephone otherwise. Then I called Rebecca Lilly's office. She was there.

We hadn't talked for more than a year. Her voice was the same, low and raspy with soft edges of humor and sex. I told her I wanted to see her and asked about lunch the next day. She agreed and said I should pick her up at home. She had been planning to take the morning off anyway. I figured she didn't want anyone connected with Harley coming anywhere near her office.

It was still early. Plenty of time for a long shower before dinner. I stripped and looked at myself in the full-length mirror, a confrontation I'd been avoiding. With some pain, I had to admit it was getting to be that time again. In the past couple of years, my spare tire had had an alarming tendency to grow, and the usual measures—a week or so of cutting down a little on food—just didn't seem to work anymore.

A salad and a chop for dinner. Beer? Tonight, at poker, okay. Tomorrow, no. If anything, wine. Because it doesn't go with potato chips. Because my mother died of a heart attack after years of being overweight. Because I like to maintain the fiction that what I do or don't do is going to make a difference in how long and how well I live.

The shower soothed me a little, and while the chop was broiling, I put in a call to Artie Perrine, one of the poker regulars, and asked him if he could make it a little early because I wanted to talk to him privately. He agreed.

Artie was an editor of *Probe* magazine, a San Francisco-based investigative monthly. I'd met him in Mendocino in 1973. He was a friend of a friend and had been up there looking for his sister, who'd gotten herself involved with some heavy-duty dealers. I'd helped him to find her and get her ass out of there. She was seventeen at the time. A few months ago Artie had mentioned that she was back up the coast again, but this time she was working as a marine biologist. He often said he owed me. I wondered how much I could collect.

Artie showed up fifteen minutes early, but so did Hal Winter, a fairly successful Berkeley attorney I'd met at a party when I first moved to Oakland. He was the second man I wanted to talk to, a good solid guy with some good solid connections with the DA's office. He didn't exactly owe me, like Artie did, but our friendship had involved a lot of give and take, so I thought he wouldn't mind doing me a favor now and then. I set Hal up in front of the Franklin stove with a beer can in his hand and invited Artie to join me in the kitchen while I dumped the chips into bowls.

I kept my voice low and he followed suit, but like I said, the house is small and there was no way to be sure Hal wouldn't overhear.

He asked what he could do for me. I told him. He leaned against the wall, looked at me from under serious eyebrows, and said he didn't see why not. He's a little guy, and sometimes he overcompensates for his size by deepening his voice and puffing up his chest.

My cover would be that I was working on a story for *Probe,* a piece about the mysterious death of a local artist. Artie would leave a free-lance contract in my mailbox the next morning.

"That ought to open doors for you, Jake," he said. He laughed, but he meant it. "The cops don't like us much, but they tend to leave us alone. They hassle you, want to check to make sure you're doing what you say, just have them call me."

"Thanks, Artie." It was funny, but now that I'd touched him on his power base I became suddenly aware of how much he'd changed since I first knew him. Back in the early seventies he was a nice kid with a thin beard and wide eyes. Now he sounded like he should have a big cigar in his mouth.

There was a knock on the door. That would be Jim Nelson, a friend of Hal's and the fourth member of the group. I started out the kitchen door, but Artie stopped me and Hal got up to let Jim in. I let Artie pull me back into the kitchen again.

"Listen, Jake," he said, "are you going to be doing this kind of thing often?"

"I don't know. Why?"

"Sometimes I hear about people in trouble. Good people."

"I might consider it, job by job. You willing to keep vouching for me?"

"Sure." He smiled slyly. "Of course, once in a while we may

have to run a little something with your byline. Just to make it look kosher. And you could probably pick up some useful information for us on some of those jobs—"

"It's possible," I interjected, grabbing for the bowls of chips. If I wasn't careful, Artie would have me working for him. He pulled some beers out of the refrigerator and followed me to the living room. The conspiratorial look on his face made me feel I'd just made a pact with the devil.

When we drew for the deal, I came up with a king. It didn't make me feel any better about Artie when he announced, in unnecessarily significant tones, that it looked like "Samson's deal." He even winked at me.

The king was the best card I had all night, except when Hal dealt a game of low ball. I drew a full house, aces over tens, and lost to Artie's two of diamonds, three and four of clubs, seven of spades, and nine of hearts.

I finished up twenty-three dollars down, a real bundle for our low-stakes games. But when I asked Hal to stay for an extra beer afterward and gave him the story about the magazine piece, he said he didn't think he'd have a problem passing along a little public information on the case for my "article." I don't know whether he'd overheard any of my conversation with Artie, but it was clear that he didn't believe a word I was saying. On the way out he punched me on the arm, snickered, and warned me to watch my tail.

—4—

Rebecca owned a condominium in a big new anthill of a building in North Berkeley. Only five stories tall but it stretched for half a block, and somehow the architects had managed to cram thirty-two apartments into it. I pushed the button for number 15 and waited.

The intercom crackled and Rebecca's distorted voice descended from the third floor.

"Who is it?"

"Jake."

"Okay." The door buzzed and I pushed and walked into the large courtyard, open to the sky so that, presumably, the exotic flora sprouting from the circular graveled beds wouldn't feel trapped. I bypassed the elevators for the sake of fitness and trotted up the uncarpeted service stairs. As I passed apartment 14, an elderly man came out, looked at me very carefully, smiled tentatively, and closed his door again. Friendly, I thought. And nosy. Rebecca opened her door before I knocked.

She hadn't changed much, just enough to show that hers had not been an easy year. Her hair was a little longer, her fingernails a little shorter, and the lines around her eyes a little deeper. The giveaway was in the two new lines at the corners of her mouth. She looked thinner and harder, and I found myself thinking that John Harley, with his wife and his house in the hills, had not been good for her.

Rebecca led me into the living room and offered me a glass of wine. I was glad it was white wine because her pale carpet was just the kind that attracts red wine like a magnet. Sure, I know the trick with the salt; I just never expect it to work. And there's a certain lack of dignity in crawling around on somebody's floor sweating and pouring salt on the rug. Especially a woman's floor. Especially a woman like Rebecca. It was this train of thought, followed while she poured and served the wine, that rubbed the edge off any regrets I still had about our relationship that never was. I don't want a woman whose carpets make me nervous.

The furniture was white and blue and yellow and red and contemporary, with two exceptions: a standard lamp with a fringed shade that might have been made in the twenties and an oak sideboard that looked Victorian.

Rebecca was wearing a pair of fashionably baggy pants, tight around the ankles; clogs; and a tight little nothing blouse, a mauve print with hardly any sleeves and hardly any buttons. She sat back and surveyed me. I'd dressed carefully in my usual corduroys, a Hawaiian shirt that, for some reason, women seem to like, and a tweed jacket.

"Too bad it's cool this afternoon," she said. "It would be nice to sit on the balcony."

I looked out through the glass doors. Like Harley, she had a view of the Bay Bridge and San Francisco but from a slightly different angle. Views like that can be expensive. We sat in the living room.

Rebecca and I had met when we were both selling houses for a living. She was still doing it. That was, in fact, how she had met

John Harley. She had sold the Harleys their house in Montclair. She told me about her relationship with him. How he had called her repeatedly until she agreed to meet him for lunch. How she'd fallen in love with him. I looked away from her eyes. I didn't want her to see what I thought of that. She told me a lot about him, too. He was wise and gentle and too kind to desert a wife who loved and needed him. She told me everything but how he was in bed. I kept my eyes on my wineglass.

"Has it occurred to you," I said, "that he might have killed her himself?" I glanced up quickly to catch her reaction. She seemed genuinely astonished.

"Of course it hasn't," she replied calmly. "For one thing, he wasn't home that morning. He was at his office."

"You're sure of that?"

"Yes. We spoke to each other. On the phone. I called him and he was there. And there are even some witnesses. A political group that's been bothering him. They saw him. They knew he was working. He told me they were picketing outside the building."

I shrugged. "I still don't know when the woman was killed."

She leaned back in her chair, frowning, thoughtful. Then she flashed me a look of understanding. "I get it," she said. "This is an intellectual exercise. You're practicing."

I laughed. "No, Rebecca. Not really."

She leaned forward again. "Oh, come on, Jake. Why would he hire you?"

"He thinks cops are stupid. Maybe he thinks I'm stupid, too. Maybe he thinks if he hires me that will convince everyone he didn't do it. Maybe he doesn't even intend to pay me."

She was on her feet, defending him. "That's ridiculous. He's not like that. He's totally sincere about this." She suddenly realized she was standing and sat down again.

"Besides," I added, "wasn't it your idea to call me?"

She downed the rest of the wine in her glass. "It was all his idea, hiring someone to investigate. All I did was suggest you."

I finished my wine and stood up. "Okay. Let's go get something to eat and talk about this some more."

We settled on Sen Ying's, Szechuan and Cantonese, a few minutes north of Rebecca's, where Berkeley disappears quietly into the town of Albany.

We were halfway there before I broke the silence.

"What time was it when you called him?"

She thought for a moment. "I'm not sure. I guess it was around ten-thirty or eleven."

"Where were you?"

"Jesus, Jake." She tried to laugh, but her voice broke. "You know how it is in my business. I was wandering around all morning. In and out of the office. I think I called him from a phone booth somewhere." I reached over and patted her hand. She pulled it out from under mine and grasped my arm. "Jake," she said softly, "you've got to help us."

The restaurant was crowded but they found us a table. We ordered white wine, sizzling rice soup, spicy pork, and almond chicken.

I had abandoned my slap-and-jab method, questioning her gently over lunch, asking her to tell me everything she knew about the dead woman. She knew a lot.

Margaret Harley had not, according to Rebecca, known that her husband was having an affair. But she had apparently felt that something was wrong and, in recent months, had begun to act suspicious in a sad way. She had been given to sporadic outbursts of bitterness about the marriage. Harley had told Rebecca that he had caught her more than once watching him in a searching, questioning way. He had begun to find it less and less possible to be in his wife's company for any length of time. He had taken to retreating to his study or working at his office. They had developed sexual problems because, or so Harley had told Rebecca, he no longer wanted to make love with his wife.

But he had vacillated about leaving her. In some ways their marriage was a comfortable one for him. For one thing, Rebecca said, Margaret had money of her own that gave John an illusion of freedom. Freedom to consider teaching less and exploring what he called other options.

Rebecca, on the other hand, felt that his fear of divorce—I thought of it as his fear of self-sufficiency—would fade as his love for her grew. She had been confident that would happen soon and, meanwhile, had been content enough to see him often and know that she was the one he really loved.

Once she started talking about John Harley, I had a little trouble getting her back on the subject of his wife. I maneuvered her around again, asking what Harley had told her about his wife's background.

Mostly he had complained that she wasn't doing anything with her talent.

Margaret Harley had been a promising young painter, achieving some recognition in her native Massachusetts while she was still in her twenties. By the time she met John Harley, she was well known and able to command high prices for her work. He had a teaching job in Boston. They had married. She had taken his name legally, continuing to sign her work "Margaret Bursky." Within a year or two of their marriage, he had received an offer for a much better job at Berkeley, and they had moved to the West Coast.

After the move, she began to paint less. In a few months she was no longer painting at all. At the time of her death, at the age of thirty-five, she had not painted for six years. While Rebecca was telling me all this, I had a quick flashback to the fake Early American furniture in Harley's rumpus room. I couldn't imagine the dead woman, an artist, living with it. The stuff must have belonged to Harley before the marriage. That shed a little more light on his personality and on their marriage. No wonder Harley's artist-wife had languished.

At first Harley had worried about his wife's apparent creative block. She had assured him that it was temporary and that she would soon pass to a new plateau in her work. When it became obvious that the problem was more than temporary, Harley had already drifted away from her. He was too involved in his own life to worry very much about hers, if indeed she had one at all apart from him.

He had told Rebecca he suspected that she had given herself too much to her married life. When that began to fail, she started looking for ways to find herself and possibly her work again. She had begun to get involved with various groups, starting, for some reason, with an astrology study group. She had moved on to a painting class that she quickly declared "low-level and useless," had taken some art history classes, which she found irrelevant, and had most recently been involved with her meditation group and her therapy group.

She had been talking lately about building a studio on the back slope of their yard. John had hoped she would. When they were both home together, her aimlessness was oppressive to him.

"Wasn't very helpful to her, was he?" I commented.

Rebecca tried to reason with me. "He couldn't very well lead her life for her, could he?"

"Certainly not. He was much too busy with his own." I forestalled an angry reply by changing the subject abruptly. "That money of hers. Does he get it now?"

Rebecca picked up a black mushroom with her chopsticks and sat staring at it, thinking. "I don't know," she said finally. "We've never discussed it. You'll have to ask him."

I reflected that they'd hardly had time to discuss it, since her death at least. "I will. You don't have any idea, I suppose, about how much money there was?"

She dropped the mushroom and picked up a piece of chicken. "There was some from her early sales, but I got the idea that there was even more from her family. I really don't know." She looked at the chicken as if she were wondering what it was and put it in her mouth. Then she took a long swallow from her glass of wine. "He didn't kill her for her money. Or have her killed. He hasn't got it in him."

"You're probably right. Why don't we forget I ever said that. How do you think she died?"

Rebecca brightened a little and looked at me straight on. "I've been thinking about that. I don't know why the police think someone killed her, but it seems obvious to me that she killed herself. After all, she wasn't very happy."

I shrugged. "They must have some reason. Tell me more about her. Was she a good-looking woman? Attractive?"

She raised her eyes and looked at me again, this time quizzically.

"She was nice enough looking, handsome, I suppose you could say. Why?"

"I just need to know all the things about her that went to make up the complete person. An exceptionally attractive victim might have been victimized because of her attractiveness."

"A lover?"

I nodded.

"Well, she certainly wasn't repulsive or anything."

I helped myself to the last of the almond chicken, waved to the waiter, and ordered another glass of wine for each of us.

Rebecca continued. "She was medium. Medium coloring, medium height, medium-sized features. Not very exciting." Like her husband, I thought. "But she certainly could have had a lover."

"Sometimes," I said, "when people suspect their spouses of playing around, they run right out and do the same. Makes them feel better. A lot better."

Her eyes softened, and she looked at me sympathetically. "Sounds like you know about that, Jake." I'd never talked about my long-dead marriage to another woman, and I wasn't going to start now.

I lightened up. "Doesn't everybody?"

The waiter brought our wine. Rebecca ate a piece of celery.

"Did she ever see you and Harley together? I mean after the sale was closed and there was no reason for you to be together?" She shook her head and concentrated on chewing what seemed to be a gristly hunk of chicken. "Did you ever run into the two of them, out in the evening or shopping or anything?" The East Bay wasn't all that big, after all. She shook her head again.

"I saw them once in a movie line but I avoided them. They never even saw me." I wondered. People who suspect their spouses seem to develop telescopic, microscopic, and panoramic vision. Well, it didn't matter.

"How hard were you pushing for marriage? Yours, I mean."

She glared at me. "He knew I wanted it."

"How often did you see each other?"

She put down her chopsticks. One of them fell on the floor. The waiter came over, looked at her full plate, and handed her another set.

"About two or three times a week. Once she went back east to visit her family, and we had several days together. What does all that matter, anyway?"

"Everything matters, Rebecca." I finished the rest of the food on the serving plates and considered what she had left uneaten in front of her. No, I'd already eaten too much. The first day of cutting down was always the hardest.

I asked her if she'd like to go somewhere for another glass of wine.

"If you don't have any more questions, I think I'll just go home, Jake. I'm exhausted and I feel a little sick."

I dropped her off and went for an Irish coffee, no sugar, at Michael's Saloon on Shattuck. I had two of them before I decided to take the case.

5

Harley wasn't in his office or he wasn't answering his phone, so I tried the home number. He was there. I closed the door to the saloon's phone booth and told him to go to his bank and draw out a five-thousand-dollar cash retainer.

"Seems like a lot of money to start off with," he grumbled. When I didn't bother to argue with him, he gave up. "Oh, all right. Meet me at my bank. It's—"

"No. I've got work to do." I also didn't want to be connected with a large withdrawal from his account. I was working for a magazine, not for Harley. I looked at my watch. Three-thirty. "Do you know the Scholar?"

"Of course. It's a bar just north of campus."

"Good. Meet me there with the money at six." A little more grumbling and we had a date. "Also, I need some information from you. Your wife's will. There is one, isn't there?"

"I think so." He sounded sulky. "I expect I'll hear from her attorney if there is."

"Okay. Let me know. The other thing I need is information about some of the groups she belonged to. What were they, where did they meet, any names you can give me?"

"Oh, yes. I thought you'd want to know that." The sulkiness had passed as quickly as it does in a child. Now he was the cooperative grownup. "The only thing I know about for sure is the meditation group. She was in a therapy group too, but she didn't talk about it." I grunted encouragement. "They met at the Earthlight Meditation Center. Do you know it? On Euclid?"

"I'll find it. Do the police know about her groups?"

"Well, they asked me, and I thought I'd better tell them. Was that right?"

"Good idea."

"Also, they asked me for her address book, and I gave it to them. And they wanted to go through her desk drawers. I didn't have any choice, did I?"

"No."

"I'd like to spend some time talking to you this evening. I don't feel we've discussed things enough. I think you should ask me some more questions, stir up my memory. We might come up with something helpful."

"We'll talk," I said reluctantly. "Later."

I returned to the bar, ordered a glass of mineral water with a twist of lemon, and wrote "Earthlight Meditation Center" in my pocket notebook.

The police probably had the jump on me there, unless they were following up other leads I knew nothing about. The address book, not to mention other personal papers, might give them a big advantage. Then again, it might not. In any case, I was stuck with talking to Harley in a few hours, whether he had any more information for me or not. His insistence that we talk didn't mean he actually thought he had information for me. He probably wouldn't feel secure in hiring me unless he could have a chunk of me now and again. I had to admit that this wasn't just his peculiarity. A lot of people seem to need personal attention from those they hire on even the most casual basis. I remembered a job I once had building some steps for some people in Santa Rosa. Just your basic wooden steps, leading down from the back door to the patio. They insisted I do it on a weekend so the husband could be around. Right away I knew I was in trouble, but I needed the money.

Well, of course, the guy didn't know anything about building steps. He got underfoot. He questioned every cut and measurement. He talked about his house and all the improvements he'd made. He wasn't trying to be obnoxious. It wasn't because he didn't trust me. It was like I was operating on his wife and he needed to be reassured that I really cared.

Harley was paying me enough so I could afford to show him I cared. I hadn't been crazy about the guy in Santa Rosa either.

I finished my mineral water and left the saloon. Before I headed north I picked up an *Oakland Tribune* and checked through it. The woman had been dead two days now. The headline had shrunk and the story had moved to page three. It said, in essence, that there was no new evidence. By tomorrow, if things stayed the same, I figured Margaret Bursky might rate no space at all.

The Earthlight Meditation Center was in an expensive section of North Berkeley, just beyond the campus. There are two kinds of spiritual enlightenment and/or self-improvement centers: the kind with money and the kind without. This one had money, or it would have been forced to move to another neighborhood long ago. The housing shortage in Berkeley and the huge student population have created a rent inflation monster that radiates south into Oakland and west into Richmond. The same is true of real estate prices.

I drove past the small business block of restaurants and shops where Euclid dead-ends at the campus, past the Earthlight Meditation Center's two-story frame house with tasteful, churchlike sign, and found a parking place without a meter a block and a half farther on.

The front door was unlocked. To the left of the entry hall was a half-open door marked OFFICE. I pushed it all the way open and went in. It reminded me of a school office. A counter to the right, a large bulletin board dead ahead, a closed door to my left where the principal would sit in grand isolation. When I came in the door, a youngish man stood up behind the counter. He was a familiar type that was beginning now to look a little old-fashioned. Some people get stuck in the decade they like best. Maybe it's a lack of flexibility or adaptability; maybe it's just whimsy. Some men never give up their crew cuts no matter how far the fifties recede into the past. This one was stuck in the sixties. He had long brown hair, down past his shoulders, a badly trimmed reddish beard, and that saintly look around the eyes that a lot of folks adopted back then. And he had that peculiar physical attitude, the one I always thought came right out of a bad movie about Jesus: shoulders slightly rounded, head thrust forward, chin upraised, eyes barely focused. I'm not saying he was stoned or anything. He was just locked into a sweetness that had gone stale.

The office itself created the same effect. It was clear that no particular school of meditation was represented here. The place was generic, maybe even neuter. The notices on the walls covered a variety of causes and preoccupations, from saving the whales to reading the Tarot. Nothing really controversial like parking meters.

The sweetly aging young man was waiting patiently for me to speak, a gentle smile on his full lips. I felt like patting his head. I tried to look harmless.

"I'm looking for someone," I said, my voice rising softly on a hopeful note.

He nodded sagely. "I'll help you if I can."

I nodded back, showing that I understood he was a nice, helpful fellow. "I'm looking for people who knew a woman named

Margaret Harley." His expression hardened and his eyes turned opaque.

"Police?" He spoke with a show of self-control. Nothing significant in that, I supposed. Just an old habit.

"No. Have they been here?" I emphasized the word *they* so he would think that I, too, disapproved of homicide investigations.

"Not yet. Who are you?"

"Jake Samson. I'm a writer."

He was not impressed. "A crime reporter?" Same category as cops, from the look on his face.

"No. Let me explain. Margaret Harley was a well-known artist once, a painter. Her name then was Margaret Bursky. She dropped out of sight a few years ago when she married John Harley. I'm doing a magazine piece on her."

His eyes were still cool. "Because of the way she died," he said in a flat voice. That made me like him a little better.

"Because of her talent and because a lot of people have wondered what happened to her." I waited while he digested that.

"We knew her as Margaret Bursky," he said, and I knew I'd won.

"Would it be possible for me to meet some of the people who were in her meditation group?"

"I don't see why not. Anyone can go to a meeting."

"When does it meet?"

He held up his index finger and consulted a sheet of paper taped to the top of the counter.

"Tonight. Eight o'clock. Room five upstairs."

"Thanks." I turned to go.

"Mr. uh . . ." I looked back at him over my shoulder. "She seemed like a really nice woman. I only met her a couple of times, you know, but I liked her."

"Right," I said thoughtfully. I made a mental note to find out just how much he'd liked her. Before I went out the office door I had a look at the bulletin board. Announcements of meditation groups and classes, business cards for all kinds of entrepreneurs—tailors, gardeners, palm readers, therapists—fliers for private classes in subjects I assumed were not available at the meditation center—astrology, body work, solar technology—and three-by-five cards listing various items for sale or apartments to rent. Nothing unusual or unexpected.

The nice young man was still standing at the counter, watching me. I nodded to him and went out the door.

So the police hadn't been there yet. Unless they were right behind me I had a chance to beat them to some of the people who knew the dead woman.

I was just feeling my way at this point. There wasn't much to go on. I needed to find out more about Margaret Bursky and Margaret Harley both. If Margaret Harley had truly lost Margaret Bursky along the way in favor of a marriage that was going bad, suicide was still a possibility and might even be the answer the cops came up with after a brief investigation. Of course, there was the bowl of fruit, but that was pretty flimsy. Maybe she was thinking about painting it.

I left my car where it was and went in search of the campus art library. It was pretty small, but I hoped I would find what I wanted in the periodicals. Sure enough, after half an hour's search through the card index, I found two references to Margaret Bursky in back issues of *Art Monthly*. One in March of 1970 and another in November of 1973, the year before her marriage. But space on the shelves had been given only to more recent issues, up to five years back.

The young woman at the desk told me they had older magazines stored in the back room and she'd be happy to find me the numbers I was looking for. That search took another fifteen minutes, during which time the desk was unattended. No matter. No one came in.

She smiled beautifully at me when she handed me the two magazines and asked what I was researching. I told her I was looking for information about Margaret Bursky.

She looked blank.

"She hasn't painted for several years," I explained. I thanked her for her help. She showed her dimples. She had short curly blond hair, green eyes, and stubby blond lashes, all of which went very well with the dimples. She looked about eighteen, but I was tempted to come back for more research in the next few days.

The 1970 issue was not helpful. The piece covered several young artists and gave only a paragraph to my subject. The more recent article, the one from 1973, showed how much status she'd gained. It was all about her. That is, it was all about her art. Had she been that secretive about her personal life? I flipped back through some of the other pieces on other artists. No, they just didn't say much about the people they were immortalizing. This was a very slick, very expensive, not very readable journal. Its level was aesthetic, its aims and language obscure, its attitude self-conscious. The material wasn't difficult, just a bit dusty. The article on Bursky went so far into the realm of gossip as to mention that the woman had been born in Massachusetts and had gone to school in New York. But it did tell me two things: She was respected in her field and she had experimented with a variety of styles. The magazine predicted that given a few more years to mature, she could be one of the century's better painters. There were two photographs with the article, both of paintings. One—a landscape—was reminiscent, to me anyway, of the French Impressionists. The other—a self-portrait—was done in quick harsh strokes of paint, very few strokes, and showed a strong intense face with dark hair and eyes. She didn't fit Rebecca's "medium" very well. I wondered whether the artist had not seen herself as others saw her, or whether Rebecca had never looked closely at the woman. Maybe this intense young artist had weathered, in a few years of marriage to John Harley, into the handsome but faded wife Rebecca had known.

I found myself staring with some regret at the face in the self-portrait. Regret that I'd never known her, that I hadn't met her in 1973. I was reminded of that old movie—what was it called, *Laura?*—where the guy falls in love with the woman in a portrait.

I got up, feeling a little depressed. The young blond woman was talking to a young blond man. Barely woman and barely man. A few years ago I wouldn't have felt self-conscious about calling them a girl and boy. They were flirting. They looked good together. I didn't think I'd come back after all.

Harley was at the Scholar waiting for me when I got there. He looked a little less damp and his color was a little better, but he still wasn't my idea of a charming drinking buddy. I slid into the booth and looked across at him. He slid an envelope across the table to me. I folded it and stuck it in my pocket, planning to count the money later.

"So, what is it you want to talk to me about, Harley?"

He looked insulted. "Well, I would like to know what you're doing and if you've learned anything."

The waitress came over and took my order. More mineral water. I wanted a beer, and I was feeling a little testy.

"Look, Harley, there's something you'd better understand." He sat up a bit straighter, his chin tilted up. "I'm not going to come around and report to you once a day. I'm going to spend my time investigating your wife's death. That's what you're paying me for; that's why I'm taking your money."

His eyes shifted away and he shrugged slightly. Good. He wasn't going to get pushy.

"The police came to my office today and asked me some more questions." I leaned forward, waiting for him to go on.

"They asked me about our marriage. Again."

"And you lied. Again."

He was indignant. "Of course I lied." He almost choked on the last word as the waitress appeared suddenly with my drink.

"What else?"

"They asked about some of the people in her address book. I didn't know Rebecca was even in the damned thing, from when we were buying the house."

"What were some of the other names?"

"I don't remember. I didn't know them." I stared at him. "Well, what do you expect? After they mentioned Rebecca's name, I got so nervous—"

"What else?"

"They wanted to know if she'd left any recent artwork."

"And she hadn't?"

He shook his head. "And they were all over the damned department talking to people. You've got to hurry."

I tossed my drink down my throat. It burned.

"Look, Harley, I've got things to do. When would be a good time tomorrow for me to come over and look through her stuff?"

"I don't know. Call me at my office in the morning." I stood up. "By the way," he added, "her funeral's on Friday if you want to come." Then he stuck his face back into his glass of what looked like a red wine cooler. Or maybe it was Kool-Aid.

I went home with my money.

The cats came running down the driveway looking distressed, stopped about three feet short of me and began to run the other way, toward the house, leading me, as cats will, toward home and their supper dishes. Just then Rosie's pickup came to a clattering halt at the curb.

"Hey, Jake!" She jumped out of the cab, followed by Alice.

"Come on back to the house while I feed the cats," I told her.

"Okay. It'll take me a few minutes to unload."

I nodded and turned toward the house again as she was lifting a six-foot stepladder out of the back of the truck.

I'd scooped out a bowl of kibble, dumped half the contents of a can of Kitty Treat into their dishes, and taken Rosie's beer out of the fridge by the time I heard Alice's tags jingling.down the path. Rosie stamped the sawdust off her boots and came inside. She examined the seat of her pants before she sat down on the couch and took the beer from my hand.

"So?" she said.

I sat down across from her, admitted I'd taken the job, and told her as much of the story as I knew.

"Bursky, huh?" She squinted at the ceiling. "I don't know what it is, but that name seems familiar." She brought her eyes back to communication level and reached down and idly scratched Alice's head. The dog grunted. "Let me think about it. Maybe I know something. Something recent." She shook her head as if to get the ball bearings moving and took a swig of her beer. "This Rebecca. Do you trust her?"

"Maybe."

"Hard to tell what she's like from your description, but I think most women are capable of killing."

I grinned at her. "I suppose that, coming from you, that's a favorable judgment."

She snorted. "You know it as well as I do, pal."

I fixed her with a disapproving glare. "Most of the killers I've known have been men, baby. You girls is too delicate, too soft. You shouldn't even be thinking about doing men's work. Like killing."

"Gosh, Jake," she said softly. "Sometimes you make me feel all tingly and subservient."

"Take off your work boots and say that, sweetheart," I muttered in my best imitation of Humphrey Bogart.

"Alice," she muttered in return, "kill." The dog wagged her tail. "Listen," she added, suddenly back in the real world, "I hate to interrupt this 1947 movie, but don't you have to get to that meditation group soon?"

"Yeah." I stood up. "Just time to make a small but adequate dinner."

She got up, too, and paused at the door, beer can in hand. "If

you get back before eleven or so, knock on the door, okay? I'd
like to hear about whatever happens."

"Sure."

"And be careful. If your relatives inherit this property, they
might not like me."

—6—

The Earthlight Meditation Center looked somehow more institu-
tional at night. I guess it was because even a house party doesn't
light up a place like that, upstairs and down. Three other people
approached the entrance at the same time I did. Two of them
went straight through the entry area into a downstairs hallway. I
could see several open doors in there. Busy night at the center.

I went upstairs and found room five. Half a dozen people were
there already, sitting on couches and upholstered armchairs. I'd
always thought you were supposed to sit up straight in a hard
chair when you meditated, feet on the floor. But I'd learned that
ten years before in Sonoma County, and maybe the seventies had
changed things. After all, you couldn't be laid back and flowing
with your feelings and totally self-centered sitting rigidly in a
straight-backed chair and making sure you were connecting with
the same floor everyone else was connecting with.

I sat on a couch next to a woman who appeared to be somewhere around forty. She was a type I've always found attractive
in a slightly offbeat way. She had long dark hair, graying, clasped
at the back of her neck with a leather buckle. Her hair looked
springy, like it would pull free and stand out all over her head if
she didn't hold it down tight. Her eyes were very dark and large,
with darker skin above and below them. A slight looseness in the
skin under her eyes. She wore three gold bracelets and several
rings on her small pudgy hands. Her skin was olive. She wore a
voluminous mud-brown dress cinched tight at her small waist
with a wide leather belt. Her legs were encased in black tights
and her feet cradled in soft leather slippers with no heels.

This woman was not a seventies or even a sixties person. She
was right out of the other side of the fifties, the beat side, the

black leotards, black beret, Chianti and lousy poetry, folk music side. Old-style bohemianism left over from the twenties. I liked it. I always had, even though I'd been barely pubescent when it had been at its peak. It was so morose.

I nodded to her. "Jake Samson."

She allowed her eyes to react in an almost-smile. "Alana Gold." Her voice was soft, almost a whisper. That's right, I remembered. It was mostly the men who were morose. The women had had their comforter roles to play.

"Have you been coming to this group long?" I asked. Very original. Do you come here often?

"Three months."

I looked around the room. Nine people, ten counting me. "How big is the group?"

"Usually around a dozen."

I decided to get right to it.

"Actually," I confessed, "I'm here to get some information." She raised her heavy dark eyebrows. "I'm doing a magazine piece on an artist, a woman who was in this group, and I need to get in touch with people who knew her."

Her expression, attentive to me a moment before, had gone a little remote. "Artist? I suppose you mean Margaret. What kind of magazine piece?" Her eyes were roaming around the room. Violent death fascinates people, but when the victim is someone they knew, it also scares them. Especially when a mysterious stranger starts dragging them into it by asking questions.

"About her work. She's been out of the public eye for the past few years, but her work shouldn't be forgotten."

Alana's attention returned reluctantly to me. She gave me the look that always reminds me of a one-way mirror: She was trying to penetrate my soul, excavating for truth, but she wouldn't let me pass through to hers. "Really? You're not a policeman?"

I smiled crookedly and dug in my wallet for my *Probe* magazine credentials. She looked at the paper and frowned slightly. "I don't know any gossip, Mr. Samson. I can't tell you anything seamy about Margaret because there's nothing seamy to tell. And I don't know anything about her work. I didn't know she was a serious artist."

Serious? A significant modifier. "Did you know she dabbled in it?"

"I had some idea . . ." A man was standing up in the middle

of the room, counting heads or checking out the women or something.

"Alana—may I call you Alana?" She nodded graciously and showed a flicker of her former interest in me. I wasn't just bull-shitting for information. Her ripe sensuality seeped out of her pores and surrounded her like an aura. "I don't know how to prove to you that I'm not out to do a hatchet job. I respect the woman as an artist. That's what I'm interested in. Did you know her well?"

She shrugged, world-weary. "I thought I knew her. But I knew her as Margaret Bursky. I didn't know she was married. We had a glass of wine together once or twice." The man who had been counting heads took on a group-leader stance, and our conversation was cut short.

"Nice to see you all here," he said smoothly, as though he were about to start selling us sets of encyclopedias. Everyone in the room seemed to settle a little more firmly in their chairs. Several people rested their heads against the backs of their seats and closed their eyes.

"Would you have a glass of wine with me after this?" I whispered. She nodded, her eyes fixed on the talking man.

"I see some new faces here tonight," he said. He was wearing a plaid flannel shirt, baggy jeans, and Birkenstock sandals with red socks. He smiled at me and at one or two others. "Beatrice, would you pass the can around?" A slight, pale woman in tight pants and platform shoes started a coffee can moving around the room. "Whatever you can afford, folks. Five or ten dollars is enough." I thought so, too. The can came to me and I tossed in a five. Then another. What the hell, Harley would be paying for it. Alana put in five. I wondered how else the center made its money. When the can got back to Beatrice again, the leader spoke.

"My name is Evan. Let's go around the room and introduce ourselves." Once again Beatrice was the starter. We all said our first names with varying degrees of aggression, flirtatiousness, or sociability.

"Now those of you who are new here may or may not have ever meditated before. It really doesn't matter. We've kind of developed our own system here. For a start, make sure both your feet are planted firmly on the floor. We're all going to be receiving and sending power to each other. But you don't want the power to slip right off the tips of your fingers, so you should clasp your hands—not too tightly—that's right. Very good, Jake." Cozy. I was willing to bet he'd trained himself never to forget a name. Everyone was shuffling into position. "Now each of you is a terminal for the current. It flows into your body. Try to keep your spines straight—that's right, Beatrice—but feel free to relax against the backs of your chairs. Nice soft chairs." His monotone was putting me into a trance. I resisted. "Now close your eyes." He paused for a second, I supposed to give us time to close our lids. "Very good. Charles, you don't look relaxed. Relax. Feel the comfort and warmth all around you." Charles was also a new-comer. With my eyes closed, I remembered that he was middle-aged, and he wore slacks and a sports jacket. He looked like a man trying to cure an ulcer. "That's good. Very good. Now everyone has a favorite color, isn't that right? A favorite color? Red or blue or maybe green or even violet or yellow . . ." I was relaxing. I couldn't help it. "Pick your favorite color. Keep your eyes closed. Imagine a round rubber ball. It's your favorite color. It's hovering in front of you." I was staring, eyes closed, at a red rubber ball. Red is not my favorite color, but the ball stubbornly insisted on being red so I stopped fighting it. "Concentrate on that ball. Concentrate. It begins to roll away from you." My ball just hung there. It didn't move at all. I gave it a push. It swung away and then back again. My rubber ball was hanging on a string. I cut the string. The ball dropped out of sight. Maybe I just wasn't in the mood for all this. But I had paid ten dollars to get into this gym, I might as well get the exercise. I found the ball, lying on the ground at my feet.

"The ball is rolling away down a wide path. . . ." I gave it a kick and it started to roll. "It is a winding path. Follow the ball. Concentrate on the ball." My path was a yellow brick road. Concentrate, Jake, I told myself, on the ball. There are no cowardly lions or scarecrows. . . .

"There is a fork in the road. Your ball rolls off to the left and comes to a stone wall about five feet tall. It disappears through a hole in the wall." I felt a vague resentment. Here I'd been following this damned red ball, and now it was supposed to disappear. It did. I was standing there facing a stone wall with moss in the cracks.

Evan's tone of voice changed. "Now, open your hands and step through the wall. That's right, open them, lay them palms up on your thighs. Good. Are you through the wall? There were a few uncertain murmurs of assent. I was still staring at a stone wall with moss in the cracks and a caterpillar crawling along the top. One of those fuzzy orange ones that look like stray tomcats. "Your hands are apart and open and ready to receive what you find on the other side of the wall. Whatever it is. You will receive it and it will travel through your mind and body and down your legs and will combine with the visions of everyone in the room." I thought about climbing over the wall but I couldn't get a foothold. I tried to imagine something on the other side and realized I was just faking it. "Your vision is unique. It is yours. It is your dream of all that is beautiful." I turned around, my back to the stone wall, and walked back along the brick road. If I couldn't go with everyone else I was at least going to amuse myself. "Receive. It is all coming to you. Clearly." I sat down on a rock just past the fork in the road and waited for the others.

"Good. When you're ready, when you're finished with your vision, open your eyes and shake your hands, shake the vision right out through the tips of your fingers and return to the world. Now stay silent. Others are still away from here."

I opened my eyes. More than half the people in the room were either shaking their hands or gazing bleary-eyed around them to see what the others were doing.

Within about three minutes everyone had finished vision number one. When the last person opened her eyes, I turned quickly to Alana again.

"Who else around here knew Margaret Bursky, talked to her pretty regularly, that sort of thing?" The leader was chatting with Beatrice. Were Beatrice and Evan an item? Who would care?

She thought for a moment. "Well, there was Billy, of course. He's not in the group, though."

"Where could I find him?"

"He works downstairs in the office during the day."

"Guy with a red beard, long brown hair?" She nodded. I would definitely have to have another chat with Billy. "Anyone else?"

"Not really. She was pretty quiet. Friendly, nice, you know. But quiet."

Evan took his group leader stance again and told us all to hold hands. We were going to have what he called a close encounter.

"Now, you're going to give yourself up totally to the forces, the vibrations, the flow of the group. You will concentrate on one thing and one thing only: the energy coming from the hands on either side of you."

We did that for a while. Alana's hand was hot. The guy on the other side of me kept squeezing mine. I couldn't tell whether this was his way of concentrating or his way of sending a message.

After the close encounter we did a couple more versions of the things we'd already done, with lots of chat from old Evan. We finished up with a healing session. We all held hands again and concentrated on the physical problem of a member of the group. I'd been right about poor Charles. He volunteered his ulcer. We bombarded it with goodwill.

When the session ended, most of the people stood around talking to each other for a while. Alana acted as though she wanted to talk to Evan, so I wandered around listening to conversations and smiling like a dope whenever anyone noticed me listening.

"Well, I never would have known either," a tall woman with a long, mouse-colored ponytail was saying, "if they hadn't printed her picture."

Her companion, a neatly dressed man with black curls on his head and on his face, nodded grimly. "Certainly seems strange, using another name. Poor thing. Wonder what happened?"

The ponytail moved slowly from side to side. "Tragic."

"Excuse me," I said with the proper mournful tone. "I couldn't help but overhear. I suppose you're talking about Margaret Harley, or Bursky?"

They turned to me and agreed, cautiously, that they were indeed talking about the deceased.

"Yes," I said, "it's very sad. Did you know her well?"

They both shook their heads, regarding me warily.

"I'm doing a little magazine piece on her and I'm looking for people who knew her, people who can tell me something about her. She was an artist, you know, a few years back."

"Yes, that was mentioned briefly in the papers, I think." The black curls waggled sadly. "But of course we didn't know that. She never talked much."

"Alana. And Billy," the woman with the ponytail said kindly, but with an air of butting me out of her tête-à-tête. "She seemed to be friends with them. You could talk to Alana now. She's here."

I smiled brightly. "Thank you, thank you very much." At least she had confirmed the information I'd already gotten from Alana. I wandered around a bit more. Quite a few of the folks were talking about their dead fellow-meditator. People were beginning to move out the door. Alana was coming toward me.

"Shall we go?" Her smile was wide and generous. She took my arm. Several people watched us leave. Well, why shouldn't she be proud to be seen on the arm of such a handsome fellow?

—7—

Alana suggested we go the Winery, a place on Telegraph Avenue. Since we both lived in that direction, we agreed to take our own cars and meet there.

The Winery was in one of those arcades created from the insides of a building. You went through the archway and there was a brick courtyard. Red, not yellow like my road. With a fountain. Each of the restaurants and shops had its own door leading into the courtyard. Skylights completed the illusion of— what? an old-fashioned dead-end brick street? But pleasant.

We chose a table in a dark corner. The waiter—she was a woman, but Rosie yelled at me once for saying "waitress" and I can't get my tongue around "waitperson"—came over instantly and lit our candle. We ordered a carafe of the house white, which she assured us was made by one of the more reliable and consistent California vineyards.

I took a few stabs at small talk, and Alana responded with practiced ease. Then I got to it.

"This Billy. How close was he to Margaret Bursky?"

She sipped at her wine. "I don't know. They seemed to be friends. Anyone could tell you that." She hesitated. "Look, I don't know much about Billy. Why are you asking me about him?"

I held up my hand in a soothing gesture. "Just trying to get a little background before I talk to him." She still looked put out.

My question had verged on gossip, after all. I decided I'd better get off the subject of Billy.

"You said you'd had an idea she dabbled in art." I tasted my wine and wondered how to approach this woman. "Where'd you get that idea?"

Alana wrinkled her forehead. "I know that intrigued you before. Why?"

"Because there doesn't seem to be a sign of any recent work. It would be great if there was some. Work no one knew existed by a fine, lost artist." Alana was a nice woman. She liked my attitude.

"I don't know. Let me think."

"Did you ever see her doing any drawing?"

"No, that wasn't it." She closed her eyes. "She used to carry this big canvas bag around with her. About this big." She indicated an object about the size of an airline bag. "It had a shoulder strap." I nodded encouragingly. "I remember once we were going to meet at the beginning of the week and she wanted my phone number. She pulled a whole lot of pencils out of the bag— maybe they were drawing pencils—and then fished around until she came up with a little notebook to write the number in. It just seems to me I remember seeing a larger notebook or drawing pad or something in the bag, too." She shrugged. "I can't be sure. But the pencils, that I'm sure of." She looked up at me over the rim of her glass. "Does that help?"

"It's interesting to speculate," I said vaguely and mysteriously. She looked at me skeptically and I abandoned mystery. "What do you think about the way she died?"

Alana cooled again perceptibly and gazed casually around the room. "What do you mean?" she murmured from an aloof profile.

"I mean do you think she might have killed herself?" I realized I was being pretty straightforward, but she was being so damned oblique and discreet I was ready to scream.

She turned to me, even cooler. "Of course not." But she wouldn't meet my eyes. Not that I have much faith in eye contact as an indicator of honesty.

I pressed on. "Did she seem reasonably happy?" I reflected that no one ever said "happy" all by itself anymore.

"Look Jake, she was my friend."

"That's very nice. But her death wasn't very nice, and I've

told you I'm writing a friendly piece, so why won't you just talk to me?"

She thought about what I'd said while she finished her glass of wine. I poured her another and refilled my own glass.

"All right," she said abruptly. "I'm going to trust you not to damage her memory. Actually, I don't really know very much." I settled back in my chair. Was she going to unwrap a little?

"When I first met her, about three months ago, she seemed depressed. She didn't talk about her personal life, but everything she said about everything was, well, colored by depression. Sometimes she would drink more wine than might have been wise. Sometimes she would pick people out in the bar or restaurant and make up stories about them, sad or peculiar stories. I assumed that those stories had something to do with her life, but it was as though she were telling me secrets somehow, and I tended to push them out of my mind later."

"Did she ever talk about marriage or art or lovers—"

She flapped her hand impatiently. "I'll get back to that, Jake. Just let me follow this process, all right?" I agreed, irritated. "For the past month or so, though, she's seemed happier. I even commented on it, making some remark about her cheerful mood, and she said something about having direction and purpose. She didn't talk about it any more than that and I didn't ask. Now, to get back to your question. I got the impression she had pretty strong ideas about marriage. I'd been talking about my own divorce, five years ago, and she said she didn't really approve of divorce. I told her my husband had been a philandering lout. That made her angry in a righteous way, but she still wasn't sure I should have left him. She was an odd mixture, you know? Conventional about some things, like divorce, and unconventional about others." She stopped and looked confused. "But is that so?" she asked wonderingly. "Isn't it conventional now to get divorced?" She shook her head. "I've lost track, I think, of . . ."

I took a chance on interrupting her again and being chastised. "How did she feel about lovers? Did you ever talk about things like that? I assume that even if she didn't talk much about her life, you talked a bit about yours."

She smiled wryly. "About my lovers, you mean? There have been one or two." She looked at me almost seductively. "I did talk about one man, as a matter of fact. She didn't seem shocked."

All right, so I'd have to be more direct. "Do you think she might have had one?"

"If she did, she never told me. But the way she felt about marriage, it seems unlikely, doesn't it?"

I reflected that either Margaret Bursky-Harley had resigned herself to the celibacy of a dead marriage or she'd been the most successfully secretive woman since my ex-wife. The level in our carafe was sinking pretty rapidly toward the one-quarter mark. I gestured at it. Alana smiled. I ordered another carafe and allowed myself some rumination time. Alana didn't seem about to press me to ask more questions.

The self-portrait I'd seen of the dead artist had shown a passionate face, with warmth, appeal, strength, and intensity. The face, and the art, had shown real sensitivity. But it could have been the sensitivity of an ascetic or even a martyr.

"So," I said with an air of renewal, "she was in a meditation group. How else did she spend her time? Any other groups or organizations?"

Alana's face closed up. The wine bearer brought us our second carafe. I was getting a little foggy. I would have to slow down, let her do more of the drinking.

"I know she was doing some therapy or other, some kind of group thing, right?" I asked.

She smiled tightly at me. That was it. She felt strange about the therapy. She was, truly, confused about what was now conventional. "Well, of course, everyone does that at one time or another, isn't that so?" Her voice was a bit higher than usual. "There wasn't anything wrong, you know. She was just exploring herself."

"Of course," I agreed, looking shocked that anyone could think that therapy served any purpose beyond that of the emotional dilettante. She relaxed. "I don't know more than one or two people who haven't done some of that sort of thing during the past ten years," I lied. "Actually, what I wanted to know was—" I had lost track of my sentence. One should not get fuzzy-brained when questioning people. It's not professional. "I still need to talk to more people who knew her. You know, find out how people saw her. And I wondered if you knew where I could get in touch with this group or the therapist. Or whatever."

Alana had finished her first glass from the new carafe. She was speeding up while I was slowing down, and she didn't seem to be feeling anything at all. She shook her head. "No, but I do know that she picked the name off the bulletin board at the center. The therapist. The card or notice is probably still up there. I just didn't pay any attention to who it was or what kind of group." Her tone was light, implying that such a group was not the sort of thing she had any use for. I remembered that I'd seen several therapists' cards on the board. Oh, well. No one ever said this was going to be easy. I wanted to talk to Billy again, so I'd be going back to the center the next day, anyway.

"Alana?" She looked at me expectantly. "If you're sure she wouldn't have killed herself, what do you think happened?"

She laughed shakily. "Well, is there any question? The poor woman fell. That seems clear enough, doesn't it?" She was asking me the question as though her own faith in the reasonableness of the world were at stake.

I peered down into my wine. I didn't for a minute believe that a woman of forty or more still thought the world was reasonable, but I didn't see any purpose in not going along with the fantasy. I looked up at her and smiled into her own anxious smile. "Sure," I said heartily, "decks are almost as dangerous as hot tubs. Dangerous place, California, hazards everywhere."

We both laughed, although I hadn't said anything very funny.

I couldn't think of anything else to ask her, and I thought I'd probably get another chance if I did think of something. We struggled through the last half of the second bottle of wine, two to one her favor. She challenged me to a California hazard-naming contest. We raced, one after another, through decks, hot tubs, smog, drought, tidal wave, earthquake, dry rot, terminal laid-backness, termites, mud slides, Mediterranean fruit flies, banana slugs, and unemployment, and then it got harder. She came up with slow strangulation by Algerian ivy. I countered with the probability that the two halves of the state, north and south, would always be bound in their unnatural union.

Although her naturally heavy eyelids were drooping very low, she managed a grin. "You win, Jake. That's the worst." It was decided that I would follow her home and she would make some coffee.

Alana drove very slowly down Telegraph toward Oakland, turning left on Alcatraz and right again just before College Avenue. Nice neighborhood. She pulled up in front of the basic brown shingle with red trim on lots of casement windows. Big dark tree in the front yard. Two flats, upper and lower. I followed her up the stairs. Converted, I thought, burping slightly with the effort of climbing, from a single-family house.

She led me into the kitchen and sat me down at a table with a red-and-white-checkered tablecloth. Bentwood chairs, four of them. New cabinets. New floor. She was weaving around on it, making coffee. I offered to help. She waved me away with a shoofly gesture.

"Nice place," I said smoothly.

She was concentrating hard on measuring the coffee into the top of the Melitta. "Thank you. Had it converted after the divorce so I could rent out part of it." Well, good, I thought. I hated to think of her without something to fall back on. She seemed softer than most of the women I'd known, as though her emotional life had been too painful and the pain had destroyed her elasticity.

She got the coffee measured and the kettle on to boil and sat down across from me. The kitchen light, stark above us, showed every line in her face. She looked tired. I guessed that I did, too, and that the bags under my eyes were standing out in high relief and my incipient whiskers were making my face look a little dirty. I took her hand.

"Alana, I want to thank you for the help you've given me. You're a good and loyal friend, and I swear to you that you will never read a bad word about Margaret Bursky that was written by me." Easy enough to promise that. I wasn't going to write any words at all if I could help it.

She looked into my eyes. "I think you're a nice man, Jake. I hope I'm right about that." The water boiled and she poured it through the coffee.

"Smells like French roast," I said.

"Of course," she replied.

We took our coffee into the living room, where one lamp was burning next to the couch. She sat down and patted the cushion next to her. Comfortable couch. I set my coffee down on the coffee table. So did she. The light was softer than in the kitchen. Neither one of us had to be disturbed by the sight of the other's life history engraved on flesh. She put her hand up and touched the back of my neck.

"I think," I said, "that you're a nice woman."

"No," she whispered, "I'm not. I won't fall in love with you. I'll just use you a few times and dump you before you have a chance to dump me. I'm not a fool, and I'm no longer fooled by romance."

Nice speech. It was either true or calculated to put me at my ease. In either case, I lied to myself, it got me off the hook. She was unbuttoning my shirt. She slid both hands inside to my chest, then moved one around to my back. She leaned slowly and smoothly back against the arm of the couch, pulling me on top of her. The hand that had been stroking my chest was working its way down inside the waistband of my pants.

— 8 —

I woke about four in the morning and couldn't drop off again. Alana was snoring slightly. I sat up on the bed and realized I wanted to be home, so I dressed quietly and left her a little note saying I would call her soon.

Tigris and Euphrates were irritated with me for being gone so long. Euphrates glared at me and grunted nasally, a kind of *inhh* sound he makes when he complains. Sometimes, when the sound doesn't quite make it out between his shiny black lips, the complaint degenerates into a silent meow. I gave them some breakfast and decided that I needed a hot bath.

While the tub was filling I hunted through my canned goods. Aha. I did have one. Nothing like a hot bath and a can of smoked oysters for whipping up a little creative thought, even at five in the morning. I opened the can and Euphrates left his breakfast in mid-chomp, his eyes glowing with greed. I carried the can, a fork, and a saucer into the bathroom and put them all up on a high shelf while I undressed. Euphrates danced around my feet, whipping up his adrenaline and grunting at about the rate of one grunt a second.

He got half a dozen oysters on the plate, on the floor. The rest, I told him, were mine.

Roughly half an hour after I stepped into the tub, the phone rang in the bedroom. It rang because I had forgotten to take it into the bathroom with me. I climbed out of the tub, dripped and puddled my way to the phone, carried it, still ringing, back to the tub, submerged again and picked up the receiver.

"Will you accept a call from Isaac Samson?" the operator wanted to know.

My father, who lived in Chicago, always called me collect. He had a theory that went like this: "If you can still afford to take a collect call, you're not starving to death and I don't have to worry about you."

"Hi, pa," I sighed. "Do you know what time it is here?"

"Sure. You think I'm a dummy? Two hours different. I wanted to catch you before you went to work." Pause. "You are working, aren't you?"

"Yes, pa. How's Eva?" Eva was my stepmother. He'd married her a few years back, two years after my mother died and he'd given up trying to run the grocery store without her. He lived in cheerful retirement with Eva, who was about sixty-five and looked ten years younger.

"She's fine, thank God. You wanta talk to her? Hey, Eva, the boy wants to talk to you." I could have done without it, since I never had anything to say to the woman, but my father's calls always required stoicism.

"Jake? How are you?"

"Fine, Eva, fine."

"So, are you dating anyone?"

"No. Not really. No one special." She tut-tutted.

"All because of that tsatske you had before." She meant my ex-wife, and she didn't mean her well. "I could see from the beginning she was no good." She hadn't known her from the beginning, only during the last year when we visited Chicago. "I hope you're a little smarter about women now. Your father wants to talk to you." The two of them were so much alike in their hit and run conversation that it seemed as though they'd been married for fifty years.

"So? Are you listening to your stepmother? You're not a kid anymore, you know."

"I know, pa."

"So I suppose you have to get ready for work now? You got a job?"

"Yeah. I got a job."

"And what are you doing this time?"

I sighed. "It's kind of complicated, pa."

"Complicated." He snorted his contempt. "Nothing is ever complicated, Jake. Complicated is something you say when you don't want to tell. It's not even a real English word." My father's concept of proper language was largely judgmental. "Something looks complicated, you look again until it looks simple. Now tell me."

"Research, pa." I was laughing. "I'm doing some research for some magazine articles."

"Magazines? Now he's a writer?"

"Listen, pa, I got to go to work. I'll write soon."

"Sure, sure . . ."

After only another three or four minutes at long-distance prices, we all managed to say good-bye to each other. I ran some more hot water and collapsed neck-deep in the warmth spreading over my legs, belly, and arms.

A little folk wisdom to start the day. Could be worse, I thought. I could have been forced to listen to the bullshit platitudes of my own generation instead of the true ones of theirs. You look again until it looks simple. . . .

In this case, though, I couldn't see any simple answers. Unless the answer was Billy. Maybe she'd rejected him. The last coherent thought I remember having before I dozed off was that I wasn't a kid anymore.

I woke up two hours later, shivering with cold, got out of the tub, toweled briskly, wincing at the agony in my stiff neck and lower back, and got dressed. I made and ate breakfast and fed the cats again. It was still too early to go to the meditation center, so I called Hal at home to find out if he'd learned anything about the case yet. He had. There wasn't much doubt that it was homicide. A few items of what the police call physical evidence. Signs of a struggle. They'd found a little plug of the dead woman's hair on the deck and a fresh, corresponding wound on her head. Her blouse was torn at the shoulder, but there were no scratches to indicate she'd torn it on a rock when she'd fallen. The redwood table was slightly out of place, a crescent of less faded wood showing at one side of the round base and a corresponding faded area partly covered by the base. They'd also noticed that the coffee cup was slightly chipped and had found the chip on the deck along with some traces of the spilled coffee. Most interesting of all, there had been no fingerprints on the cup. None. Not even Margaret Harley's. Someone had picked up the cup, wiped it clean, and put it back on the table. There was a pretty good thumbprint on the fruit bowl, but the police hadn't been able to trace it yet.

I thanked Hal and said I'd keep in touch. It was nearly nine o'clock, but I remembered a sign on the meditation center door that said they didn't open until eleven.

Rebecca might be in her office. I wanted to know if the police had followed up on finding her name in Bursky's address book. Bursky. I decided not to call her Margaret Harley anymore, at least not in my thoughts.

Rebecca's realty company was in Oakland, near Lake Merritt. I didn't call. It was just a few minutes from my house.

She wasn't there. There was only one person in the office, a woman, and when I asked about Rebecca she looked at me with her face squeezed up in a "should I tell you, it's really very puzzling" look. She decided in my favor.

"It was really strange," she said. "The radio was on, and all of a sudden she stood up and stared at it like she'd heard something terrible and went tearing out of here like a crazy woman. I've had it on ever since, but I can't figure out what it could have been."

"May I?" I asked, striding to the radio and turning it up. A few odds and ends of news stories and then there it was, being repeated, an update.

"No word yet on injuries in that campus fire. The firefighters are still trying to get it under control. About all we've been able to find out is that it started in Chandler Hall, in one of the offices of the political science department. We'll keep on it and keep you informed. . . ."

I was out of there and in my car in maybe three seconds. I had to be sure I still had a live client.

Half a mile was as close as I could get by car. The police had barricaded the roads close to the campus and only emergency vehicles were getting through. A campus is a crowded place, and they weren't taking any chances.

The smoke was visible for some distance, a dark blot on the sky. By pushing rudely through the mob I was able to get fairly close to Chandler. Smoke was gushing black and smelly out of three second-story windows in a row. I didn't see Rebecca anywhere. The whole area stank of melting plastic. I didn't argue when a line of cops pushed us all back. I was still in the front row.

The fire was at the political science department's end of the second floor, but I couldn't be sure whether one of the windows was Harley's.

I turned to the young man standing next to me. He looked like a student. Short-cropped hair and straight-legged jeans and pale yellow shirt. A vision of the eighties, via the fifties. He was watching the fire with his eyes half-shut and his mouth half-open.

"Do you know what offices those are?" I pointed at the smoking windows.

"Sure." He was half-smiling. "The one in the middle, that's John Harley's office. The ones on either side, I don't know."

"What about Harley?" I persisted. The kid narrowed his eyes even more and closed his mouth. He barely opened it again to speak.

"You a friend of his?" Jesus, I thought, what movie did he get that line out of?

I clenched my jaw heroically and muttered something incoherent but macho-sounding.

The kid turned his eyes back to the firefighting scene. "I hear he got out okay."

Maybe I blinked because the next time I looked for the kid he was gone. Funny, I thought. Usually the people who push their way to the front line at a disaster stick around until it's all over.

Another hour passed before the fire was completely out and most of the crowd had scattered. That's when I saw Harley, trying to push his way into the building. Not even singed, from what I could see. But when I got up closer to him I could smell the smoke on his clothes. He was clutching his briefcase.

They wouldn't let him near his office. It wasn't safe yet and there were things that had to be done before anything could be touched. That's what they told him. They said he should check back with them in an hour. I offered to buy him a cup of coffee. He fumbled along after me.

"God!" he kept repeating. "God! I couldn't get anything out of there. I don't know what's been destroyed, what's left. I almost got caught. It was coming from two directions at once."

I got him calmed down enough to tell his story coherently.

"Those two rooms on either side of me. The storage rooms. It was sudden. This roaring sound and heat, and then I heard someone scream 'Fire,' and then my walls, on both sides of me, they were on fire and I barely made it out the door. Someone tried to get me, Samson." His thin lips bit off those last words like a parakeet nipping at cuttlebone. I cocked my head, still listening to him. "I'm not sure, but I think a few minutes before the fire, I heard someone go into those rooms. First one side and then the other."

"Why would anyone want to get you, Harley?" I felt, somehow, that the question did not sound sincere.

"Isn't it obvious?" he asked. "I have a strong liberal reputation. Apparently they think I'm dangerous to their movement." He patted his briefcase and stuck out his chin, a martyr to righteousness and what he saw as his own fame. "They were probably after this. My manuscript. It's going to be the definitive work—"

I didn't care. "Did Rebecca find you?" I interjected. He looked at me, and I saw a flash of anger in his eyes.

"Yes. Can you imagine her, actually coming here?"

I shrugged. "She was worried."

He nodded, accepting the inevitability of her devotion. "I should have called her, I suppose, if only to keep her away. I made her leave." I didn't comment on that but told him I needed to go through his wife's effects and see if the police had left anything that might be informative. We agreed that I would meet him later at his house.

I left Harley with the cops, who wanted to know why he thought someone might start a fire in his department. There wasn't much question but that it was arson. Everything flammable in the two storerooms had been piled against the walls connecting with Harley's office and doused with gasoline. The arsonists had even, obligingly, left their gallon cans behind.

An hour after that the police and several radio and TV stations received a communiqué from CORPS claiming responsibility for the fire and saying that they meant it as a message to all the corrupters of American youth.

Everyone rushed to broadcast the news. But within a couple more hours there was a second message, also from CORPS, denying that it had anything to do with the fire.

9

The first announcement was broadcast right around the time I got to the Earthlight Meditation Center. I walked in just in time to hear it on Billy's office radio. He held up his hand for silence, and we listened together. The announcer liked the word *communiqué*. He used it three times.

Billy smiled ruefully at me and shook his head. "A little excitement on the campus, huh?" He paused, shook his head again, and then gave me a politely inquiring look. "What can I do for you today?"

I smiled back at him. "I've been hearing some stories about you, Billy." I hadn't heard much, but I wasn't going to tell him that.

"Oh?" he said. No expression at all. Not hostile, not scared, not even puzzled. Just blank.

"About your relationship with Margaret Bursky."

He rubbed his eyes, long-suffering. "What is it you want? I have work to do, you know." He turned away, heading toward a bank of file cabinets.

"Just hold it, Billy. I want to talk to you," I barked. I was gambling that he'd respond to that kind of treatment. He did. He skidded to a stop and turned around.

"Who the hell are you, anyway?" He was trying to snarl. He was also trying to cover up, with bravado, the fact that he had followed orders and stopped walking away from me.

"I want to know why you lied to me yesterday. About your friendship with Margaret Bursky."

He stopped trying to snarl and looked merely offended. "I don't have to answer your questions. I think you should leave."

I tossed him my best wolfish grin. "Come on, Billy. Maybe the police don't have to know how close you were to the woman."

That got to him. "You can't blackmail me, you bastard. I told them we were friends." And now he had told me that the police were already onto the meditation center.

I patted the air with my hand in a calming gesture. "Hey, relax, Billy. It just seems to me that if you knew her all that well you could tell me a lot about her. Anonymously."

His expression changed again, this time to a funny, sly look that, taken to its extreme, usually indicates a kink in the brain. Cool people like me, we don't let people catch us looking that way. The look faded quickly, but I knew he was playing a game with me. I gazed at him steadily.

His eyes slid away from mine. "We were friends. That's all." The slyness was deliberate, I guessed. He was trying to give me the impression that he was hiding something. I knew that ploy. Artie Perrine used it every time he bluffed at poker.

"That's what I figured," I told him, enjoying the quick wash of disappointment that crossed his undistinguished hairy features. "After all . . ." I narrowed my eyes and gave him a look that fell just short of disgust. He was appropriately insulted.

"As a matter of fact, we were very good friends," he said huffily.

I raised my eyebrows and pursed my lips. "Then why didn't you tell me?"

"What makes you think I tell everyone everything I know?" he snapped. I couldn't believe how childish this guy was. "I don't see that it's anyone's business." His voice broke. "It's so hard to talk about." He shook his head and covered his eyes. "I just can't. Not yet. Maybe in a few days."

I gritted my teeth. "Perhaps one more question?" He looked up at me, the picture of crucifixion. "Her therapy group. Do you know the name of the therapist?" He shook his head, turned, and walked slowly toward his desk. If he knew anything at all, I couldn't let him off the hook for "a few days." I had an idea.

"One more thing?" He raised his shoulders in resignation. "Have a meal with me and just give me your impressions of the woman—as a close friend." He stood up a little straighter and turned to face me. He was smiling. I should have known from the beginning that the way to this guy's information, if he had any, was through his stomach. I suspected there'd been times in his life when a free meal was the only kind he could get. The love of handouts was habit-forming.

"Of course," he said. "Tomorrow night? By then . . ." He raised his shoulders again, implying that he might, in another thirty hours or so, have his emotions under control. I had the feeling they never had been.

"I'll call you," I said. He returned to his desk, looking cheerful. I went to the bulletin board and copied down the names and phone numbers of the four therapists who'd pinned their cards there. One in Berkeley, three in Oakland. With any luck, I could see them all that day and squeeze in a visit to Harley's, too. Since I was in Berkeley, I called the nearest one first. His name was Harold Feldman. I told him I was doing a magazine article and would like to talk to him. His voice and his telephone manner were pleasant, youthful, and nonthreatening.

"What kind of article, Mr. Samson?"

"I'd rather discuss it with you in person, if you can find the time." It's too easy to cut someone short on the phone. Even though face-to-face visits would mean time wasted on dead ends, they also more than doubled the odds of coming up with something. Feldman thought it over.

"Tell you what, Mr. Samson. I've got a free hour right now. But there's only about forty-five minutes of it left."

I told him that would do and I'd be right there.

Feldman plied his practice in a house converted to several small professional offices. There was a lawyer, another therapist, a family counselor, and a consultant, whatever that might mean. He responded immediately to my knock on his half-open door, leaping up from behind a desk and coming to meet me halfway. He shook my hand. A little guy, about my age, but wide-eyed like a kid. Not many lines on his face. Bright blue kid eyes, pinkish tan skin, light brown hair that covered about three-quarters of his head. He looked healthy and he looked like he had a lot of leisure time. We sat in comfortable chairs with no desk between us. Just two pals.

"So, Mr. Samson. What is it you want to talk about?"

I told him what I was after. He looked disappointed and shook his small round head.

"No, I'm sorry, I didn't know the poor woman."

I thanked him, shook his hand again, and left. He'd been startled by my abruptness. I figured he hadn't had very many two-minute sessions.

The second therapist had her office over an antique shop in North Oakland, a couple of blocks past the Berkeley line. I knew I'd met her before, but I couldn't remember where.

"You're Jake," she said, with a kind of wonder.

"Well, yes . . ." Then it hit me. A year or so ago. Rosie had gone out with her for about a month. I'd met her once or twice. But the romance had gone the way those things go sometimes. She'd wanted the whole thing with Rosie; Rosie hadn't wanted the whole thing with her. Her name was Jill. I'd liked her a lot and had been sorry it hadn't worked out.

She hadn't known Margaret Bursky either.

"It was nice seeing you again, Jill," I told her as I got up to leave.

She smiled. A very pretty smile. Rosie had rocks in her head.

"How is she doing, Jake? I see her around sometimes, you know, but we don't talk much."

I chewed my lip. I didn't think Rosie was doing all that great, but I couldn't very well say that. "She's fine. Doing fine."

Jill held out her hand, and I took it briefly in a friendly shake. Life sure was scummy sometimes.

The third one was the one. Oh, boy, was she the one.

She stood about five foot eight. She had long blond Anglo-Saxon hair. Very pale blond. Maybe even farther north than Anglo-Saxon. She had cheekbones that looked like soft triangles, blue gray eyes, and golden skin tinged with pink highlights. She looked like an ice maiden until she smiled. Her lips were full, her teeth were perfect, and there was this dent that appeared magically in her left cheek. Devastating. She also had a long white neck dipping down into her shirt, the shirt unbuttoned to the top of the gentle swell of breast. She was wearing gray tweed slacks and a mauve silk blouse. She damned near stopped my heart.

I'm not normally a total sucker for good looks. I like good-looking women, of course, but beautiful zombies don't appeal to me. I'm not a necrophiliac. This woman was so alive, so warm, she vibrated and pulsed and got all kinds of answering vibrations and pulsations from my blasé carcass. Her name was Iris Hughes. She could have been called nasturtium, and it would have been all right with me.

Margaret Bursky had been in her Thursday night group. And she wouldn't tell me anything else. I thought fast. If she wouldn't talk to Jake Samson the writer, maybe she'd talk to Jake Samson the investigator. I decided to trust her, since there were no witnesses. I admitted that I was working on Bursky's death but didn't tell her who I was working for. Ethics are ethics. I used the word *murder* just to touch things up a bit.

The word hit her pretty hard, but she recovered quickly. "I'd heard that the police thought it might be homicide," she said, ice maidenishly. "But what proof is there?"

"I wouldn't call it proof. But there are some very good indications. Did you like her, Dr. Hughes?"

"Not doctor," she answered absently. "Just a master's degree at the moment. Yes, I liked her. She was a troubled woman and her troubles had caused some bitterness. But she was a good woman. A lost one, Mr. Samson."

"Jake. Do I call you Master?"

She gazed at me for a moment and decided to be amused. "Only if you really want to." She paused. "Maybe she killed herself."

"Hell of a stupid way to do it. She might not have died."

She nodded, still gazing at me, Lord. "Why should I help you, Jake? I'm willing to cooperate with the police as far as I can, but why you?"

I didn't answer, just looked back at her and tried not to wreck my composure on those sharp iceberg eyes.

"The thing is," she continued, "I don't really know anything that would be useful. I certainly wasn't aware of any threat to her life."

"Could I join your group? Get to know some of the people who knew her? I'd drop out again—"

"No."

"Is there any other way I could meet them? I've trusted you enough to blow my cover. You can trust me."

She was thinking. "It is possible that some of the members of the group might be of some help." She was thinking about it hard, studying my face.

"Someone tried to kill her husband today, too," I added. "I don't know who might be next." I didn't really think we were dealing with a mass murderer, but I hoped that implication might push her over the line. It did. She stood up and walked to a file cabinet in the corner, opened a drawer, took out a sheet of paper, and carried it back to her desk.

"This is a list of the names and addresses of the people in the group. I could be coy and go out and get a drink of water or something, but if I'm going to do that I might as well just hand you the list. Should I be expecting the police to visit me, too?"

"Yes."

She pursed her lips. Somehow, on her, it looked good. "If they really want this list, they can get it," she said thoughtfully. "Of course, you're not the police."

"I'm cuter."

She smiled gently. "Do you really think so?" I'd asked for that. Then she took a pen and a piece of paper and began to copy the list. It wasn't very long. She slid it across the desk to me.

Five names, not including Margaret Bursky. Addresses and phone numbers for four of them, address only for the fifth.

"I am trusting you, Jake. If I find out it was a mistake you're going to be in trouble for operating without a license. And for breaking and entering and rifling my files. Clear?"

"Very." I tucked the list in my wallet. "Now tell me, do you like movies?"

She grinned. "You are kind of cute at that. But I can't go out with you." She waved the list at me. "I can't afford to get involved. I can't afford to lose clients. I may anyway, when you start nosing around."

"I don't expect this investigation to last forever," I said stubbornly.

"Okay," she laughed. "Call me when it's over."

I walked down the carpeted stairs wondering how I could get her to change her mind, climbed into my car, turned the ignition key, and sat there stupidly for a moment, listening to the radio.

It was then that I heard the second message from CORPS. The one that said they'd had nothing to do with the fire.

—10—

The denial from CORPS brought me back down to earth, down as far as Harley. It was time to meet him at his house.

Harley was drinking what looked like a whisky and soda. He wasn't holding up well. I noticed the faint smell of smoke still coming from his tweed jacket. He offered me a drink and I turned it down.

"Where did she keep her personal things, Harley?"

My businesslike approach straightened him up a little.

"In her desk, of course. In her room."

"Her own bedroom?"

He flushed slightly. "Sometimes it was that, yes." He led me to it and stood in the doorway. The room held a single bed covered with a blue chenille spread, a nightstand, a reading lamp, a few prints and two Margaret Bursky paintings on the walls, an oval braided rug, a small bookcase, a desk, and an empty easel near the window. One of the paintings was a landscape, the other an unrecognizable mass of primary colors that I liked very much. Both were dated 1970.

I started with the bookcase. Several art history books, a dozen or so books about individual artists, mostly dead ones, complete with color plates, and a few novels of the best-seller variety. Nothing there. I tried the desk. A few snapshots of the happy couple in better times, a lot of odds and ends like old checking statements and check registers, out-of-date auto-insurance policies, a few letters that were years old, a few travel brochures, a file folder that contained tax returns from 1969 to 1972. The kind of detritus everyone collects and forgets to throw away. The only thing I found that was unique to her was an old drawing pad with yellowed pages that contained what looked like studies for a landscape. If there had been anything more significant in those drawers, the police had it now.

The nightstand came next. Nothing in there but a box of tissues and a bottle of aspirin. I tried the closet. Two robes on hangers, one heavy and one lightweight, and one nightgown. A pair of slippers. And something I'd been looking for. The canvas shoulder bag that Alana had described to me. I pulled it out into the light. Harley was still standing in the doorway, watching me. He seemed reluctant to actually enter the room, and I wondered if he ever had.

Alana said the bag had contained notebooks or drawing pads. Not anymore. All I found were half a dozen drawing pencils, two pens, and a couple of those erasers that artists use, the kind that look and feel like silly putty.

"Did the police take anything out of this bag?" I asked Harley, hoping he'd noticed.

"I don't know. I don't think so. Like what?"

"Like sketch pads."

"I didn't notice any of them carrying anything like that."

Well, I thought, that was that. Nothing more to be gained here. I stuck the bag back in the closet and closed the door.

Then I spent half an hour touring the rest of the house, looking at everything that was left of Margaret Bursky. A few more paintings, a few more letters and old photographs in the dresser she shared with Harley, even old shopping lists left in the hall table. When I thought I'd seen all there was to see, I thanked Harley for his time and prepared to go.

"You're leaving?" he asked, following me to the front door. "That's all you're going to do?"

"Nothing more to do, for now," I answered. He didn't want me to leave. He was probably afraid someone would set fire to the house with him in it, and wanted to share the experience. I said I'd keep in touch and escaped to my car.

— *11* —

There was a small shopping center at the bottom of this particular set of hills. I pulled into the lot near a phone booth and took out the list I'd gotten from Iris Hughes. Not very likely that they'd all be at home in the middle of the afternoon, but I thought I'd give it a try.

The first name on the list was Debbi Lawton. That's right, Debbi, spelled with an *i*. She would be young and probably silly in other ways besides the spelling of her name. I guessed she'd be at work. I dialed her number.

"Hello, this is Debbi speaking. I'm not able to come to the phone right now, but if you'll leave your name and number . . ." I waited patiently, listening to the spiel about how she'd really love to talk to me, until the recording talked itself out. Then I left my name and number.

The second name on the list was William Cavour. He was home. He lived in the upper Elmwood district of Berkeley—the kind of area where the neighborhood movie theater runs French and Russian films. Not movies, films.

Much to my surprise, the house wasn't cedar shingle. It was stucco, freshly painted a dark blue with white trim. The front yard looked like it had been done with manicure scissors, and the house looked large. Little round bushes lined the flagstone walk. When I'd called, someone besides Cavour had answered the phone and asked the purpose of my call. I'd told him it was personal. He had put Cavour himself on the line. When he'd heard it was about Margaret Bursky, his voice had chilled noticeably, but he had been polite and had said he would see me.

I pressed the doorbell. Chimes played the first four notes of "Lara's Theme" from *Doctor Zhivago*.

The man who came to the door was of medium height and muscular, with very short-cropped blond hair. He was dressed to show off his muscles. His pants and T-shirt were very tight. He asked for my credentials, and I showed him my letter from *Probe* magazine. Without another word, he led me down a hall and into a really beautiful room.

The ceilings were a good twelve feet high. No aluminum-framed, sliding-glass, cut-a-chunk-out-of-the-wall remodeling had been done here. The original French doors led out to what may well have been the original patio. I never did get a good look at the patio, so I couldn't be sure. And not just the original doors, but the original oak finish. Oiled. On all the woodwork. The forest green walls and yellow oak were a backdrop for the furnishings. Whoever had done this room was not afraid to mix periods and had done it well. The rugs were Oriental and very thick. There were some early Victorian pieces—a large corner cabinet and a desk—that were really early Victorian, with clean lines, sturdy craftsmanship, and the look of well-worn age. Along with that were a couple of items that looked like good copies of medieval stuff: a straight-backed chair that served as side chair for the desk, upholstered in royal blue velvet, and a chest against the wall near the French doors.

Everything else was contemporary, and I knew where I'd seen it before. At a showing of hand-made, artist-designed furniture at the Oakland Museum. The colors were lush, the woods glowed, and the man standing with his back to the doors, silhouetted, walked toward me wearing a smoking jacket that might actually have been Edwardian. With it he wore jeans. His feet were bare.

"Mr. Samson." He extended a firm right hand, looked carefully into my eyes, and invited me to sit on a chair made of brown leather hung from a framework of very hard gnarled wood I couldn't recognize. It was comfortable. He pulled the side chair around to face me.

Cavour's medium-long brown hair, brushed back over the tops of his ears, was just beginning to turn gray, as was his moustache. The lines around his eyes were not deep, but there was the slightest suggestion of crepe on the lids and on his throat above the burgundy ascot. He was somewhere around fifty, maybe older.

He didn't waste any time. "What is it you want to know? And, incidentally, where did you get my name?" He crossed his legs and clasped his long-fingered hands over his denim-covered knee.

"I got your name from Margaret Bursky's personal papers."

He looked skeptical but didn't argue with me. I gave him the story about the magazine piece. While I was talking, the phone rang in another room, twice before it was picked up.

"Very nice," he said when I told him the article would be a positive one. "But I don't see how I can help you with that. I despised the woman."

I must have shown some shock.

He smiled. "Don't look at me that way, Mr. Samson. You and I have both lived long enough to know that dying improves no one's character. I believe in good manners but not to the point of being a hypocrite."

I cocked an eyebrow at him. "I don't communicate well in epigrams, Mr. Cavour."

He laughed out loud, showing beautiful teeth that looked like his own. Then he relaxed. "What do you think? Was she really murdered?"

"Hard to say," I replied. "Tell me why you hated her."

"You're thinking I wouldn't like any woman, isn't that right, Mr. Samson?"

"No. I don't think in stereotypes either."

"Good, because it isn't true. Perhaps I don't like them the way you do, but I pride myself on my feminism." He said it simply, with no hint of oratory. I believed him. "I didn't like Margaret Bursky because she didn't like me. She did think in stereotypes. She was a judgmental, bigoted bitch." He flashed his handsome smile again. "You can print that if you like." The phone rang again. It was picked up after the first ring.

"So she didn't approve of your sex life. Okay, what else?" I was thinking that if what this man said was true, Iris had a regrettable tendency to speak well of the dead.

Cavour quirked an eyebrow and stroked his moustache. "I don't believe you're a writer. Are you a policeman of some sort?"

I shook my head. "Strong and silent, eh? Like a drink?"

As a matter of fact, I thought a drink would be a great idea. He got up and left the room, returning almost instantly.

Then the man who'd answered the door appeared, strode muscularly to the large cabinet in the corner, opened it and revealed a full bar, sink, tiny refrigerator and all. I accepted white wine. Cavour had a brandy in a gigantic snifter. The butler, or whatever he was, was interrupted once in his drink-pouring by the phone. He went immediately to answer it, was gone for only a minute or two, and returned to serve our drinks. I was getting curious about that telephone.

Cupping the snifter carefully, Cavour swirled the brandy. "What is it you're really after?" he wanted to know.

"I want to know about her life. The people she associated with. I want to find out if she was getting back to her art or if she had abandoned it for good. If there's any work of hers to be found, I'd like to find it. I want to get to the people who knew her best and form some sort of picture of the woman. How she lived. Why she died."

He sniffed the brandy but didn't drink any. "All I can tell you is what I learned about her in a group I'm sure you know we had in common, a therapy group. Of course, one is not supposed to tell those secrets. But she's dead, after all, and she seems, surprisingly enough, to have been some kind of public figure." He sipped his brandy. I tasted my wine. It was icy cold and very good. "Let's see . . . her art. She was beginning to work at it again. Once I even saw a sketchbook. Not what was inside it, of course." He snorted. "We weren't that close. But I saw the book itself. She was carrying that canvas bag of hers, and half of the book was sticking out the top."

"Did she ever talk about her husband, her marriage?"

"Never. I didn't even know she was married. She talked only about her past as an artist and her attempts to recapture her ability to work." The phone was ringing again. This time it rang three times. I tossed him a questioning look. "Roger will get it," he assured me. Roger did, in the middle of the fifth ring.

"What was her relationship like with the rest of the group? The two of you didn't get along, but what about the others?"

"I won't tell you by name," he said, sipping again at his now-warmed brandy. I waited. I had finished my glass of wine. Roger reappeared and looked at our glasses. I nodded. He poured me some more wine. The phone rang again as he was leaving the room.

"She didn't approve of one of the women, and the other she seemed to be indifferent to. Of the men, besides me—well, it was odd. She seemed close to this young boy. A student. A very peculiar type. He doesn't like me either."

"Not a very compatible group," I remarked.

"You're right." He laughed. "But there was some interesting counterpoint."

I tried a quick jab. "Just how much did you hate her, Mr. Cavour?"

"Oh, now, Mr. Samson." He shook his head at me. "That's what I thought you were after. As I said, I despised her. But not enough to kill her. I'm able to insulate myself quite well against people like Margaret Bursky, even when I choose to dip a toe in their mud. I like my life just the way it is. Can you imagine me in prison?"

I couldn't. I finished my second glass of wine. I guessed I believed him. When I stuck out my hand, thanking him for his help, he clasped it warmly in both of his.

"Good luck, Mr. Samson. In whatever it is you're doing." He escorted me to the hall. We passed a room where Roger sat, talking on the telephone.

"Yes," Roger was saying, "he has been given your phone number. I think you'll like each other."

I turned to Cavour. "Call boys?" The question was casual and, I thought, nonjudgmental, but he looked at me with distaste. I realized he wasn't having any of that "we're all sophisticates together" stuff. Not from me. He'd been through a war I'd never had to fight.

"Certainly not, Mr. Samson. I run a legitimate dating bureau. Relationship-oriented."

"Seems to be doing well."

He hadn't forgiven me for my lapse of taste, but his manners remained impeccable. "Of course. Many of us prefer equal, non-paying relationships." He opened the door and I went out, feeling like a clod.

I tried reaching the two others whose phone numbers were listed but had no luck. The fifth, someone named Edward Cutter, had no phone number, just an address. I decided to visit him and check him out.

Cutter lived in a run-down four-flat west of Grove Street in South Berkeley. The house was covered with crumbling gray imitation-shingle siding. The yard was trampled dirt with a few dusty and disheveled sections of what used to be a boxwood hedge. The sidewalk was cracked. The wooden steps leading up to the two doors were worn concave and smooth in the middle. There were two door bells next to each door. Three of them had names taped beside them, and none of the names was Cutter. I leaned on the nameless one. A window slid open above my head, and a male voice mumbled, "Who ya looking for?" I raised my eyes to a familiar face. I couldn't tell whether he recognized me, so I played it like poker.

"I'm looking for Edward Cutter."

"Yeah? Who wants him?" He didn't sound hostile, just chilly.

"A friend of Margaret Bursky."

He threw me a suspicious look. "Wait a minute," he said, turning away from the window.

He was my friend from the campus fire. The young guy who'd been standing in the front row. The one who had known it was Harley's office that was burning and hadn't looked at all sad about it.

—12—

The door jerked open in front of me, but he didn't step out of the way. He stood blocking the entry.

I detected a tiny shift in his regard, and then it was gone. He'd remembered me but he wasn't going to admit it.

"I'm Cutter."

"Can I come in and talk to you?"

"No. You can talk to me right here. What do you want?"

I gave him the stuff about the magazine article. If anything, he looked colder, more rock-faced. He was crossing the line into hate.

"Fucking leeches," he muttered, challenging me in direct eye-to-eye confrontation.

I ignored his student demonstration. "I hear you were pretty close to her," I said smoothly.

He was having a little trouble staying focused on my eyes, but he managed. He shook his head. "I don't know who told you that. I didn't hardly know the woman."

I sighed for the days when people who'd gotten as far as college usually knew how to speak the language. "You did know her. Look, can I come in and talk to you? She deserves this article, the recognition—"

He grunted. "What the hell kind of difference is it gonna make to a dead woman? You want anything else?" I started to open my mouth. "You make me sick. I got nothing to say. I didn't know her. Fucking leech." And he slammed the door in my face.

I was elated. Either this guy was just crazy or I'd gotten my first break. He was hiding something. And he certainly fitted Cavour's description of a peculiar young man, a student, who seemed to be close to Margaret Bursky.

It was nearly five o'clock, and I realized I hadn't had any lunch. I was hungry and energized and felt like eating, drinking, and celebrating. Iris? I thought it would be better strategy to take her at her word, at least for a while. There was Alana, but the thought of her made me uncomfortable, as though the strength of my reaction to Iris nullified the mild pleasure of Alana's company. Sometimes it is not easy to be a combination of romantic and nice guy. Not only self-destructive and naïve but also frustrating as hell. Could it be I was meant to marry and have babies?

I dialed Rosie's number. No answer. Maybe Rebecca could tear herself away for an hour or so. I rang her office. She said I'd just caught her and that she'd be delighted to have a drink with me. Even dinner.

She was waiting at the restaurant when I got there, a hamburger and beer place, but a good one. She ordered wine. I went off my diet.

Rebecca looked weary and tense around the eyes, and the corners of her mouth were even more deeply cut.

"Relax," I told her. "He lived through it, didn't he?"

She shrugged dismally. "It's all such a mess. You'd think that at least now we'd be able to"—she stopped short and glanced at me with just a touch of guilt—"you know what I mean."

"Give it time," I said meaninglessly, and took a big bite of my hamburger, following it up with a long wonderful swallow of beer.

"You're looking happy," she accused me.

"Things are moving along."

She leaned back in her chair, making a visible try at relaxation, and studied my face. "You're making progress?"

"I think so."

"Tell me." She leaned forward, eager.

But I wasn't ready to tell her. Telling her would be like reporting to Harley and I wanted more to go on. "Not yet."

"Why not?" She was disappointed, maybe even angry.

"Because I don't have anything definite yet. I'm just following some leads that may go somewhere. And of course there's the fire. The police are going to think it's a pretty strange coincidence, a man's wife gets killed and next thing you know someone's trying to cook him. This is going to stir them up a little for sure."

Her mouth twisted in an ugly grimace. "The police. They would have been just as happy to snoop around a little and let it go at suicide. They've got enough to do. But now, oh, hell." Suddenly there were tears in her eyes. I checked my hand for catsup and reached across the table to grasp her shoulder. The tears didn't spill. She drained her wineglass and ordered more wine.

"Look," I said, "it's going to be okay. I'm going to clear this thing up, and you and Harley can ride off into the sunset. Hey, what are friends for?"

"Don't you mean what is money for?" she shot back at me.

"Rebecca, I'm on your side."

"Terrific. But are you sure you know what you're doing?" She was close to tears again, but I didn't touch her. Sure, she was upset, but I was beginning to feel a little cranky, too.

I let myself go. "Listen, bitch, you want to change your mind about my doing this job, you just let me know. But Harley owes me for the time I've already put in."

She peered at me as though she'd just realized I was sitting across from her. "No. No, that's not what I'm saying." She slumped. "I'm sorry. Of course I want you. I guess I'm just angry with Harley and upset about the fire." I looked unconvinced, so she added one more trouble for good measure. "I'm feeling a little crazy around business, too. It's been rough lately.

There's a deal I've been trying to close, a contingency thing. I need the money, and it's dragging on. If I seem irritable, that's a big part of it." She sighed, deep and long, and reached her hand across the table to mine. I realized then that the woman was close to the edge. It was all just too much for her. All that and business problems, too. And Harley, far from being a pillar of strength, was adding to the strain, helping to drain her of her stamina. She was trying to hold up both of them, and he wouldn't even let her close enough to do it right.

I got the feeling that if I wasn't careful I'd get the blood sucked right out of me. I wasn't about to try to do this job with the pair of them wrapped around my neck. I finished my beer and told her I had to get going. She nodded absently.

"You will tell us, Jake, when you have something definite?"

"I'll report directly to Harley, Rebecca," I said. That wasn't good enough for her, I could tell. She'd said "us"; I'd said Harley. But she let it go, and I left her sitting there chewing her thumbnail and staring into her wineglass.

I made a quick stop at home to water my begonias and feed the cats. Rosie still wasn't there. I put in another call to Debbi Lawton. She was home and invited me to come right over.

Debbi lived in one of those straight-edged apartment buildings erected in the fifties, the kind that hasn't aged gracefully. It was pink stucco with six door bells and a carport that seated six. I rang her bell and she buzzed me in the door. She was second floor left rear.

She showed me into a nearly characterless living room that was saved by human clutter: a pile of magazines in a chair, an unframed poster rolled up and leaning in a corner, dirty ashtrays and rings on the Plexiglas top of the coffee table. The living room windows had a view of the carport roof and the pleasant tree-shaded yard of the house next door.

Debbi gave me a very bright smile and offered me a drink. I asked for coffee. I was a little muzzy-headed from my encounter with Rebecca and needed to sharpen up. I had plans for the evening.

"All I have is instant," she said with a "we bachelor girls are just so flighty" expression on her face. I smiled and said that would be fine. She trotted to the other side of the bar that divided the living room from the tiny kitchen area.

I'd been right about Debbi. She was young. About twenty-three, I guessed, with the slightly dulled bounce of the aging cheerleader. She was pretty, with even features and a body with no apparent flaws. Light brown hair, medium height. I stifled a yawn and told her about the magazine article. She was still smiling, but the smile looked a bit strained. Lord, I thought, what is the idiotic convention that teaches women they must smile constantly? I have never understood. Is it supposed to be attractive? Is it supposed to keep up the morale of the unsmiling male? Or are they baring their teeth?

She brought a tray into the living room. One cup of coffee, one glass of orange juice. She set the tray down in front of me, on the coffee table, and sat next to me on the couch.

"If you want a screwdriver, too," she said, flourishing her glass, "don't be shy."

I mumbled my thanks. The coffee was too hot to drink. Nice apartment, I said. Thanks, she said, but she didn't believe in apartments. She wanted to buy, make an investment. She was looking around. We talked about ourselves for a while. She was one of that new breed of young people coming out of school with business degrees and corporate ambitions. Very steady, very work-oriented, very much a part of what my age group used to call the establishment. It was inevitable. A law of nature. There's always a conservative reaction to radical chaos, and vice versa. She was two years past graduation and two years along in her five-year plan for corralling her own key department at the downtown Oakland office of her home conglomerate. I thought it was all admirable. She thought my work as a writer was admirable. We sat there like two aliens from different galaxies, smiling and nodding at each other in different languages.

I brought the conversation around to Margaret Bursky. I told her I had some of Bursky's private papers and that was where I'd found her name.

She raised both her eyebrows. "Whatever would I be doing in her private papers?" she wanted to know.

"Well, she just mentioned you."

"In whatever context?" The question was friendly, but the skin on her face looked stretched.

"As a member of the group—"

She turned pale. "What group?"

"The therapy group."

She stood up abruptly and walked to the kitchen, ostensibly to make herself another drink. But I caught a glimpse of her averted face. It was flushed. "That's supposed to be confidential," she said in a hard, tight voice.

"I assure you," I said in what I thought might be a corporate manner, "that this article concerns itself only with Margaret Bursky."

"Well, I don't see why!" she flashed at me. "What was so damned wonderful about her anyway?" She marched back into the living room with her second screwdriver and faced me squarely, free hand on her narrow hip.

"She was a fine artist."

"Hah!" She swallowed a whole lot of orange juice and vodka. "She was a dirty old woman. She had no business messing with men half her age. You want to know about her? I'll tell you about her. Always so damned prissy and mealymouthed. Like she'd never even heard of sex. And all the time she was leading him around like—"

"Him? Who?" I interjected. "Who was she leading around? Billy?"

She stared at me. "Billy? Who's Billy? I'm talking about Ed. Eddie Cutter." She practically spat the name at me.

My coffee had finally cooled. I drank some. "They were lovers?" I asked.

She studied my face, her eyes narrowing. "I don't know." Her voice was bitter. "How would I know? They certainly weren't talking about it if they were. And they certainly weren't about to tell me."

I ruminated. It was not easy to ruminate in a small space filled with passion, but I ruminated anyway. To Alana, the woman had been sexless. To Debbi, she was a sex-mad hag. Once, to the art world, she'd been a creative, innovative painter. Now, to a middle-aged gay gentleman, she was a narrow-minded bigot. Who the hell was she? Probably all of them. I guessed, if you'd asked four people about me, you'd come up with four different references, too.

As I ruminated, Debbi regained her control.

"Sorry I blew up, Mr. Samson. May I call you Jake?" Some of that old smile was back. I smiled, too. "It's just that some people seem to think that being an artist excuses anything. Anything at all." I nodded sympathetically. That was certainly true. And there were the posturing nonproducers who stretched that premise to its limit. But I had often thought that if you were cursed with a creative compulsion and the insecure life it could bring, you maybe had the right to a little leeway.

I stayed another fifteen minutes, by the end of which she was working on her third screwdriver and flirting heavily. An old-young woman-girl, angry, bewildered, and stuck in her own contradictions. Trying to solve her own puzzle and ashamed, apparently, that she was getting help from a therapist to do it.

—*13*—

Dusk had given way to full dark when I drove back to Edward Cutter's apartment building. I parked just down the street on the other side and began to watch for signs of life at his windows. A light was on in the front room. I thought I saw a shadow of movement across one of the drawn shades, so I settled down to wait.

About an hour later the light went out. A few minutes after that, Cutter burst out the front door, climbed into an old battered blue Chevy two-door and drove off.

When he'd turned the corner, I got out of the car and approached the house, reconnoitering. I was carrying a glass cutter and a tire iron, the cutter in my pocket and the prying tool tucked inside my jacket under my arm. Only one of the other apartments showed light from the front, the second floor west. Cutter's apartment was second floor east. I strolled up the driveway, casually, like I belonged there, and around to the back of the house.

The place was a burglar's dream. No lights at the back. Precarious-looking wooden porches, roofed and shadowed, stretching across both stories. There was music coming from a well-lighted house across the back fence, but no people were in sight. I squinted up at what had to be Cutter's back door and could just barely see that there was a window next to it.

This was as good a time as any. I headed up the creaky wooden stairs to the second-floor porch.

The upper pane of Cutter's back window had been broken and patched with plywood. That was good and bad. I wouldn't have to deal with any tricky window locks, but it was going to take some time to get the plywood off.

I jammed the prying end of the tire iron down inside the frame and began to push at the wood, nailed from the inside, very slowly and gently. Splintering wood makes a hell of a noise.

The wood itself wasn't the problem, though. The silly fool had nailed half-inch plywood with two-and-a-half-inch spikes. Careful as I was, a couple of those nails squawked like chickens giving birth.

Finally the bottom of the plywood was free and the sides loosened enough for me to reach in and unlock the bottom half of the frame. When I pulled my hand back out again, I ripped my index finger open on one of the exposed nails. Blood dripped on the sill. I didn't bother to wipe it up. Cutter would be able to tell someone had been there whether I left some of myself behind or not.

The lower frame was stuck, but I levered it up with the prying tool and crawled inside. Then I unlocked the back door so I could get out fast if I had to.

The flat had the usual layout, with the back door opening into the kitchen. It could have smelled better. The odor was easily traced to a sinkful of dirty dishes. A long hallway led from the kitchen to the living room, with bedroom and bathroom opening onto the hall.

I started in the living room, at the front of the flat. The room was dimly lit by the street lamps outside. There was just enough light to get an idea of the contents of the room. The windows were covered by cracked old shades. No curtains. The usual furniture. A desk. Pictures of some kind, of varying sizes, on the walls.

The stomach flutters that had begun when I was working on the window were now accompanied by a heavy heartbeat and an aromatic sweat. All the signs that tell you when you're doing something dangerous and probably stupid, like burglarizing someone's apartment or falling in love. I had a little talk with myself. Jake, I said, you are bigger than Cutter and probably stronger. He doesn't look like he's ever done much physical work. If he surprised you, you could just punch him out and go.

I aimed my pocket flash at the desk. The first drawer didn't yield much. A savings passbook that showed eighty-eight dollars in the bank; several months of checking statements, all of which showed a consistently survival-level income; a request to register for the draft; a few letters from his mother.

The second drawer was more interesting. It held some leaflets distributed by CORPS. Lots of them. Under those were some old publications from the Save Our Children campaign of a few years back, and some newer stuff put out by the Moral Majority. The guy was on some interesting mailing lists. Down at the bottom of the pile I found some fliers announcing a Nazi party rally in Chicago. And I found a notebook with just a few pages filled that looked like notes or plans. It was hard to tell with a quick glance, since the style was not lucid. I ripped out the pages and stuck them in my pocket. The leaflets I left alone. All that junk is the same.

A car door slammed outside, and a fresh flood of sweat soaked my armpits. I waited. Nothing. Nothing but new and awful thoughts. Maybe all Cutter had to conceal was a crush on a dead woman. Maybe he'd see the faint light of my flash from outside and call the police from the corner liquor store. Credentials from a magazine wouldn't go far in a defense for breaking and entering.

I went through the rest of the drawers more quickly, anxious to work my way toward the back door. No photographs of Cutter and Bursky. No photographs of Cutter wearing a swastika armband or holding an apple pie in one hand and a flag in the other. A picture of his mom. She looked like a nice woman.

There was an appointment calendar on the desk. I took it.

Then I picked my way to the other side of the room and examined the bookcase. Boards on bricks. After hearing him talk, I hadn't been sure he could read, but there weren't many books. One novel, written years ago by a woman who had the idea that superior people had more rights than other kinds of people, including the right to live and prosper. I've never cared much for inferior people myself, but I figured that my ideas about inferiority might not tally with hers. There were a lot of pamphlets written by people I'd never heard of, a few books about World War II, a biography of Joe McCarthy, a few history textbooks, and notebooks that held scribblings from history and political science classes. The notes were sprinkled with question marks, exclamation points, and words like *bullshit*, *commie*, and *fag*. I didn't look to see what he might have done to the history books.

A few newsmagazines, ranging from moderate to very conservative, tossed casually on the couch like throw pillows, completed the intellectual decor. I raised my flashlight to the walls. Several copies of the CORPS fliers I'd seen in his desk were hanging from nails bashed into the damaged plaster, spaced artistically around the room. And two very good reasons why Cutter had not let me come into his apartment to talk to him. Two drawings, unframed and taped to the wall. Apparently he hadn't wanted to punch nail holes in them. One was a portrait, in ink, of Cutter himself. The other was a drawing of the house Margaret Bursky had shared with John Harley. Both drawings were signed MB. I took them down, swept my light briefly around the room, and headed for the bedroom.

Cutter had used a less aesthetic approach in there. The walls were bare. His dresser drawers were unremarkable, except that they smelled about as good as the kitchen. Shirts, underwear, pants, socks. I found a cheap bracelet in with his underwear but I didn't guess it was his. After all, I once found a bra in my sock drawer and I still don't know how it got there. A couple of ties. I looked in the closet. More pants, more shirts, a couple of jackets, some shoes on the floor. I scanned the shelf above the clothes rod. A large paper bag. I brought it down to eye level and looked inside. Sketch pads. Three of them. I opened one and glanced at the first drawing. No signature, but a genuine artist had done it and I knew of only one artist in this case. Besides, the style was very familiar. I stuck the drawings I'd taken from the living room in with the sketch pads, tucked the bag under my arm and decided to get out of there. I closed the back door carefully behind me, tiptoed down the stairs, sauntered around to the front of the building, walked slowly to my car, and took off without the squeal of tires. If I hadn't quit smoking a year back, I would have stuck three cigarettes in my mouth at once.

That was when I began to worry about the effect my burglary might have. Maybe it would stir things up too much, make the waters muddy, send felons fleeing in all directions. The only reason I was bothering to worry about that was because I didn't have to worry any more about getting caught in the criminal act.

The important thing was that I had evidence of Cutter's involvement in the case and I had it in my hands. And maybe, somewhere in the papers I'd taken, I'd get more. The second, and even more important thing was, I'd gotten out with my ass and my freedom intact. I should have felt clever and groovy and macho, like one of those lean fast-talking types in the old movies. But they had never even looked nervous, and I had been terrified during the whole adventure.

I headed straight home with the booty.

—14—

Rosie's truck was out front and the cottage lights were on, so I knocked lightly on her door. I heard her footsteps and Alice's.

"Hi. You alone?"

She nodded. "Come on in. I've got some information for you." She paused and looked me over carefully. "You okay? You look a little flushed. Glittery around the eyes."

"I'm okay, but I'd love a beer." She got me one. I sat down with her at the kitchen table. "I burglarized a house tonight."

"That's more exciting than my news." She laughed. "You tell first."

I told her about Cutter, and about his apartment, finishing up with: "I haven't even looked at the stuff yet." Rosie was pleased. I hadn't seen her look that excited since just before she found out the gorgeous dark-haired "writer" she was seeing was dedicated to group sex and was barely literate.

We decided to look through the spoils together, but first she wanted to tell me what she'd learned.

"It's really only a sidelight on Bursky's character," she said modestly, "but the name was familiar and I remembered where I'd heard it before. A friend of mine used to work for a feminist art quarterly down in L.A. It ran out of money and folded a few months ago. Anyway, I called her today and asked her what it was I remembered her saying about Bursky. It turns out they wanted to do an article on her, a kind of 'where is she now' story." I nodded. Apparently Bursky hadn't been forgotten by everyone. "Well, they wrote to her up here, asking if they could talk to her. She wrote back, and she wasn't friendly. She said she wasn't an artist anymore, at least not a working artist, and even if she were, she would not have her name connected with a feminist journal." I made a face. "Yeah," Rosie said. "She said she opposed everything the movement stood for. She used words like *immoral, rabble-rousing* and *antifamily*. She said she was a wife and proud of it, and she didn't see any reason to associate with lesbians and whores. Those are the words she used. Can you believe it?" Rosie was shaking her head in wonder.

"Sure I can," I said. "And that clears up the mystery."

She frowned at me, puzzled.

"She was murdered by a lesbian whore who worked for the feminist art journal."

"Very funny. Let's see what you've got."

We sat side by side on her couch and pulled the largest sketchbook out of the sack. Most of the drawings were portraits. There was a pencil sketch of Alana and one of Harley. The one of Harley was softer-looking than the man himself, with a weaker jawline than he actually possessed. But neither Harley nor Alana had known she was working at her art, so, if I were to believe them, the drawings had been done from memory. I wondered how many of those suspicious looks Harley thought his wife was giving him were actually just the squint-eyed gaze of an artist studying a subject.

I gave Rosie personality sketches of the people I knew as we went along. There were several pencil drawings of Cutter. Even one of Billy that wasn't very successful. I wondered if that was because she didn't know his face as well as those of the others or because she was in love with him and couldn't quite tell what he looked like. But that came under the heading of useless and probably erroneous speculation.

The drawing of Iris, on the other hand, was pretty good. I began to talk about her, and I guess I went on too long because Rosie jabbed me in the ribs and made me turn the page.

"For God's sake, Jacob, we can talk about that later." She was smiling. "Why do you think Bursky gave all this stuff to Cutter?"

"Maybe she didn't want to keep it at home. Didn't want Harley to see it. Some of the faces might have been familiar to him. Like Cutter's. She wouldn't have wanted that. Or maybe she was just shutting her wandering husband out of her life."

The next drawing was a tiny sketch of Cutter's house, just a few lines, really, but recognizable nevertheless. We turned another page and out slipped a CORPS leaflet, the notice of a rally to be held outside Chandler Hall the week before her death. Why would she be carrying a thing like that around with her? Even with what Rosie had learned about her, I was having trouble believing that Margaret Bursky could go along with a group like that.

But then, what the hell was she doing with a guy like Cutter? Not just a kid but a nasty, dangerous kid who was maybe involved with even nastier and more dangerous grownups.

And what about CORPS' connection with the fire at Harley's office? Did they do it or didn't they? Was it a political gesture or were they really out to kill Harley? I passed on these questions to Rosie. She said she'd be happy to come up with some answers for a year's free rent. If she came up with the right answers, I told her, she could have a year's free rent. But I guessed I'd rather come up with the answers myself, so how about a race?

"Look, Nero," she snarled, "stop eating that orchid and listen to me. Either I'm working for you or I'm not."

"Very well, Archie, you may consider yourself an employee."

"I'm terribly glad to hear you say that, dear Mr. Poirot."

"Not at all, my dear madame Marple."

"Gosh, Dad, I sure hope we can clear this thing up."

"Don't worry, Ellery, with your brains and my connections as a ninety-two-year-old policeman. . . ."

We turned another page of the sketchbook, and another. Two more portraits, of men I didn't think I'd seen before. Except that one of them, a very rough sketch, kicked up some little memory. I stared at it for a good thirty seconds. Rosie waiting patiently. Then I knew who he reminded me of. The other new guy in the meditation group. Charles. The one with the ulcer. Or at least it looked like him. I couldn't be sure.

After that, we came to the blank pages. I picked up the book and shook it. No more fliers. The smaller sketchbooks yielded nothing much: a drawing of the Earthlight Meditation Center building was the only one I could place, and the rest looked like studies or exercises. There was nothing else in the bag. I put the books back inside of it and took the meeting notes and calendar out of my pockets. We started with the calendar. There were appointments with a lot of initials and a couple of names I didn't recognize, most often someone named Frank. And there were several meetings with MB. I skipped through the book to the date of her death. He either hadn't had or hadn't written down an appointment with her that day. I didn't expect any little reminders to "set fire to the PS department," and I didn't find any.

We turned to the pages I'd ripped out of his notebook. They seemed to be personal notes, a spotty little diary about his political life. I should have known a bunch like CORPS wouldn't have someone actually writing down the minutes of their meetings.

There were no more than a dozen barely legible, badly misspelled, and heavily abbreviated pages. No dates or anything like that, and only initials for names. Initials yet. The kid was playing at spy. But those few pages held quite a bit of information, even if I still didn't know enough to decipher it all.

We read through the pages once, quickly, and I filled Rosie in wherever I could. Then I took out my own notebook and began to organize the scribbles.

First heading: what seemed to be names, represented by single initials. I listed all the initials, starting with the two that I thought might connect with the two full names on Cutter's calendar: *F,* maybe for Frank, and *A,* maybe for Arthur. Then there was an *H,* a *J,* a couple of *S*'s, an *R,* a *B,* a *D.* Of course, I couldn't be sure the initials all stood for names. *F* could stand for fire, *R* for rally, and *H* for hellfire, for all I knew. We decided to go back to them after we'd made a few more notes.

Second heading: place names. King Street was mentioned. That was the street Cutter lived on. And Chandler. Chandler was mentioned several times. Various other campus and Telegraph Avenue locations—restaurants, coffeehouses, street corners. He had met *F* several times at Telegraph and Dwight, at the tiny triangular park, a little island of dope dealing and bad music.

The only other important place name was the name of the street where the Harleys had lived. Virgo Street. Bursky was becoming more incomprehensible to me every minute. I already knew they were pretty well acquainted, but to give that crazy her address? I couldn't believe a sane woman would do it. I was beginning to think that maybe she had killed herself. But the address was one of the later entries. It wasn't something he'd known all along.

Okay, so those were the names and the places. Now I wanted to connect them with events. The first entry had to do with a meeting, group unnamed. The contributions of three people were mentioned, *M, F,* and *J. J,* it appeared, said it was time to do something really "sicnifigant," something that would attract a lot of attention. This information was followed by the notation,

"F—F was worried about the plan. *J* said we could always deny it. Why should we?"

"Fire?" Rosie wondered. "And someone with the initial *F* was worried about that idea?" I thought that sounded reasonable. And CORPS had denied setting it, after someone had claimed responsibility for it in the group's name. Cutter? Possibly. The notes made it sound that way.

Then *J* ordered *F* to go check out Chandler. This was followed by the notation, "*M*—said already checked out Chandler." *F* said he would do it anyway.

It wasn't too hard to figure out what was being discussed. But was this *M* Margaret Bursky?

That seemed to be all there was to that particular conversation. Another entry followed half a blank page. The character lineup was *M*, *F*, and *J*. This time, *F* had apparently come to see *M* at King Street. Margaret? At Cutter's house?

F said he'd checked out Chandler. Then, "*F*—told *M* he was still worried, *F* too dangerous and be careful. What a jerk. *F* said *J* going out of town, *F* in charge. Shit. Why not me?"

This last seemed to pinpoint *M* as "me"—Cutter himself. If that were so, Bursky wasn't in it yet. It was possible that Cutter had, indeed, gone so far as to give himself a code initial. I wouldn't have been surprised if he'd referred to himself as 007.

There was more complaining about not being left in charge. Then there was a full blank page followed by a little story about *M* and *M*. *M* told *M*—Cutter told Margaret?—about *F* and "*M* got all upset." After that, there was a speculation: "Why should *M* care anyway? She ought to help!"

Rosie and I looked at each other. "She" could be Margaret Bursky. Not liking the idea of setting her husband on fire even if he was philandering.

"What if she threatened to tell the police?" Rosie asked. I wondered the same thing myself.

There were two full pages of rambling stuff about how the corrupters were trying to destroy American institutions, then another break. I couldn't see any immediate significance about the next few pages, just *M* talking to an *S*, an *A* and a *B* about *F*, at three different locations and at three different times. I got the impression he was drumming up enthusiasm for *F*—probably fire—and against *F*—probably Frank, the guy who'd been left in charge. I couldn't tell, in all the confusion of Cutter's mind, whether he'd had any luck at all. There was some babble about more meetings with *F* at Dwight and Telegraph, with *F* passing on some incoherent orders about protesting and picketing and leaflets.

Cutter saw somebody named *R* somewhere on Telegraph Avenue and said it was "funny *R* pretended to not know me." I couldn't imagine what that could be about, and it probably didn't matter. The pages were full of odds and ends that had oozed out of Cutter's mind to no apparent purpose. Things like "*D* called me again some people cant take a hint I guess." I thought of poor Debbi, who might have been the one who couldn't take a hint.

Then he wrote, "went to Virgo to see *M*. Ha! It wasn't easy."

The item wasn't dated, any more than any of them were. What wasn't easy? Did he have to be so damned cute? Was he saying he'd killed her or sacrificed himself by going to bed with her? Or that he had convinced her it would be fun to cremate her husband?

The last notation said "*S*—watch out for him." Could be Samson.

Rosie and I talked things over for a while. From what was in the notebook, it looked pretty good for Cutter setting the fire—"*F* said be careful"—and giving the group public credit for it which was later rescinded by the higher-ups.

His reasons for going against the group policy could have been purely political or what passed for political in his mind: the desire to take credit for a protest against Harley's politics and his corruption of American youth. Or they could have been personal. Harley was unfaithful to his wife and Cutter had some kind of attachment to that wife and wanted credit for avenging her.

The police should be tipped off somehow, I reasoned, but I was reluctant to get them on Cutter's trail just yet. They seemed to be a day or so behind me on the Bursky death, and I preferred to keep them that way.

Rosie said I couldn't do it, couldn't play it that close to the chest with these nuts running around. No telling what they'd do next. At least if I tipped the police they could keep an eye on Cutter. If they had any spare eyes. I tried another idea on Rosie. First thing in the morning, I said, I would make copies of the notebook pages and send the originals to the cops. That would delay them for a day and give me a little more time with my prime suspect, but I'd still be passing on what I had.

I admitted the plan was dangerous. If I were a cop, I'd bust my ass for it. Withholding evidence in a murder case, not to mention operating without a license. Not to mention breaking and entering. Quite a list. But ten thousand dollars was a lot of money, and things were beginning to break. And I hadn't had this much fun in years. Besides, I was a writer, I told myself. This was my story.

I'd find a way of dealing with all those details when the time came, I was sure. Rosie looked doubtful, but then Rosie is a skeptic. I changed the subject by telling her I'd seen her old friend Jill that afternoon.

She nodded and changed the subject back again.

"Tell the police now," she insisted. "He's dangerous. How would you feel if someone else died because you kept this to yourself?"

We compromised. I would call the cops in the morning and tell them what I was sending them. Anonymously and without using Cutter's name.

I hate it when other people are right.

—*15*—

Next morning I made copies of the diary pages at a place up near the campus, printed Cutter's name at the top of the first page of the originals, stuck them in an envelope, and mailed them to the Berkeley police. From a Berkeley mailbox.

After that I called them from a Berkeley telephone booth. Anonymity, I reasoned, might as well include operating from a town I didn't live in.

The cop who answered the phone tried once to get my name, gave up, and listened to what I had to say. Which wasn't much. Just that I was mailing them some material written by someone connected closely with the campus fire. Nothing about Bursky. They could figure that out for themselves.

What I felt like doing then was wandering around, having

another look at the Harley house, having another look at the charred campus building, turning my mind loose, and hoping some connections would come clear.

But what I did was wander over to King Street, to Cutter's apartment building. A return to the scene of my crime.

His car was nowhere in sight. I parked, walked up to his front door, and rang the nameless bell. No answer, but maybe he was playing hard to get. I strolled around to the rear and climbed the stairs to his door quietly. No sign of life. The plywood had been knocked back into place, but somehow, in the process, he'd broken the lower pane. Clumsy. I banged on the door for a while and finally conceded that he probably wasn't home.

My next step required a decision that was giving me some trouble. The funeral. The cops were sure to have someone there, and showing up wouldn't do much for my low profile. But at the same time I had the same reason they did for being there: the possibility of learning something new.

I sat in my car thinking it over for a while, hoping Cutter would show up and make the decision for me. If I was busy talking to him, I couldn't very well go, could I?

So I waited and let my mind skip around among the suspects. Cutter. He certainly looked like the best bet, but there were still other possibilities. There was Billy, although I doubted if he could organize a trip to the Laundromat. Debbi. A pretty respectable type, but the façade covered a passionate soul. And it seemed to me that any woman who was hot for Eddie Cutter was capable of almost any insanity.

A lot of people could have killed Margaret Bursky or at least could have wanted to. Including her husband. Including Rebecca. Including, maybe, someone who hadn't even come into it yet. I was beginning to wonder if maybe I was in over my head.

Sure, I knew a lot more than I had a day ago, but a collection of facts is only a collection of facts.

Cutter made my decision for me, after all, by failing to show up. I went to the funeral.

There were only a couple of cars there ahead of me that I recognized: Harley's and Alana's. A chubby guy who looked like he could eat lunch on a coffin ushered me into the elegant foyer, down a short passage, and into a small room with a couple dozen folding chairs facing a closed coffin and a dais. Harley was sitting in the front row looking mournful. I nodded to him but sat down one row back, next to Alana. She gripped my hand briefly. Her nose and eyes were red. I wondered if I should say something about seeing her again but I decided not to. After all, she had said she wouldn't fall in love with me and would dump me before I dumped her. No obligation to say or do anything.

Billy came in, looking brave, followed by three people I didn't know who seemed to be together. Evan, the meditation group leader, arrived and took the empty seat on the other side of Alana. Then came Iris, just ahead of a tall, authoritative-looking, cadaverous man who I guessed was either the mortician or the minister. Iris sat in the row behind mine. The tall man positioned himself at one end of the back row.

No one else showed up until, right at the stroke of eleven, the real mortician entered the room with the real minister, who advanced to the dais. So the tall man was either a friend of the family or a cop, and he looked more like a cop than any of the other people I didn't know. I tried to avoid looking at him and tried to pretend I wasn't avoiding looking at him. I would have preferred looking at Iris, but she was behind me.

Evan was murmuring something I couldn't catch to Alana when I felt a light touch on my shoulder and turned halfway around, just enough to catch Iris's breath on my ear when she whispered "Hi." Then she sat back and we all listened solemnly to the minister. Harley was crying.

Iris left the instant the service was over, and Alana smiled good-bye and went off with Evan. I saw Billy heading toward me and raised a hand to hold him off for a moment so I could have a word with Harley, who had just had a word with the tall man.

"Who is he?" I asked, nodding toward the tall man's back as he walked toward the door.

"Sergeant Hawkins. Police. I think it's Ralph Hawkins."

The other people I didn't know were standing a few feet away eyeing Harley. I assumed they were waiting to mumble their condolences. "What about them?"

"My colleagues."

"Where's her family?"

"There's hardly any family. A couple of old people back east she cared about, a couple of young ones she'd all but lost touch with." He glanced toward the door. "I have to go talk to Hawkins now."

I didn't let him go. "What about?"

"He said they had an anonymous tip this morning about the fire." My call, I thought. "He said the caller gave them a name, and they want to know if I've ever heard of the man."

"A name for the arsonist?" We weren't talking about my call, after all.

"Yes. I have to go. I'll be at my office later if you want to talk to me."

"I do," I said. I needed to find out more about that call. Someone else had dropped a tip to the police that morning. Rosie flashed through my mind, but I dismissed the thought. We'd made an agreement, and I knew she would stick by it. I reflected that maybe someone in his own group had done it, hoping to take the pressure off CORPS and put it on an individual.

Harley left and Billy ambled over to join me. We left the chapel together.

"When do you want to talk to me?" he asked. Translation: When's the free meal?

"How about lunch, right now?" He agreed, but he didn't look terribly pleased. Probably counting on dinner.

We met at a restaurant he suggested, a fondue place near the campus. He ordered the steak and a half bottle of burgundy. Not the house burgundy either.

"You're on an expense account, right?" He smiled innocently. I grunted something affirmative. "Now," he said, sighing contentedly and settling back with his first glass, "what can I tell you?"

"What was your relationship with Margaret Bursky? How did you feel about her?" The question was abrupt, and he wasn't ready for it. He sighed again, louder, just to make sure I heard.

"You know, Samson, those are two separate questions." I stuck my tongue in my cheek and waited. "You want it straight?" I cocked an eyebrow and nodded, still waiting. He wasn't going to answer without lots of preliminaries. "How did I feel about her?" I sipped my Perrier with a twist of lime, patience incarnate. "I loved her." I looked at him, wondering what was coming next. "What was our relationship? That's a little harder." The waiter, a skinny little guy with black hair and long clean fingernails, brought our fondue. Mine was cheese, because I wanted cheese. With a big pile of sourdough bread. Billy forked a piece of steak into the hot oil and kept it there too long.

"She just didn't see me that way, you know?"

I tossed out what I hoped would be a leading question. "Political differences?"

He shook his head, overcooking another piece of steak. "Not that I know of." He screwed his face into a puzzled expression. "That's an odd question."

"Just wondering. I didn't mean anything by it." Casually, I skewered a hunk of bread and dipped it in the cheese. "By the way, do you like fruit?" I was thinking of the bowl of fruit on Harley's deck. Billy didn't even blink.

"Not with fondue," he said. Then he paused, fiddling with his fondue dish. "You know," he said sadly, "she never told me she was married." The flame under the oil, smothered by his fidgeting, went out. "Damn." He looked around for the waiter, spotted him at the other side of the room, and waved at him. The waiter, serving another table, nodded in acknowledgment.

"No, she didn't tell me anything at all. Just that she wanted us to be friends. I even asked her if there was someone else. She said there wasn't. Billy shot an impatient look across the room at the waiter, talking to a customer. Then my gentle companion did something I would never have expected him to do. He stood up, marched across the room, and tapped the waiter on the shoulder. I couldn't hear what he was saying to the man, but he didn't act friendly. He stalked back to our table, followed by the waiter, sat down, and pointed imperiously at his fondue dish. It was duly lighted, and the waiter left.

Maybe, I thought, Billy could organize a trip to the Laundromat after all. If the Laundromat served food.

"You were saying?" I prodded. His face was still congested with irritation. He slumped back in his chair again and took a deep breath.

"I really loved her. I would have understood if she'd only told me the truth about being married. Although I don't really see what difference that makes."

I lost a piece of bread in the viscous mass of cheddar and fished around for it. "So I guess you were pretty pissed off about the whole thing, huh, Billy?"

He looked shocked. A little drop of oil glistened in his beard. "Of course not! I could never have been angry with Margaret. I told you, I loved her." This man, I was thinking, didn't know much about love.

"So, why are you telling me all this now?" I had talked to him twice before. The first time he'd said he barely knew her. The second time he'd said they were good friends. Now he was saying he had loved her. Maybe the next time I talked to him he'd tell me they'd been lovers for five years.

"Well, I was pretty upset at first, afraid to get mixed up in it. But then the police came to see me anyway. And I don't really have anything to hide. What the heck, Samson, I don't mind being in your article. As someone who was close to her. Someone who kind of loved her from afar. You could mention the meditation center, too. Her story is a story that should be told, and I would be proud to be part of it." Some suspect, I thought. He wants publicity. Then he leaned confidingly across the table. "Listen, Samson, what do you really think about that fire at her husband's office?"

"I think somebody doesn't like him. Did you tell the cops you loved her?"

He looked at me like I'd just said meditation gave you warts.

"I told them we were friends. After all, that's all it amounted to. Friendship. They could see it was hard for me to talk about it, you know?"

"Yeah," I said. "I know." I waved at the waiter and asked for the check.

"About this article," Billy asked, "when will it be printed?"

I shrugged. "Hard to say."

"Well, listen, you, uh, you haven't even asked for my last name. For the article. It's Wolter." He spelled it, and I wrote it down dutifully on the back of a hardware store receipt I found in my pocket.

—16—

Billy was not ruled out completely, but he'd moved way down on the list for the time being. His aggression with the waiter had been surprising; still, I couldn't imagine a killer being so anxious to talk about his private life. And as an unsuccessful lover, at that.

I drove over to King Street again. No sign of Cutter's car yet. I sat there for more than an hour, reading through his diary pages, before I got restless enough to start pawing through my dash compartment looking for something more interesting to read. I found a book of crossword puzzles I'd bought for a friend in the hospital. He'd been released before I'd gotten to see him and I'd been carrying it around ever since. Scratching a little deeper in the accumulated papers and debris, I found a pen. Then I put the diary pages at the bottom of the other papers, closed the glove box, and began to pass the time more pleasantly.

Another two hours and a dozen or so puzzles later, Cutter showed up. I decided just to keep an eye on him and see if the police came to visit. See who else came to visit. Wait for him to go somewhere and maybe meet someone. It was time to meet some of the other characters in his book.

Two more hours passed. I'd gotten there around two and it was now nearly seven o'clock. My legs and back ached from sitting, and I couldn't get up and get out of the car. He might see me. I was getting hungry. I was considering driving down to the corner and stretching my legs when Cutter came out his front door.

Considering that someone had broken into his flat the night before and taken away some items that connected him with arson and homicide, Cutter looked unconcerned. He was wearing the same emotionless expression he'd affected the other times I'd seen him. Or was it an affectation? He didn't check out the street, didn't look around before he got in his car. The perfect automaton. Hitler would have loved him.

I waited until he'd driven almost all the way up Alcatraz to Grove before I started my car and began to follow him. He turned left on Grove, heading north. At Ashby he turned right. He was working his way east, toward the campus.

Sure enough, he was on his way to University Avenue. Then he cut over to the north side of campus. I was a block behind him when he parked on Euclid and got out of his car. I swung past him and parked in a red zone. When he crossed onto the campus grounds, I got out of my car and started after him on foot.

I've never done a lot of tailing, and it's pretty tricky. If the guy doesn't look behind him, you're okay. If he knows your face and is worried about being followed, and has half a brain, it's damned near impossible. But Cutter never turned around. He just kept on marching down the campus paths. I wondered if we were headed for a demonstration.

We walked for a while. A lot of it seemed to be uphill, and I was beginning to realize that I could be in better shape. I didn't get tired. I just knew I was walking. He turned up the steps to the Greek Theater, the giant amphitheater donated to the university by a newspaper mogul. I'd been there only a couple of times before, once for a country-western concert.

Cutter went through the turnstile area. The place was deserted. It was nearly sunset. Crouching on the steps, I watched him go toward the theater itself. There was no reason to go through it to get somewhere else. I guessed we'd reached our destination.

Like I said, I'd been there twice before, once for a concert. The other time I went to meet a woman in the eucalyptus grove above the theater. A very spectacular place to get romantic, looking down the tiers of the immense semicircle with the moonlight illuminating the fake antiquity of the seats and the big stage at the bottom with its Greek columns. As far as I know, no one in my family was ever Greek, but that night I had gotten carried all the way back. I figured it was either a strong genetic memory or an indelible mark made sometime in my childhood by a Hollywood production.

I decided not to go right into the theater. Anyone already in there couldn't miss someone coming in after him. I went up above, where I'd been that other night. From there I could see and not be seen, with any luck at all. I cursed myself for not carrying binoculars. If he'd come to meet someone I didn't know, the distance down to the bottom of the half-bowl would make it awfully hard to recognize the person again.

I got down on my belly next to a fragrant eucalyptus and looked down. I saw Cutter, his back to me, sitting alone on the lowest tier. There were leaves and strips of bark on the ground beneath me from the perpetually shedding trees. My clothing would smell medicinal. Well, I thought philosophically, eucalyptus was supposed to be a flea repellent. I looked at the trees. The time I'd come for the concert it had been sunset, too. The dull moss green leaves had been lit from within, like they were today, by the rust red glow of the trunk and the branches, a glowing shadow of red. As the sun drops lower, the red glow fades to mauve and merges, finally, with the moss of the leaves. And then it's night.

This time I didn't get any further than mauve.

"Don't move, Samson," the voice behind and above me said. A deep male voice. I moved my head, twisting my neck as far as it would twist, and saw the man with the gun. Someone I knew but not very well. It was the man named Charles, the other new-comer at the meditation group the night I'd gone. The one in Margaret Bursky's sketchbook. We'd given only our first names that night. He'd picked up my last name somewhere else.

"Hello, Charles," I said calmly, gazing up from the ground into the gun's good-sized muzzle. It looked like a .38.

"I told you not to move, Samson. Eyes front." I did as I was told. There was still no one down below but Cutter.

Charles took a deep breath and then bellowed, "Hey, Eddie!" Cutter looked around, startled, unable to place the sound. "Up here!" Cutter turned and saw us and started climbing the eigh-teen tiers of concrete. He came up fast. He was breathing hard when he got to the top. He glared down at me. I shrugged as well as I could and smiled.

"I guess," Charles's voice was heavy and sarcastic, "that you didn't know you were being followed, right, Eddie?"

"Shit," Eddie replied in a strangled voice.

"I saw him come in after you, dummy. I was looking for cops."

"Listen, Frank, how the hell could I know—" Frank, I thought. The *F* in Cutter's notes. The *Frank* on his appointment calendar.

"Forget it," Frank, alias Charles, cut in. "We've got him any-way. Roll over, Samson." Reluctantly, I turned over on my back, the leaves crackling under me.

Frank was wearing the same sports coat and slacks he'd had on the night the meditation group met. He still looked like his ulcer was bothering him. He had little lines of pain around his mouth and eyes, and his left hand rested protectively over his stomach.

"Okay, Samson. Where'd you put the stuff you took from the dummy's apartment?"

"Listen, Frank," Cutter began to protest.

"And you had to tell him my name, too, didn't you?" Frank turned partway toward Cutter, abruptly, threateningly. Cutter looked a little less emotionless than usual. Then Frank turned back to me.

"Answer me!"

"I don't know what you're talking about. I'm a writer—" He kicked me hard in the side. I couldn't keep from crying out. That made me mad. I started to get to my feet and he planted his toe on the point of my chin. The vertebrae in my neck made a cracking sound—a sound I heard just before I blacked out for a fraction of a second. I'd been punched in the jaw a few times in my life, but I'd never been kicked there. It makes a difference. The pain was so bad and so generalized that I couldn't tell what damage had been done. But I could still move. And I could see that Cutter had turned his head away. Squeamish?

"What did you do with the bag, Samson?" My eyes flicked to Cutter's face. I couldn't be sure, but he seemed to be warning me or pleading with me. My head was clearing a little. "The bag. Where is it? The pictures?"

I didn't think Cutter would beg me to keep quiet for my own sake. And why wouldn't he want to get the bag back? Then I realized that he wasn't worried about the drawings. Frank hadn't said a word about the really interesting item—the diary. Cutter's own contribution to the evidence. That had to be it. He hadn't told Frank about the notes. Frank wouldn't have liked it if he'd found out the kid had been writing little stories about all his friends. He might turn his gun on his own lackey. This Frank was no student playing at politics.

Nevertheless, he did know the drawings existed, including, presumably, the one of his own ugly face. Even if he didn't know for sure that I had them, he seemed to be willing to gamble my life on the possibility.

I, on the other hand, preferred staying alive to holding on to the drawings. But they were at my house. My nice private house. My castle. A good place to kill me once he had what he wanted. And Rosie might be home. Taking them there could endanger her. If I'd been physically able to manage it lying down, I would have kicked myself.

I didn't have to. Frank got impatient with my slow thinking and kicked me in the balls. I rolled up like a snail, gasping, blinded in a deep red and watery universe.

"The bag," he repeated. I couldn't talk, but he knew that. He waited.

When the first shock of pain had passed and I was able to feel other things, like the tears still gushing out of my eyes, I asked him a question.

"Let me stand up? I'll get the bag for you if you'll let me stand up." Oh, how badly I wanted to be up on my feet, level with this bastard, away from *his* feet.

He smiled slightly and nodded, stepping back, pointing the gun at my gut. I struggled to my feet, nearly falling to the ground again.

"I took the bag for the story. The drawings. There aren't any others, none that she's done recently. So I took it. Okay?"

Frank glanced at Cutter. "Search the boy, Eddie. Let's find out who he is."

Eddie obeyed, and I was very glad I'd tucked the diary pages away in my car. I didn't care how much trouble they gave Eddie, but I sure didn't want Frank to know I knew as much as I did. I was also glad I had no investigator's license. All they found on me—driver's license, credit cards, library card, letter from *Probe* magazine—was stuff that showed I was what I said I was. Jake Samson, writer. No evidence of any other kind of work.

"Okay, Samson, maybe you are a writer. Maybe that's why you've been nosing around. But you can't have the drawings." He smirked. "I just can't tell you how sorry I am about that." He seemed more relaxed, now that he'd beaten me. Almost happy. I was beginning to think that, if he did believe me, he might let me live. He could figure that it was more dangerous to make another corpse, a reporter's corpse, than to take a chance on my writing about a couple of guys who took back some stolen property.

Okay, so now what? I was on my feet, but I still couldn't stand up straight. My chin and jaw felt stiff, partly with blood, I thought. Something, probably a broken rib, stabbed me when I moved. As for the rest, well, walking would not be easy. And through the physical pain something just as strong and primitive was prodding me. My territory was about to be invaded and the prospect was sickening. I made a desperate, futile try at stopping that invasion.

"Let me deliver the sketchbooks to you, anywhere you say. I'll go right now and get them. I know what I did was breaking and entering. I don't want trouble. I'm not out to get anyone." I faked a catch in my voice, hoping they'd actually fall for it. Frank just laughed at me and Cutter exploded.

"Well," he sputtered, "Someone's sure out to get me. And the cops—"

"Just shut up, dummy," Frank growled. Then he laughed. "Besides, we took care of her."

Cutter turned to his boss. "We don't know she called them. Maybe he did." He jerked a thumb in my direction. He certainly had grounds for suspicion. Who else would have called the police? Yeah. Who else?

"And how would he know anything about it?" He gave me a Richard Widmark sneer. Apparently I had succeeded in failing to impress him.

So Frank thought he knew who had turned Cutter in that morning. A "she." A member of CORPS? Someone he'd "taken care of." How?

Frank said "Let's go," and stuck his gun in his pocket. He kept his hand in there, too. He shoved me to get me going and we started to walk. My mind was moving a little more smoothly than my body. Cutter knew the cops had gotten a tip about him. That meant one of two things. Either he'd gotten a tip himself and was evading them and their questions or he'd already been questioned and left alone. For the time being. I knew the police couldn't do much with an anonymous phone tip except question him and maybe watch him, and they didn't seem to be watching him very carefully yet. I wondered how much further they'd take it when they got my package of diary pages in the mail.

Although the pain was easing everywhere but in my neck and my ribs, I moved as slowly as I thought Frank would tolerate. He tried once or twice to hurry me along, but he didn't push very hard. I hoped that was because he'd exhausted his need to torture me.

He stopped our parade at the first water fountain, pulled out a handkerchief, and washed the blood off my chin. After all, a shambling wreck being herded along wouldn't attract that much attention in Berkeley, where people have seen even worse wrecks getting by on their own. But blood might have raised a few eyebrows.

—*17*—

We made our way across the campus, earning no more than a few curious glances. Just three pals out for a walk. We emerged into Berkeley proper. When we passed Cutter's car, he turned toward it, but Frank growled at him again.

"I'm not riding in that heap. We'll take mine." Cutter nodded, sullen but not really rebellious. We passed my car. There was a ticket on the windshield. One more item for the expense record.

Frank's car was big, new, and gaudy. He ordered Cutter to drive while he sat in the back seat with me. He took the gun out of his pocket again and held it on me.

Cutter drove fast. We reached my house in ten minutes. With great relief I saw that Rosie's pickup truck was not there. She was out. If I got rid of my two escorts fast enough, she would be safe.

The cats came running down the drive. I didn't want Tigris and Euphrates anywhere near Frank's gun. Or his feet.

"Shoo!" I hissed at them, stamping my feet. "Get out of this yard." They skidded to a stop. I added, "Damned cats. People ought to keep their lousy pets in the house." Then I clapped my hands and made threatening gestures. The cats were puzzled rather than frightened by my behavior, but I stopped them long enough to get to the house with my two friends and close the front door behind us.

"I'll just go and get the bag," I said, heading for the back room I use as an office.

"You hold on," Frank said. "Eddie, go with him." I was half a room ahead of Cutter and managed to kick a box file in front of the cat door before he caught up with me.

I picked the bag of sketchbooks off the floor and handed it to him on my way out of the room.

Frank waved his .38 at me. "Sit down and sit still while we have a look." Cutter pulled the sketchbooks out of the bag and glanced through them. He nodded to Frank, who opened the front door, held it so Cutter would exit first, and turned back to me.

"Don't pull any shit, Samson. Don't forget we know where you live." I nodded, trying to look grateful for being allowed to live. I figured I would just have to get Frank before he got me.

The first thing I did after they left was stay sitting down. I was having trouble deciding what to do with the next hour or two of my life.

A few years ago everyone I knew attributed indecisiveness to something or other in Libra. Since I'm a Libra, that's as good an excuse as anything, but in this case I guessed I could fall back on the fact that I'd been kicked in the head.

I wanted to stay home. I wanted to talk to Rosie. I wanted my car. I wanted to see Iris Hughes and let her see me, battered but brave.

I also wanted to go to the hospital.

Cats, on the other hand, are single-minded. They wanted to get in the house. I moved the box file, and they bulled through the cat door looking huffy. I started to feed them. Then I noticed, for the first time, a note on the refrigerator from Rosie, saying she had taken care of them. I fed them anyway. I called a cab.

The cab driver took a look at my face and said yeah, he thought going to the hospital was a good idea. He dropped me off at the emergency entrance and said he hoped I didn't fall off any more ladders. A couple of X rays and a lot of poking and probing later, I emerged with a taped midsection and two stitches in my chin. A cracked rib, they said. I was lucky the fall I'd taken—the doctor eyed me suspiciously when he said "fall"—hadn't done more than take a small chip off one of my canine teeth. My chin was one big bruise.

The second cab driver, the one who took me to my car, didn't even notice I was messed up. She chatted happily and nonstop about how she really didn't have to do this for a living but that it amused her.

I slipped the parking ticket out from under my windshield wiper and stuffed it in the dashboard compartment. Then I drove to a bar on Telegraph Avenue and had a couple of beers to clear my head. I didn't feel like eating dinner. When my head was sufficiently cleared, I went to the phone booth and looked up Iris Hughes in the directory. No luck. The only listing was for her office.

Next I called Harley to find out about his conversation with Hawkins, the detective I'd seen at the funeral. Hawkins had asked him if he knew someone named Edward Cutter. He said he didn't. He was incensed because the police had done no more than question Cutter, a "perfectly good suspect," and let him go.

I had a cup of coffee and plotted my next steps. If Cutter hadn't disappeared by the next day, the cops would probably go to see him then, too, when they got the diary pages in the mail.

The diary connected him with more than the fire. It tied him to Margaret Bursky as well. It also tied all those mysterious initials to Margaret Bursky. If she had been closely involved with Frank and his crew, I could imagine a whole list of potential killers, including Frank himself. After all, the notes had hinted that perhaps Cutter had told Bursky—the other *M*—about the fire and *M* had "got all upset." Frank certainly didn't mind a little violence. I wondered how far CORPS would go in protecting itself from the law.

But Bursky had been involved with a lot of people. There were still two members of the therapy group I hadn't talked to. I had a lot more work to do. Anger and pain weren't the only effects of the beating I'd taken. My adrenaline was racing. I wanted to keep going.

I made another call. A woman answered and told me that, no, her husband wasn't in, hadn't been in for two weeks, and wasn't expected in for yet another week. He was out of town on business. If that was all true, he didn't have anything to do with anything and would be back too late to tell me anything he might know. Too bad. That left Jayne Doherty. I rang her number and told her my reporter story. She thought it was all very exciting and invited me to come right over.

Jayne Doherty lived in a tiny cottage in back of a medium-sized house in the Temescal section of Oakland. The neighborhood is a little farther from the Berkeley line than my own, part of the same old Italian section that still had quite a few old Italians left in it, along with their well-kept yards and prolific vegetable gardens. It's the kind of area where solar and wind energy are nothing new—everyone uses them to dry their clothes, and grandmother's clothesline is passed on from one generation to the next. The influx from more expensive Berkeley, as well as from other parts of Oakland, has changed the character somewhat in recent years, adding a racial, sexual, and ideological mix that seems to work rather well.

I went through the gate at the side of the house and was lunged at, fortunately from behind a closed window, by a large dog that had no discernible breed but lots of sharp-looking teeth. By the time I'd passed the house, Jayne Doherty, alerted by the mutt, was standing in the door of her cottage watching me approach.

She was a big woman. About five ten or so and maybe a hundred and sixty pounds. Or more. Not fat for a woman that size, not if she knew how to use her body, not if she had some muscle under the softness. She knew how and she did have. I could tell by the way she moved that she could probably heave me right over her shoulder if she wanted to.

She had shoulder-length light brown hair streaked with gray.

It had just the slightest wave to it, so you couldn't tell how much was her and how much was hairdresser's art. She was wearing those off-white drawstring pants with a plaid cotton shirt tucked into the waist. She was nicely constructed. Medium-heavy breasts and a substantial belly with no spare tire. A warm smile that revealed a slight gap between her front teeth, freckles on her face and arms, and dark blue eyes. She was about my age, maybe a little older. She was pretty damned sexy.

The first thing she said to me was "Jesus, what the hell happened to you?"

I shrugged and smiled. "Car accident."

She shook her head sympathetically, waved airily at a comfortable-looking chair, and disappeared into the kitchen. It was easy to tell it was the kitchen, since the cottage had only three very small rooms, and you could see into both the others from the living room.

She came back with a bottle of red wine and two glasses. The wine was too sweet and I made a mental note never to buy that kind.

We were about two minutes into our conversation when the phone rang in the bedroom. She was gone a full five minutes, and from what I could overhear, she was talking pretty juicy stuff. This woman liked to chat about other people's private lives. If she knew anything at all, she'd be a valuable source. I sipped the sticky wine and waited.

Then I heard the dog snarling and barking and crashing against the window frame again. In a few seconds someone knocked on the door.

"Get it, will you, Jake?" she called from the bedroom. I opened the door to a boy of about sixteen years, a very pretty boy with an incipient beard and a couple of small adolescent pimples. He was of medium height and muscular build, and he had pale blond hair and dark brown eyes. He scowled at me.

"Where's Jayne?" he asked threateningly. Just then she emerged from the bedroom.

"Denny, sweetheart!" She gave him a kiss. On the lips. "Go fix yourself a sandwich or something, will you, darling?" She smiled ravishingly at me. "He's always so hungry." The boy tossed me another scowl, muttered something, and disappeared into the kitchen.

"Now, Jake." She plunked herself down on a cushion on the floor with surprising grace. "Sorry for the delays." She winked at me. "You know how it is." I said yes, I knew how it was.

"You want to know all about Margaret Bursky. What can I tell you?" She thought for a moment. "She wasn't exactly the most talkative member of our group, but heavens, she hardly had to talk at all. The dynamics in that group! I've dropped out, you know. Too many crazy people!" She laughed uproariously.

I heard the refrigerator door slam, followed by the clashing of dishes and cutlery.

"I've met a couple of members of the group," I said, and waited for her to take it from there.

"Have you met Eddie?" I nodded. "And Debbi?" I nodded again. "What a pair. With Bursky right in the middle." She leaned toward me. "Was she really murdered?"

I said I didn't know and asked what she thought.

She laughed again. "I think little Debbi would have been only too happy to give her a push." At the tail end of that slanderous statement, Denny came out of the kitchen with a sandwich on a plate. "Are you hungry, Jake?" I shook my head. "Anyway, I guess I don't really mean that. Debbi is so conventional. I can't imagine her doing anything that imaginative." She paused and turned to Denny, who had sat down beside her on her tuffet. "Mr. Samson is a reporter, Denny. He wants to know all about that Margaret Bursky. You know, the one who was killed?" The boy nodded, and his expression became slightly less hostile.

"Well," he said with a full mouth, "I was wondering what the hell he was doing here."

"Denny, dear." She spoke dismissively, if affectionately, and turned to me again. "He tends to be jealous," she said by way of explanation. I was glad he'd decided to eat first and beat me up later.

"What exactly was Debbi's relationship with Margaret Bursky?" I asked.

"Yes. Let's see. The group was about to break up the last time I went because of all the personal interaction, and Iris was going to move everyone into different groups. Maybe I could rejoin, come to think of it, if she's going to do that."

I tried to get her back on the track. "What personal interaction?"

"Well, Debbi and Eddie, of course—my God, doesn't that combination of names bring back the fifties?" She erupted again in that body-shaking laugh. Denny finished his sandwich and turned hot eyes on her. "Debbi was very interested in Eddie. They belonged to that group together. That other group. I never did get it straight what kind of group it was, but Debbi joined a few weeks ago. Something political. I don't know whether she joined because she meant it or because of Cutter. Love does such strange things." She jabbed Denny in the ribs with her elbow and he giggled foolishly. "Anyway, Eddie was interested in Margaret. She seemed interested in him in some way, but I don't know what it was exactly. Maybe they were lovers."

"Was Bursky involved in that other group, too?"

"I don't know. Wait a minute. I think I overheard something. Yes. She was going to a meeting or something. Maybe. Or she had. Or she was interested in it. Anyway, Debbi was just about ready to kill. I guess it's not in such good taste to say that, but what the hell? Are you still hungry, Denny?" He shook his head. "I was really surprised to find out that Margaret was married. She certainly didn't ever say anything about it. Just about painting. All the time. She was obsessed with it."

Doherty looked thoughtful. Denny put an arm around her shoulder. "I suppose that's what you're really interested in—the painting?"

"I know she did some drawings, that she was beginning to get back into it. Did she ever give any drawings away, that you know of?"

"Aha! I can certainly answer that. She wouldn't even let anyone see them. I know Eddie said he wanted one once, and she said he couldn't have any. That no one could because she wasn't ready for that yet. Whatever that means." Denny whispered in her ear and she gave him a lewd look. "Why don't you go in the bedroom and watch television until I'm finished here," she said with an unmistakable undertone. He gave me a suspicious look, mumbled "okay," and went into the bedroom. He didn't close the door, and we had to talk over the rumble of the late news.

"So," she said, with an air of wrapping things up, "what else can I tell you?"

"Did you ever get the impression that Cutter might have been angry or upset with her?"

She looked at me peculiarly. Maybe she thought that was an odd question for a reporter to ask. "No. I don't think I ever saw him angry at all, at anything. Debbi was the angry one. Little bitch, actually."

"How did Margaret Bursky behave toward Debbi?"

Again that curious look. "She ignored her." Jayne Doherty's answers were getting noticeably shorter, her eyes wandering toward the bedroom.

"What were your feelings about Margaret Bursky? What did you think of her?"

She shrugged. "Attractive. Kind of soulful. The mysterious artist type. I imagine that sort of thing turns young men on." Her eyes wavered once again. Denny was laughing at some old movie. "Older men, too, I suppose. She was all right. But depressive. Very depressive. It depressed me to be around her. She probably killed herself." Doherty stood up. I was getting my signal to get out of there and let her get on with her evening's entertainment. My head was throbbing and my ribs were aching, and I thought I might as well leave.

"If I come up with any other questions, may I call you again?"

She looked at me vaguely. "Of course. Any time." I put my glass down on the coffee table and took my leave.

I must have been tired because I forgot about the dog and damn near jumped out of my skin when it went into its act.

My conversation with Jayne Doherty had given me some gap-fillers and some questions. I'd known that Debbi was jealous of Bursky and Cutter and that she disliked the dead woman. Now I knew that Debbi was in Cutter's political group and that Bursky, too, had gone to a meeting of CORPS.

But all that Debbi and Eddie stuff was just so much confirmation of earlier information and guesswork. What was really interesting was Bursky's refusal to let Eddie have any of her drawings. I had been assuming that she kept her stuff at Cutter's so Harley wouldn't see that she'd been drawing pictures of people who hated him. Now I knew that was unlikely. So how did he get them? And when?

I looked at my watch. It was very late, but I called Debbi anyway. She sounded groggy, yet she denied that she'd been sleeping. I apologized for the lateness of the call. She said that was all right and why didn't I come right over? I was surprised.

She seemed awfully eager to get me over there. Maybe, I thought nervously, Frank had decided to kill me after all. Maybe he was there now, at Debbi's, waiting. I dismissed the thought. I wanted to see her anyway.

—18—

Debbi was alone and she was in worse shape than I was. She looked like the loser in a badly matched heavyweight bout, with a bandage over one eyebrow, a black eye, a purple cheekbone, a grazed and swollen jaw, a cut lip, and a red nose. I figured the nose was red from crying, because it didn't look damaged. She had a little trouble walking and held her left arm up against her rib cage.

I was remembering three things. Debbi had been involved in CORPS, the person that Frank said he'd taken care of was a "she," and Frank was partial to jaws and ribs.

"So," I said, "you're the one Frank beat up."

She didn't look surprised that I'd guessed what had happened to her. Her eyes were blank with the special blankness of exhausted fear. She didn't answer me and she didn't say anything about my own injuries. I followed her in and sat down.

"How come you told the cops about Eddie Cutter?" I asked gently.

She looked at me, one eye bright with tears, the other half closed. "I didn't."

And I didn't believe her any more than Frank had. "Because you're in love with him?"

"He's a rotten bastard." Somehow, coming out of Debbi's mouth, the words were shocking.

"Last time I talked to you, you told me you didn't know what there was between Eddie and Margaret Bursky. That wasn't true, was it? Were you protecting him?"

She answered indirectly. "It didn't last long enough to be called an affair."

"How long did it last?"

"Just a week or so. Then she stopped it. She said it was wrong."

"How did he feel about that?"

"He was a little angry, but I don't think he really felt much of anything else. I don't think he feels anything at all about anybody." The tears spilled over, and she winced when she wiped them off her bruises.

"When did Frank beat you up?"

"Want some wine?"

"No. Why does he think you called the police about Cutter?"

"I want some wine."

I could see then that some of her unsteadiness had to do with alcohol. The bottle she poured from was three-quarters empty. She drank her wine in three gulps and poured more, then stayed behind the bar so it formed a barrier between us. She was scared and she wanted company, but she didn't want to talk about Frank.

"Okay," I said. "Forget it." I got up to leave.

"You already know, so why ask me?"

I sat down again.

"Who killed Margaret Bursky?"

"I don't know, really. I don't know. But I think Eddie did it. Listen, I can't talk to you. Frank would kill me."

"No one will ever know you told me anything. If you know too much, they may kill you anyway. If they're caught, they won't be able to."

"Maybe they followed you here."

"Nobody followed me here." I was pretty sure of that. Beatings make me cautious.

She shook her head. I couldn't tell whether she was trying to clear it or whether she was denying something—my reliability, her safety, her willingness to go even further in implicating Cutter or the group.

"Why do you think Cutter killed her?"

"I can't talk about this. I can't get mixed up in it. I'd lose my job. You think they want someone who's mixed up in something like this? They'd fire me if they knew I was in a political group, let alone involved in a murder." Her panic about her job seemed a bit overdrawn, but I guessed it could be real. As real as her switch from protecting Cutter to accusing him of murder?

"Are you still in a political group?" She shook her head. I tried a different angle. I would make statements, and she would confirm or deny. "So. You called the police and told them Cutter set the fire because he was involved with Margaret Bursky."

"No!"

"You didn't tell the police, but you think he killed her?"

"That's right. I don't know who told them. Frank was so sure it was me, but it wasn't." Maybe she had and maybe she hadn't. The other half of the question was more important. I repeated it.

"Why do you think he killed her?"

"Look, won't you have some wine with me? I don't want to keep drinking alone."

She was a miserable sight. The respectable young woman, the rising executive. The establishment baby. With her face all marked up. Involved with people who broke the law. And now she was drinking alone, too. I accepted some wine, even though I didn't think I was up to drinking.

She brought it to me and sat with me again.

"Why do you want to know about what I think? Are you really just a writer?"

"If you have proof he killed her, why haven't you gone to the police?" I knew the answer but I wanted to push her to talk more.

"I told you. How many times do I have to tell you?" Drink was pumping up her spirit. She was exasperated with me. "I can't get mixed up in this. I just want to get out of this crummy mess with my job and my life."

"But you don't want someone to get away with murder, do you?"

She tried to sneer. It hurt her lip. "Why should I care?" She wasn't convincing. She had hesitated, and there had been a different kind of pain in her eyes. I wondered if I had, as the therapy addicts say, "pushed a button." A law-and-order button. Maybe she was a total innocent. Maybe she hadn't joined that group only because of Cutter. Maybe she had believed that they represented American virtue. I looked at her sadly. She looked at the floor.

I decided to follow the law-and-order line.

"You don't want to be involved, but you want the crime punished, isn't that right, Debbi? Those people, CORPS, they're just a bunch of criminals. Maybe they didn't set the fire, as a group, but they're protecting Cutter. Frank is, anyway." I knew the fire had been a group idea, but I wanted to find out if she had anything to add to what I already knew. I waited for what seemed like a long time for her to say something. She didn't. I went on. "That's why Frank beat you up. If Eddie killed her, I'd bet Frank knows about it. That's arson, assault, maybe even murder. You're a responsible citizen, Debbi. You can't just let it go." She didn't answer. She was still looking at the floor. "Tell me what you know, and I'll do what I can to see that the right people are punished. Without involving you, if possible." That made her raise her head.

"I joined that group because I really believed . . ." She poured herself another drink. "I really did. I thought Eddie was like a soldier, some kind of soldier."

"Soldiers are for killing."

She looked at my still-full glass, probably hoping she could refill it. "He was there that day."

"The day she died? He was at her house?"

"Yes."

"How do you know?"

"He was supposed to meet me for an early lunch. He called to say he couldn't make it, that he had to go see Margaret."

"Did he tell you why?"

"No, but I thought it had something to do with the fire."

"She didn't want him to do it, right?"

Debbi nodded. "You already know a lot, don't you?"

"Was she in that group?"

"Kind of. She'd started coming to meetings. Of course, no one knew who she was. She would sit there and listen to our plans for picketing the political science department and go along with them completely. She loved it."

"But not the fire. She didn't love the idea of the fire." I didn't ask how she herself had reconciled arson with law and order. Whatever her reasons had been, she didn't seem to have them anymore.

"No. But Eddie thought he could convince her because they'd been, well, lovers in a way. A one-week stand," she added scornfully.

"And he still didn't know who she was?"

She shook her head slowly, as though it hurt. She was far from sober and she was beginning to look pale.

"When did he find out?"

"When everyone else did. After she was dead. Excuse me." She stood up abruptly and lurched to the bathroom. I could hear her being sick.

I was remembering his notes. He had known before that. He hadn't been able to understand why she cared, why she wouldn't want to help with the fire. And he had gone on in a diatribe against infidelity. He had known she was Harley's wife. But he hadn't told anyone. Why had he kept her secret? Loyalty to her? After all, that bit of intelligence might have increased his standing with the group, and he was certainly interested in that. He had wanted to be left in charge.

So he had been the dead woman's lover, however briefly. She had broken it off. She had disagreed with the plan to set fire to her husband's office. He was half crazy, judging by his written ravings. He had gone to see her the day she died. Pretty good case. On the other hand, he hadn't told the group who she was. Also—and this seemed important to me—he may have been half crazy, but he hadn't helped Frank beat me up. And it was Frank, not Eddie, who'd gotten to Debbi. Finally, I had only Debbi's word that he had been on Virgo Street the day of Bursky's death. How good was her word when she had reason enough of her own to want Bursky dead? And why would he tell her where he was going if he planned to kill the woman?

What about the drawings? How had he gotten them? And was he crazy enough to kill someone and display her artwork on his apartment walls afterward? It dawned on me then that I had actually done the guy a favor by stealing everything in his apartment that connected him with Margaret Bursky. The police must have been there the next day to question him. If they'd gotten into his place, they could have seen for themselves that he knew her. Well, there was nothing I could do about any of it now. I didn't even have the damned drawings anymore. Frank did.

Debbi returned, looking a little better. I stood up, preparing to leave. Maybe I could get to Cutter before the police grabbed him again. I needed to find out if he'd told them about my burglary.

Debbi looked scared. "You're not going, are you?" She was pleading.

"I have to, Debbi. I still have things to do tonight. Work," I said lamely. It was after twelve. She didn't believe me. Writers don't work after twelve.

"Please. Don't go. I'm afraid to be alone." She was all messed up, drunk, crying, scared half to death, but she still had some dignity. "He might come back. He might decide to kill me." She had taken hold of my shoulders. If she had looked pathetic, I might have been able to go. But she didn't. She looked like a frightened woman. Frightened for good cause and asking my help. I glanced with some misgivings at the couch. It didn't look comfortable, and the way my body felt, that was a big consideration. She caught my look.

"No, not there," she said. "I don't want to be alone."

I didn't feel much like sleeping with her. I guess I didn't seem too enthusiastic because she blushed and let go of my shoulders.

"I don't mean anything by it. I'm not asking you to do anything. I just want someone near. I couldn't, anyway."

So I decided to go along with her. Maybe I wasn't too eager to be alone myself that night. I would try getting to Cutter early in the morning, before the mail was delivered and the cops picked him up again.

Debbi took a nightgown out of a drawer and disappeared into the bathroom. I stripped down to my shorts and climbed into the queen-sized waterbed. It felt good, like the womb. Warm, firm, and soft, like flesh. I wasn't used to sleeping in my shorts. I wasn't used to sleeping in anything. But I was drifting peacefully when she came back. The nightgown came to her knees. It had short sleeves and was buttoned up to her neck. She stumbled on a throw rug, caught herself, and got in beside me. The minute she lay down and relaxed, the tears came again. I could feel her shaking with sobs. I reached over and patted her shoulder. She came close and pressed against my side, crying on my upper arm. Then she lifted her right leg over my thigh. Just cuddling, I thought. I could feel the hem of her nightgown. It was moving up as her thigh slid over mine. It moved all the way up until I felt her pubic hair brushing against me. She was not crying anymore. She was biting my neck. Her grip tightened and her hips began to move. Then she reached down and touched me.

"You don't have to do anything," she said, and she climbed on top of me.

—*19*—

When I awoke the next morning, Debbi was gone. I didn't think she worked on Saturday, so I guessed she'd fled out of embarrassment. It was nine o'clock. I jumped out of bed and almost yelled. The cracked rib reminded me of its existence.

Dressing quickly, I cursed myself for oversleeping. There was a good chance the police, like nearly everyone else, didn't get their mail until late afternoon, and I comforted myself with that thought.

Debbi had left a note on the dresser. I thought, wryly, that maybe she should have left a ten dollar bill, as well. The note said, "You're a nice man. I don't usually like nice men." I'd been nice, all right. So nice I'd forgotten to ask her where she'd been the morning Margaret Bursky was killed.

Cutter's car was nowhere in sight when I got to his street. I rang the bell, banged on the door, and checked out his back window again. He wasn't there. Sharp hunger pangs forced me to think about food, and I headed for a little restaurant down on Adeline, which was run by some friends of Rosie's. They served a great breakfast, when you could get a place to sit down. I was in luck. There was an empty stool at the counter.

"What'll you have, Jake?" Marcy, a woman I'd met a couple of times with Rosie, eyed my bruises but didn't say anything. I ordered, we joked around a little, then she left me to brood while she took care of business.

Okay. What came next? I used the restaurant pay phone to put in a call to Hal at home. The cops hadn't gotten to Cutter a second time. Not yet. He was still running around loose. That was all he knew.

One question kept going around and around in my head. Not so much who killed Margaret Bursky as why Debbi was still alive. If Cutter or someone from CORPS had killed the artist for some transgression or other, why had they just knocked Debbi around a little?

Once again I considered the possibilities. Bursky had been killed in the heat of someone's passion—maybe Cutter's, maybe Debbi's, maybe Billy's, maybe even the passion of some unknown person named *X*. Or her death had been an accident, a little error in timing or judgment by someone who was only trying to scare her, possibly Frank. Or she had torn out her own hair and jumped. She was dangerous to the group, and they had pushed her over the edge with picket signs. Any other possibilites? Probably an infinite number, but those were the only ones I could come up with before breakfast.

The food came and I wolfed it down. Two pancakes with just a touch of cinnamon; two eggs, over medium, with sausage; orange juice and coffee. That made me feel better. I felt so much better that I called Iris Hughes and asked her to have lunch with me. She wouldn't, but she was curious about what I'd been doing and invited me to her office during her free hour between eleven and twelve. Goody.

I hadn't been home for a long time, and it seemed like a good idea to check my answering machine and have a word or two with Tigris and Euphrates. Maybe even Rosie, if she was around.

She wasn't, but she'd left a note: "Where the hell have you been? I'm worried and pissed off. Why don't you ever call your old mother? The cats have been fed and soothed again. Alice sends her regards."

There were some messages on my machine, too. One from Rosie, with a phone number where she could be reached. One from a man who left a number but no name, and whose voice didn't sound at all familiar. One, heaven help me, from Sergeant Ralph Hawkins of homicide. One from John Harley. And one from, of all people, Eddie Cutter. Cutter said he couldn't be reached by phone and would call me back. That left two important ones, Rosie and the cop. Rosie first. She was relieved to hear from me and sympathetic about my wounds. We made a date to have dinner together that night so I could fill her in. Then I called the number Hawkins had left. Unfortunately, he was at his desk.

He told me to stay put and that he'd be at my house in half an hour. He had some questions to ask me.

I made a pot of coffee and called the no name whose voice hadn't sounded familiar. He said his name was Jared.

"Last or first?" I asked pleasantly. There had been, I recalled, a very important *J* in Cutter's notebook.

"Either," he said cryptically, "and both." Sure, I thought. Just what I needed this morning before some cop dragged me off to jail. A mystery man. He said he wanted to see me, and I told him he'd have to wait his turn.

"I don't suppose you'd like to tell me what you want to talk to me about?" I asked politely. Hell, maybe he was just a prospective client, offering me five thousand to find his striped tie in his underwear drawer.

He came on like Sydney Greenstreet. "We have," he said in a fruity voice, "mutual acquaintances. You seem to be involved in a matter which concerns me, and I think we'd better discuss our mutual interests before you come up against some real trouble."

A threat. Terrific. I had thought I'd be dealing with one nice harmless murderer, and I seemed to be meeting a whole flock of vicious birds. Well, wasn't that just the way of it?

I told him I could make a tentative appointment to see him at three that afternoon, and I gave him the name of a bar that always had customers at that time of day.

Then I called Iris and told her I couldn't make it at eleven. I didn't tell her it was because I'd be talking to the law. Hell, I could be mysterious, too. I told her I'd be free to have a drink with her later that evening. She agreed to have Sunday brunch with me the next day. A small victory but a victory nonetheless. I took a badly needed shower to celebrate.

Hawkins was even more impressive close up than he'd been from across the room at the funeral. He looked even taller standing in my doorway. The bones of his face were clearly outlined, his skin a yellowish olive, his brown eyes tired. He was wearing brown denim pants, a brown-and-yellow-checkered flannel shirt, and a baggy lightweight safari jacket, which he didn't take off. He eyed my battered chin with something that looked like disgust. When he introduced himself, he included his rank.

I offered him coffee; he accepted and sat down in my most comfortable chair. Euphrates joined him instantly. He patted the cat absently on its head, the way one pats a dog. Fortunately, Euphrates likes dogs and enjoys being treated like one. He settled down, purring, in Hawkins's lap. When I came back from the kitchen, the man's fingers were resting lightly on the cat's shoulders.

He thanked me politely for his coffee, set the cup down on the end table beside him, scratched Euphrates' neck, and turned a glittering hard look on me.

"Okay, Samson, what the hell do you think you're doing?" The look and the question were all the more startling because his body seemed so completely relaxed.

"Don't give me that innocent look. You've been running around questioning people, saying you're a writer—let's see your credentials, okay?" He didn't get up. I did and I handed him the letter from *Probe*. "We'll check on this, you know," he said darkly. I nodded, secure in my cover. How could anyone prove I wasn't working on an article? If it didn't get printed, it could always be because it wasn't good enough. "I've been tripping over you for days, Samson. When are you going to have everything you need and get the hell out of my way?"

"I didn't know I was getting in your way, Sergeant."

He glared at me. "That's a pile of shit, pal."

I frowned thoughtfully back at him.

"Come on, why don't you just tell me what you're doing and why? We don't want any civilians getting hurt, you know." He sneered, but that was just part of his act. I figured he was trying to get me mad enough either to say something stupid or do something even stupider. He was dying to put me somewhere out of the way for a while. He didn't care whether I was working on an article. He didn't care what I was doing as long as I stopped.

"Who did that to you?" He dropped his eyelids halfway and focused on my chin. I started to answer, but he cut me off. "You fell, right?" I nodded. "Last night," he added. He was trying to impress me with his omniscience so I'd give up and talk to him. I wasn't too impressed. If he'd talked to someone who saw me before the beating and someone who saw me after—like Jayne Doherty—he'd have before and after pictures of my face.

"What do you need from me, Sergeant?" I asked, trying to look like a man who was not feeling patient but was trying to act like he was. Just so he wouldn't know I would have talked to him for six months if I could have found out what he knew that I didn't. If anything.

"I want to know who you've talked to and what they've told you."

I gave him a lot of what I had, with a few exceptions. I didn't tell him I'd broken into Cutter's apartment. I didn't tell him I was the anonymous diary donor. I didn't tell him I'd followed Cutter to the Greek Theater, met Frank, gotten kicked around, and had then given the drawings I hadn't taken in the first place back to the people who didn't have any business having them. I didn't tell him I'd gotten a phone message from Cutter that day. I didn't tell him I'd gone to bed with both Alana and Debbi and was dying to go to bed with Bursky's shrink. I saw no reason to hide the fact that someone named Jared had called. Maybe, if he heard the name, Hawkins would give something away. He didn't.

"Does that worry you?" he wanted to know. "This Jared guy calling?" He reached for his coffee and drank it straight down. Either he liked it cold or he was used to forgetting he had some.

I shrugged. If I admitted I was worried, I'd be halfway to admitting I'd had an experience that made me think there was cause to be scared. Hawkins was tricky, but I was sharpened by tension and physical pain. On the edge.

He didn't push. "Sounds like you've got enough to write your story, Samson. Why don't you get out of the way?" He said it without inflection, just so I wouldn't know how much weight he was putting behind it.

"Want some more coffee?" He shook his head. "I can't drop it yet," I told him. "I have to follow through with these people, find out what was really going on."

"And find out what really happened to her?" he said softly.

"Sure. Of course. What kind of story would it be—"

"Jesus, you're an asshole," he muttered.

"You're probably right," I admitted.

He sighed and gazed at the back of Euphrates' head. "Okay, Samson. I'm going to believe you're writing an article, even though I don't believe it. I'm going to believe you haven't been withholding evidence or obstructing an officer in the perform- ance of his duty. You do know, by the way, that you could go to jail for that. For a year?" He paused for effect. I nodded agreea- bly. "I'm also going to believe you're not operating privately without a license and fucking up a case against a killer because you don't know what the shit you're doing. Even though I don't believe it. And I'm going to try very hard to believe you're not going to get yourself, or me, or anyone else killed." He shifted his gaze back to my face, like he was shooting icicles.

"What do you think about that, Samson?"

"I'm glad you believe me."

"I don't want you to think I'm against freedom of the press or anything." He smiled viciously. "I just want you to know I'll slice your ass for sandwiches if I find out that all those things I'm believing aren't true."

I ignored the challenge. "Of course. Sure. Listen, I want to cooperate with the police. If I get information—not that anything I get could be useful to you—I'll pass it on. Maybe you'd be willing to do the same?" I expected that he'd either not answer or he'd take my head off for that one. He stayed quiet for a second before he answered me.

"You get any information you don't pass on, and you'll be writing a firsthand exposé of what it's like to be in jail. And I'm telling you only what I think will keep you from fucking up, if that's possible. You've got nothing coming from me, Samson."

"I understand that," I replied gravely.

"Good," he said. He put one hand in Euphrates' armpits and one around his butt and lifted him gently to the floor. Then he stood up. He didn't brush the striped hairs off his pants. He looked me over carefully.

"Tell me something, Samson, were you one of those types back in the sixties who used to call cops pigs?"

"No."

"You're the right age."

"So are you. You want to know what I was doing in 1968?"

He looked bored. "Nam?"

"I was wearing a Chicago police uniform and bashing heads."

"Couldn't take it, huh?" His face revealed no surprise. I wondered if he'd already checked far enough to know about my short career.

"No," I agreed. "I guess I couldn't."

He nodded. "If anything," he said, "it's gotten worse." I knew he wasn't talking about police violence. He was talking about the alienation, the frustration, the exhaustion of being a cop. But he didn't punch me on the arm, buddy-style. He didn't shake my hand. He just threw me another warning look and went out the door.

—20—

I couldn't call Cutter because I didn't have a number. Of the recorded phone calls left on my machine, only John Harley remained.

"I want to talk to you," he blurted out the second I identified myself.

"You are."

He growled at me. "They came to see me again this morning."

"Hawkins?"

"No, his partner. They work in pairs, you know." I knew that, but I let him hang on to his superiority. "He read me off a list of initials. He wanted to know if I knew anything about them. Who they might be. But that's not all. He wanted to know if I'd been faithful to my wife. He wanted to know if there was any reason my wife would have had to wish me harm. How would they get information like that, for God's sake?"

"From Cutter," I told him. I didn't explain further that the information came from Cutter through me. "I know about the documents they got the initials from." I tried to sound reassuring. "They were something Cutter wrote, something that didn't say anything about you and Rebecca specifically. And the same papers implicate him pretty heavily. He wrote that he went to your house, Harley, and the visit seems to have been recent. Also, you might be interested to know, he had some drawings that belonged to your wife. I don't know where they are now, but he had them."

"So the case is solved? Why isn't he in jail?"

"It's not solved."

"If they put Cutter in jail, the case is solved," he said mulishly. It occurred to me that he was probably right. They might be able to whip together a pretty good case against Cutter if, for example, Debbi talked. "And," Harley added, "you didn't solve it." From his viewpoint, that was true. He didn't know I'd sent the diary pages that could help get Cutter. He wouldn't be able to see past the fact that the same pages hinted at his own trouble with his dead wife.

"I'll tell you what, Samson. I think you're stalling. I think you should have come up with something concrete by now. I've already given you five thousand for your work. I consider that money spent. But maybe you're just not the right man for the job."

He was giving me a tempting opening. I could back off, not get killed, not get turned into sandwiches by a smart cop, leave Harley and Rebecca and Debbi and Cutter to the police. I thought about it. For a minute.

"Listen, Harley, you can consider yourself bound by our original deal. I find the killer and you pay me a total of ten thousand dollars."

"Why don't you think it's Cutter?"

"I don't know that it isn't Cutter. I also don't know that it isn't one of several other people. I'm still investigating. So are the police."

He sputtered something at me.

"Another thing," I added for good measure, "you can damned well stop getting hysterical every time somebody pokes you with a dull stick. If you don't let me handle this and stick to our deal, I'll get out, all right. And I'll give the cops everything I know about you and Rebecca."

"That's extortion." He actually sounded shocked.

"No, it's not, Harley. It's a promise. You have to trust me, so don't give me any more reason not to trust you."

He puffed and grumbled a little, but he did back off. This was not the first time in my life I'd been forced to reflect on the advantages of legitimacy. If you operate legally, you can also claim the protection of the law. Like taking recalcitrant debtors to court and waving nice, tight, lawyer-made contracts at the judge. But when you've lived on the edge of things for years and like the objectivity of the position, you get a little funny about your independence. I just can't get comfortable about working under the eye of the state. Maybe my mother was bitten by a cossack.

I told Harley I'd keep him informed. He said he'd be in his office working that afternoon. I hung up.

There was nothing I could do until three o'clock, and I decided to give my rib a rest. Tigris strolled in from her bird watching, said hello, and followed me to bed.

Half an hour later I was roused by a persistent, medium-loud knock on the door.

There was a peephole, and I used it. Cutter was on my front porch, looking over his shoulder, peering into neighboring yards, doing an impatient little dance. No one else that I could see, just Cutter. I opened the door, pulled him in, and locked the door again.

He stumbled, caught himself, glared at me, and dropped down on the couch, half-reclining.

"Who invited you?" I wanted to know.

He didn't move. "It wasn't my idea to beat you up." He

blinked and rubbed his eyes. "I didn't go home last night. I came here looking for you and waited around out in the street." He yawned, showing lots of fillings. "I tried to go home this morning, once, but the police were there. I called you and left a message on your machine. I left my car on the street, walked around. I called you again a while ago and the line was busy. Then I came by and saw this car out front. Looked like an unmarked car, so I took off again. . . ."

I was impressed. I'd had no idea he could string so many words together. Nevertheless, I interrupted his monologue by grabbing his shoulders and hauling him into a sitting position. He pulled back but stayed sitting.

His look was sullen. About as close to emotion as he ever got, I figured.

"Samson, why are the cops after me again? Did you give them my diary?"

"Yeah."

"Oh, shit. That's really gonna be it then. Everybody's gonna want my ass now, boy. All those names—"

"Just initials. Tell me, Cutter, that *J* in the book. Was that someone named Jared?"

"Fuck you."

"Pretty important man, right?"

He repeated his instructions.

"Sure, Cutter. I'll give it a try. But first I'm going to let the cops know where they can pick you up." I turned toward the telephone.

"Hey, man!" He jumped up, all renewed energy. "Whattaya want to do that for? What did I do to you anyway?"

"You mean besides standing around and watching me get kicked in the balls? You mean what besides that?"

"I would have helped if I could. After all, you didn't tell him about the diary. But I couldn't stop him. He had a gun. I couldn't stop a gun. And you told the cops." His lower lip was actually sticking out. "Look, let me stay here for a couple hours, catch my breath. I can pay for it." He switched from the pout to a more familiar look, the look that, I supposed, made Debbi think of him as a soldier. "You're looking for information. I got information."

"Why should you tell me anything?"

"Got anything to eat?"

I went to the refrigerator, took out two slices of bologna,

shoved them between two slices of bread, and stuck the sandwich in his hand. He looked at it distastefully but took a big bite anyway.

"I repeat, Cutter, what is it you want to tell me?"

"The police already questioned me about the fire. Now maybe they want me for the killing, too. I got a feeling. And Frank said if they found out I was close to her, you know."

"You said you had information for me."

"Got another sandwich? And some milk?" I went to the kitchen to get him the food. While I was pouring the milk, I heard the front door open and close. I shot back through the door fast, but there he sat.

"That cat," he said, "the one that bothers you. It was in the house. I shoved it out."

"Thanks," I said, and went back into the kitchen for his sandwich and milk.

He drank half the milk down. "Okay," he said. "I didn't kill her. Here's the truth. Her husband. He did it."

"How do you know that?" I practically yawned in his face.

"He was having an affair." The phrase sounded strange coming from his barely literate lips. So he was a bit of a prude, too.

"So?"

"So he wanted to get rid of his wife. It's always the husband anyway, right? Well, he was betraying her with another woman." The more he talked about sex the less he sounded like himself. "He's totally corrupt. He killed her. You can bet he did. Because of his woman."

"You know who the woman is?"

"I sure do. Margaret knew, too."

"How?"

"It happened like this. Margaret wasn't telling anybody she was Harley's wife, right? She was ashamed, probably. And I didn't know yet either. We were having coffee together and talking about things, and I mentioned that I'd been down at the Marina and I'd seen Harley and this Rebecca walking around down there. She didn't cry or anything, but I could see that she was holding something in. Then she told me. That she was Harley's wife and that she thought he was betraying her, and now she was sure of it. He wanted someone else. He killed her."

"Jesus, Cutter, haven't you ever heard of divorce?"

He shrugged. "That's got to be what happened."

"Terrific. That's very helpful, really," I sneered. "Now you answer some questions."

He gave me a wary look and swallowed the last of his second sandwich.

"Did you tell the police about Harley's girl friend?"

"They just asked me about the fire. I didn't volunteer nothing."

"Who's Jared?"

"Forget it, man."

"How did you know Rebecca's name?"

He shifted a little and glanced toward the door like he wanted to use it. "I don't know. You hear stuff. Everybody hears stuff."

"Okay," I said, feigning patience, "then tell me how you got Margaret Bursky's drawings. She sure didn't give them to you."

"Yes she did."

"How did Frank know the portraits existed? Did all those people sit for them?"

"No. She did them all from memory. She told me she had them."

"And you told Frank?"

"Not until after she was dead. After you took them."

"When did she give the sketchbooks to you?"

His eyes were shifting. His fingers were drumming. He was crossing and uncrossing his legs. "Couple days before she died."

"You're lying. I'm going to turn you in." I grabbed the front of his shirt. His breath smelled of bologna. I didn't see him reach into his jacket pocket, but I felt the gun pressed against my side a second later.

"Okay, Samson. I don't like doing this, but you don't give me any choices. And I need help. I got to get away. I'd just take your car, but you'd call the cops so I'm taking you, too."

"Gee," I said, "this is just like television. Do you think it's the American thing to do, coming to visit a man, eating his food, all with the idea of stealing his car? Not to mention his person—"

"Shut up. I'm not stealing your car. You're gonna drive it." He poked the gun into my side, hard, just missing the cracked rib. "Walk in front of me. I'll have the gun on you, in my pocket. Don't try nothing."

I half-expected him to rasp "Or I'll waste you," but he didn't. We had started down the path when I heard a familiar-sounding engine. Rosie's pickup. She parked in front and came through the gate, Alice at her heels. She was carrying a couple of six-foot-long two-by-fours, probably for her latest home project.

"Don't stop to talk," Cutter whispered. "Say you got to rush. Or I'll take her, too."

Rosie and Alice were just a few feet away from us now.

"Can't stop to talk, Ellery," I told her. "I'll be back soon." Cutter, the dummy, was still behind me. I bared my teeth at Rosie and rolled my eyes in a silent, if grotesque, plea. Her eyelids barely flickered. She'd seen the drawing of Cutter. Would she know him?

"Sure, darling," she said, by way of letting me know she wasn't playing herself. "See you later."

I had gone about three paces beyond her when I heard a crack, a grunt, and a thud. I turned to find Cutter on his face in the driveway and Rosie finishing her follow-through with one of the two-by-fours. The other one was lying across the back of his neck. The gun he'd been holding was on the ground.

Rosie picked up the gun. "I hope," she said, "that he is who I think he is."

—21—

At the very least, Cutter was an arsonist, and even if he wasn't a killer, I was a little put out by his attempt to kidnap me, as well as by his refusal to answer the questions I'd wanted him to answer. In the space of a couple of minutes, I went over all the reasons for and against turning him in.

If he told the cops I'd stolen the drawings, he'd have to admit he had had them. He might not want to do that. But there was a very good chance he'd be eager to tell them about Harley and Rebecca, if they started pushing at him about Bursky's death. Did that matter? How did I know the police didn't already have that information? If they'd taken Cutter's diary pages at all seriously, they were already looking for the woman Harley was seeing.

Then there was Hawkins. If he caught up with Cutter and found out I'd had the kid and let him go, I'd probably wind up in jail myself. All in all, I didn't have a choice. Not morally and not in practical terms either.

Cutter groaned and rolled over, focusing his eyes first on me and then on Rosie, who was holding the gun on him. I left the two of them that way and called the police.

Hawkins got there in about ten minutes with two uniformed cops. While the uniforms cuffed Cutter and tucked him into the back of their squad car, Hawkins chewed his lip and thought about what kind of trouble he could give us.

I forestalled him by introducing him to Rosie. She transferred the gun from her right hand to her left and shook his hand.

He grunted. "You got a permit for that gun, Miss?"

She looked at it, startled. "It's not mine. It's Cutter's."

He nodded and took it from her. "I'd like you two to come down and make a statement. You can take your own car." He turned and began to walk toward the street. We followed. Before he got into his car, he turned and called out to us.

"Who hit him with the two-by-four?"

"I did," Rosie said, a little defiantly.

He looked at her and smiled.

We didn't finish until just after three. Rosie and I had taken separate vehicles so I could go straight to my appointment with Jared.

I'd gotten all the way to the door of the bar before I remembered that I didn't know what Jared looked like. Apparently, though, someone had described me to him. The minute I walked in, a large man got off his barstool and came to meet me. He didn't shake hands; he just said, "Samson?" I nodded. "Jared," he barked, and herded me to a booth in the far corner.

His face was familiar, as Frank's had been. Jared, too, had been immortalized by Margaret Bursky in her sketchbook.

He was a little taller than me and a whole lot heavier. Where Frank was soft-looking, this man was big and fat and solid. He was wearing, of all things, a cheap brown business suit and a plaid tie, and the suit was older than his paunch. The jacket was buttoned, and it stretched across his belly.

Even with that terrible example of obesity right there in front of me, I ordered beer. He ordered bourbon and water, no ice, like he'd spent his life in cheap motels with no ice machines.

A couple of minutes after we sat down, another man got up from the bar and joined us. He was even bigger than Jared. There were no introductions.

I gazed into Jared's muddy hazel eyes. The pouches under

them and the deep lines that ran from his nose to the sides of his mouth put his age at somewhere around forty-five. The pouches weren't dark and came from time, not dissipation. He had very little gray in his mousy brown hair. His face was red, shiny, and round, like a nasty Santa Claus.

He was taking a good look at me, too.

"Aren't you going to ask me why I called you, Samson? What kind of a name is that, anyway? Samson? Your first name's Jake, isn't it? Jewish?"

Great, I thought. I was going to love this guy. "I don't know what kind of name Samson is because it originated at Ellis Island. But I'm Jewish."

He nodded, feigning disinterest. I didn't ask him what kind of name Jared was.

"Well?" he said.

"Okay." I shrugged. "What did you want to see me about?"

He took a long swallow of his bourbon. "I want to know what you're after."

"I'm sure you already know that. I'm doing a magazine piece on Margaret Bursky. That's what I'm after."

He smiled. "Going to stick to that, are you?"

"That's right."

"Okay, Samson, let me put it this way. I don't have any problem with you doing a magazine piece on what's-her-name. But I do have a problem with some of the things you might say in that article. And I have a problem with your temporary possession of some drawings. I wouldn't want any mention of them to appear in any magazine." I started to speak, but he held up his hand. "And I wouldn't want anything about CORPS in there either, and that nonsense about the fire."

"Who the hell are you?" I snarled. "I'll write what I please." I thought I was striking the proper attitude for a reporter who was being told not to write his story.

"How much do you get for an article, Mr. Samson?" All of a sudden I was "mister."

But the question caught me. "Two thousand dollars," I said, wondering if that was even close to what writers actually got.

He laughed. "Hardly seems worth the effort." I stared deliberately at his off-the-rack brown suit. He turned a little redder. "What would you take to drop the whole thing?"

"I don't think I can drop the whole thing," I said, with just the slightest edge of slyness in my voice and an upward, open-ended inflection.

His eyes narrowed. A traveling salesman looking shrewd. "I'm going to trust you, Mr. Samson. I think you can do a nice little story about the woman without getting into anything political. After all, it's a story about art, right?"

I returned the shrewd look. "Could be."

"For, say, a couple of thousand on top of what you get for the piece itself?"

I laughed at him. "Not enough. Double it."

"Four thousand dollars?" He contrived to look both angry and admiring at the same time. "I'll compromise. Three."

I stared at my beer, pretending to think it over. Then I reached my hand across the table. "Deal," I said. We shook.

"One more thing, though," he added. "I want to see a copy of the article before it's printed."

"No problem. No problem at all." I smiled, looking smug. "What if I decide not to write it at all, later I mean. Will you make up the difference?"

"The two thousand?" I nodded. He pursed his fleshy lips. "Not worth it to me. Who cares about an art story? How much longer until you finish it?"

"Couple weeks, maybe," I told him.

He shook his head. "I don't think so. I think you'll finish a lot sooner than that."

"I can certainly try," I said cheerfully.

"Good. Another thing." He seemed to enjoy adding provisos. "I hear you turned in some kid named Cutter today. You pull anything on me and you're dead." He smiled broadly and swallowed the rest of his bourbon.

"Don't worry about it," I muttered through my teeth. "I need the money." I hesitated before I added, as though I hadn't been thinking about it all along, "But where can I get in touch with you when the article is finished?"

He stood and threw some money on the table. Enough for both our drinks and a small tip. His friend stood up, too. "I'll get back to you." Then they both lumbered out of the bar.

I ordered another beer to get the taste of Jared out of my mouth.

Running through my mind was the line in Cutter's notebook about *J* going out of town and *F* being placed in charge. Out of town where? In charge of exactly what? There was too much I still didn't know and only three people, other than Jared himself and the dead woman, who could fill me in: Cutter, Frank, and Debbi.

Eddie was pretty much out of my reach. I didn't know where to find Frank. And I wasn't terribly anxious to see Debbi again right away. I was glad I was having dinner with Rosie. I needed to talk the thing out a little.

Obviously, Jared, like Frank, was no student. And Jared was in charge or delegated leadership to Frank. So, just as obviously, CORPS was a student group run from the outside, from the big adult world in which some very obnoxious people had organized some very obnoxious groups. Like the groups whose propaganda Cutter'd had in his desk. I wondered which one Jared represented.

And I wondered if any of those groups had any reason for killing a depressive, unhappily married artist who had a habit of doing portraits from memory. Jared had made it clear that he didn't want her connected with CORPS in my imaginary article.

But I also remembered that he had specifically mentioned the fire. Not her murder. Just the fire.

—22—

Hal Winter had been home that morning, but his machine was answering the phone that afternoon. The trouble with answering machines is that they leave you in limbo. Oh, sure, you get to leave a message, but what if the guy you're calling is a thousand miles "away from the phone"?

Cutter had been in custody a couple of hours, and I was itching to know if he was talking and what he was talking about. I calmed down, hoped for the best, assumed that Hal hadn't taken it into his head to leave town, and left a message that Cutter had been arrested and that I'd be home around five. Please call.

Then I phoned Harley. If I wanted him to keep paying the bills, I was going to have to baby him along. He was still at his office, so I went over there. I hadn't seen the place since the fire. It was an ugly sight.

I could see right through parts of the smoke-blackened walls, past the skeleton of charred studs, into the rooms on either side. Soggy, sooty sheetrock lay in chunks all over the floor and hung precariously from the ceiling.

Harley was standing at the file cabinet in the corner.

"I was just going through things to see what could be saved," he said sadly. I looked in the file drawers. Wet papers. The cabinet itself had held up pretty well considering the rush of fire that must have hit it. Some of the contents, at least, looked salvageable. I remembered that he had also had some papers stacked on a bookshelf against the wall. A wooden bookshelf. There was nothing left there now but charcoal and ash. He'd always had his desk piled with papers, too, and its metal surface showed blistered paint with little black scraps stuck in the blisters. His chair was shoved into a corner. It still stank. It was a burned and melted mass of plastic and stuffing.

I felt sorry for the man. He looked so lost. His whole personality was tied up with this office.

"Come on, Harley," I said. "I'll buy you a cup of coffee and we can talk about the case."

For the first time since I'd arrived, he looked directly at me. He stared at my face, still bandaged and purple with bruises.

"Looks a little like your office, doesn't it?" I quipped.

He didn't even smile. "I hope that didn't happen to you in the line of duty."

"It did. But don't worry about expenses. I've got medical coverage. Coffee?"

He shook his head. He wanted to stay with his debris. Nothing was going to make him perk up, I thought, so I tried the big news out on him.

"The police have got Cutter now. This time they'll be able to hold him. He tried to kidnap me."

He brightened just a little. "Will they charge him with Margaret's murder?"

"I don't know about that."

"It has to be Cutter!" he cried. "If the police can't prove it, you have to. Otherwise, they'll keep looking. And I think they actually still suspect me."

"Relax," I said. "That's what you hired me for." I didn't feel sorry for him anymore. The old familiar distaste was returning with every word out of his mouth.

"Well, they asked me again what time I went to work that day and when I went home. I think they even asked those Nazis what time they saw me leaving the building."

"They have to ask those questions. You're probably all right."

"I don't understand. You said Cutter had information about my marriage that he gave to the police. You said he had even been to my house and that he had some of Margaret's property in his possession. What was he doing at my house if he wasn't killing my wife?"

"I don't know when he was there. I do know that he knew your wife pretty well. And that she was probably involved with him through CORPS."

He didn't say anything, and he didn't look very surprised.

"Even so," I continued, "I still don't know that he killed her. There are other possibilities."

Harley looked angry. "Like who? Don't give me that. Our deal was that you would find the real killer before the police implicated me because of Rebecca. It sounds like the police caught Cutter anyway. Maybe you don't want to admit he's the killer because you didn't catch him."

I ignored the bullshit and decided to tell him that Cutter knew about his relationship with Rebecca.

He gaped at me. "He saw us together?"

"Yes. And he told Margaret."

He gave that a couple seconds thought. "But he couldn't have known who she was," he said resolutely. "I could have been talking to a student."

"You're wrong, Harley. He knew. He mentioned her by name."

"But he'll tell the police!"

"Maybe. Probably."

"You were supposed to prevent this." He banged his fist down on what was left of his desktop. "You shouldn't have turned him in. You've really—"

"Shut up, Harley," I said softly. "It couldn't be helped."

He rested his elbows on the desk, blackening the brown suede patches of his jacket, and covered his face with his hands. I thought he was going to cry.

"They must have been following me around, watching me. Those Nazi bastards." He took his hands away from his face. He wasn't crying. "If the police ask me, I'll deny it, that's all. It's his word against mine. The word of an arsonist and a killer. I'll say he's trying to avert suspicion from himself. He can't prove anything." The look he gave me was half terror, half impotent rage. "But you'd better. For God's sake, do something. That's what I'm paying you for. Make sure they charge Cutter. I can't take much more." His voice rose hysterically, then sank again to a near whisper. "It's all been too much. I'm pretty tough. But first my wife, and then my office, and now . . . I don't know what to do anymore."

"Just try to leave it to me," I said with more confidence than I was feeling. I told him I'd get back to him soon and left him to his charred remains.

On my way home, I turned my mind loose, hoping it would be creative. But I kept getting stuck on Harley. On his insistence that I concentrate on hanging Cutter. Maybe that had been the object all along. A fall guy. And an amateur detective with lots of evidence against the fall guy dropped in his lap. Except that Harley hadn't exactly directed me to Cutter. Or had he? Maybe he'd known all along about his wife's affiliations.

I drove through Berkeley mumbling to myself. No, the whole idea was stupid. Harley wasn't dumb enough to discount the police or think they'd be influenced by whatever I might come up with. Nor was he clever enough to come up with such a convoluted scheme. He was an average jerk with more than the average amount of arrogance and selfishness. Just another of Margaret Bursky's bad choices. The woman was no judge of character.

The first thing I did when I got in the door was make another try at reaching Hal. He was home and he'd been busy.

"Yeah, Jake, I just tried to call you. Cutter's got his whole body in a sling."

"Well, yes, I assumed he was in a little trouble. After all, he tried to kidnap me."

"Right, right, but that's not all they've got him on. He's confessed to the arson. Conviction on either of those charges would put him away for a while. Even if the fingerprints aren't enough to go on for anything else. Like homicide."

"Fingerprints? What are you talking about?"

"Oh, sorry. Guess I got a little ahead of you. When they took him in today, they put him through the usual routine. They'd been waiting for word from Sacramento on those prints they found on the fruit bowl. They don't have to wait any longer. The prints were Cutter's. On the bowl they found on the deck the day she was killed."

"Sounds like he's had it," I admitted.

"Could be. It sure gives them something to work on."

"They're still looking at other suspects, then?"

"You bet."

I was remembering Harley's fear. "What about the husband? Is he clear?"

"Hell, no. His campus alibis won't do it. They can't pinpoint the time of death that closely. He could have killed her before he went to work. And there is a money motive."

"Yeah?"

"Yeah. She left him half her money. At least a hundred thousand."

"Where'd the other half go?"

"Divided three ways between some ditsy meditation center, a few relatives back east, and a political group called CORPS."

That explained why Harley hadn't been surprised when I'd told him his wife was involved with CORPS. I'd asked him to let me know about the will, but he hadn't bothered. Probably afraid I'd start suspecting him myself. So, I thought, Bursky had managed, in death, to stab her husband in the back. An act worthy of the woman whose self-portrait had so fascinated me. A great joke, if she'd meant it as one: leaving money to her husband's enemies.

—23—

Rosie had a look in her eye that I didn't like. We were having dinner at a Japanese restaurant on Claremont that had the best fried oysters in the East Bay. That's what I had ordered. Rosie had shrimp teriyaki. We were working on our second bottle of sake by the time I'd finished filling her in. She chewed a piece of carrot thoughtfully and met my eyes straight on with a funny little smile. I wondered what was coming.

"There are two sides to this, at least," she said. "The political and the personal. Two different possible reasons for the killer. Personal hate or political necessity."

"Three," I corrected. "There's the money. There's also the possibility of a combination of all three. A political connection, a personal one, and good old greed."

Rosie brushed that complication off with a wave of her hand. "Doesn't matter. Not for the point I was about to make."

"Which is?"

"There's only one of you, and everybody knows you by now."

I thought I could see what was coming. I didn't like it, but there was no way I could express my hesitation without putting our friendship in danger.

"Okay, Rosie, what do you want to do?"

"Join CORPS."

"Well," I said, grinning, "you're certainly a likely candidate for membership in a right-wing group that believes in traditional American values."

She grimaced. "What am I anyway?" she asked. "A Peruvian or something?"

I laughed. "Maybe not. But you're the enemy to them and to what they're trying to do."

"What are they trying to do?" she asked wearily.

"The question is, who's doing what? Jared seems to have pushed for the fire, but who is Jared? Where does he go when he leaves town? Where does he come from? We just don't know enough."

"Right," Rosie said triumphantly. "That's why I'm joining CORPS."

"I don't know, Rosie," I said slowly, still smiling. "Do you think you can act like one of them?"

"Hey, what is this? Don't you think I'm an American either?"

I gave up. After her performance with the two-by-fours, the big brother stuff was even more ridiculous than it would have been normally.

Once she'd won her point, she was perfectly willing to let me take a break from the case and have a nice, friendly, relaxed dinner. In fact, she was eager to change the subject. We talked about our personal lives for a while. She mentioned a date she'd had the night before, smiled a little and said she'd had fun but wouldn't tell me any more than that. I figured if she was in love she'd say so. She encouraged me to keep trying with Iris if I was "all that hot for her." We batted the cheerful nonsense around for a while until I realized my eyes were closing and my body was going numb. We called it a night. She promised to keep me informed, step by step, on her progress with CORPS.

When I got home, there was only one message on the machine. From Rebecca. Just asking me to call her. I didn't want to, but I guessed she must be upset about Cutter being able to identify her. So I took the phone into the bedroom, undressed, got under the covers, and dialed her number, yawning. She answered on the second ring.

She said she just wanted to talk, that she was feeling lonely. Not a word about Cutter. Apparently she hadn't heard from Harley yet. I asked her how come she was so lonely.

"Oh, it's John. He won't see me. He won't even let me call him. He says he doesn't think it would be smart to take a chance on being seen together until this thing blows over."

"Well," I said, almost choking on a yawn, "that seems reasonable."

"Don't be silly. He saw me when his wife was alive. We were a big secret then, too." Oh, wonderful. She had called to have someone to argue with. "I feel as though I was just a supplement or something. And now there's nothing to be a supplement to." A fascinating topic, but I really didn't give a damn at the moment.

"Rebecca . . ." I began, with something that sounded oddly like a whine. She caught the tone.

"Listen, Jake, I really am about to go out of my mind with boredom. How about dinner tomorrow night?"

Very flattering. I mumbled "Sure," agreed to meet her at the same place we'd gone to before, and fumbled the phone onto its cradle. It wasn't even ten o'clock when I fell asleep, and it was ten in the morning when I woke up. Tigris was standing on my chest glaring into my eyes. Euphrates was standing in the bedroom doorway, waiting to escort me to the kitchen.

I fed them and took a shower while the water boiled for my coffee. By the time I'd shaken off my heavy sleep, gotten dressed, and watered a few plants, it was nearly time to meet Iris for brunch. I wondered how many restaurant meals Harley would be willing to pay for. If I kept eating out at the rate I'd been going, the five-thousand retainer could be eaten up very quickly.

Now that my mind was beginning to function again, the conversation with Rebecca was replaying itself in my mind. Her mention of the "big secret" of Harley's relationship with her. But Cutter had known.

Cutter was getting more and more interesting, and I was anxious to see what I could pull out of Iris by way of information about him. Without blowing the date.

The place she had wanted to have brunch was one of my least favorite. It was fairly new and was the latest, maybe even the last, stage in the evolution of the health food business. If Safeway Markets had designed a restaurant, it would look like Simple Simon's.

Everything was very slick. Slick lighting, slick ferns, slick art on the walls, slick furniture, and slick food. The place was big enough to house an old-fashioned family cafeteria, and I found myself wishing for that wonderful dingy look and that wonderful overcooked food. But the nostalgia was brief. I was having trouble holding on to those memories of old tastes and old aromas. Nothing at Simple Simon's smelled anything like veal cutlets, gravy, and real mashed potatoes.

No question about it. My tastes were handed down through generations of heart attack victims.

Iris wasn't there yet, so I took a small table with a view of the door, ordered a glass of carrot juice, and told the waiter there would be two of us.

She arrived at the same time as the carrot juice and looked almost as expensive. She was wearing tan slacks, sandals, and a beautifully garish silk shirt in a tropical flower print. Her pale blond hair fell straight and heavy to her shoulders. I waved; she smiled and strode to our table. I don't know if anyone else in the room was watching her. I was watching her too hard myself to notice. She slipped into the chair across from me and gave me an amused look. I checked to make sure my mouth wasn't hanging open and handed her a menu.

"So," she said, "Eddie's in jail and you put him there. Is that how your face got that way?" She was eyeing my bandaged chin.

I looked at her carefully. No, there was no criticism in her expression. "Uh uh," I answered. "But I thought turning him in was a better idea than being kidnaped."

"Much better." She smiled. The waiter came back and we both ordered large salads with yogurt dressing.

"How did you find out about his arrest?" I asked. "Was it in the papers today?"

"I don't know. I don't read the papers. They depress me." She lifted her eyebrows slightly, so I could tell she was making a joke against herself. "No. He asked if he could see his therapist, and they let me visit him. Who hit him with a rock?"

"It wasn't a rock. It was a pair of two-by-fours. My tenant. And my friend. She's a carpenter."

"Interesting weapon. He wasn't badly hurt, though."

I smiled sweetly. "I'm so glad."

"Of course, I'm not his therapist anymore. Now that he's confessed, he won't be coming to my office. Not for years."

I crushed a cherry tomato in my mouth, swallowed, and said, "What do you know about his confession?" I added diplomatically, "Whatever's public, that is."

"Just that he started the fire." She stabbed a lettuce leaf with her fork and held it midway between plate and mouth, studying my face. "If you're wondering about the murder, he didn't confess to that. He says he didn't do it. Just the fire."

"Did he say who put him up to it?"

"He says no one put him up to it, that he did it all on his own, all by himself. That CORPS wasn't involved. Only Eddie. He says it was a political statement and there was nothing personal behind it. So," she concluded, "I guess that solves the fire."

I didn't correct her. "Iris, this is important. I just want your opinion. Maybe you can't give it to me." She met my eyes, and the gray ice flashed with wariness. "Do you think Cutter is capable of killing, was capable of killing Margaret Bursky?"

"If I don't answer that," she shot at me, "you'll assume it's because I think he's the killer." This woman was sharp. She couldn't be maneuvered without letting it happen. "For what it's worth, I don't think he has ever killed anyone."

I pushed one more time. "What about Debbi?" She looked at me coldly and spoke through her teeth.

"Drop it, Samson."

"Okay." I showed my palms in surrender. "We can change the subject. I'm awfully glad you agreed to have brunch with me."

"No more business? Just pleasure?" she asked, and the gray eyes looked a little warmer.

"Pleasure," I said, tasting the word.

She smiled. "Slow down, pal."

"How slow can I be? I lead a life of great danger. I get beaten up, kidnapped, threatened by the police and by—" I almost mentioned Jared, but I decided I'd keep him to myself for a while. "Every day could be my last, my dear." I crinkled my eyebrows Gig Young fashion. Urbane.

She laughed. "Sounds like fun. A little self-indulgent but fun. I'm free Wednesday night."

This was only Sunday. I wondered whether she was busy with work or with men, but of course I didn't ask. I agreed blandly to Wednesday night, giving the impression that I was tied up until then, too. I probably would be.

"Why have you changed your mind about going out with me?" I wanted to hear something wildly complimentary, but I should have known better.

"Doesn't matter anymore. You've seen most of the people in the group; they've talked about it among themselves. They know you've been to see me, too. Nobody's even hinted an accusation at me. I guess you've brought adventure into their lives. This whole thing has."

I nodded. That was nice.

"And besides," she said, "you are cute."

—24—

Iris and I separated at Simple Simon's door with the promise to talk to each other before Wednesday.

I was feeling pretty good, so I left my car in the municipal parking lot and took a walk through downtown Berkeley, mulling things over. Exercising heavy mental discipline, I even managed to think about the case, instead of Iris. Business is business.

Downtown Berkeley is pretty small and runs to old buildings and old businesses. Walking down Shattuck toward University, you pass auto dealers, glass suppliers, sound equipment stores. Then you start seeing restaurants, Chinese and Italian, mostly, and movie theaters. Berkeley has lots of movie theaters. There are always hordes of students wandering around, bearing their packs with that air of rugged bravado that implies a recent return from the wilds of Yosemite. Packs full of address books, old letters, a textbook or two, a stale sandwich, some notes, maybe some dirty underwear. The usual business people of all varieties.

A few of the burnt-out relics of the sixties you see everywhere else in Berkeley, but not as many as you see on Telegraph Avenue. They cling to the campus, as though it's the only memory left in their drug-fried minds.

The case simmered in my own mind. Did Iris's refusal to say anything about Debbi imply that she thought she was capable of murder? And Cutter's confession was so much garbage. The fire wasn't his idea, just his recreation. I stopped to get a couple of Sunday newspapers, tossed everything but the news sections into a trash can, and sat down on a bus-stop bench to paw through them. I checked out the *San Francisco Examiner and Chronicle* first and found a story on page three, just a few inches, about Cutter's arrest and confession. The *Oakland Tribune* had a bigger story, at the bottom of page one. Unfortunately, I was in the story as his intended kidnap victim. Magazine writer Jacob Samson. But there was, at least, no mention of Rosie. I wondered if Hawkins had kept her out of it. If so, I was grateful.

The publicity made me so nervous I decided to go home and take a nap.

About six o'clock Rosie knocked on my door, and I pulled on a pair of pants and let her in. I couldn't believe my eyes.

"Where did you get that?" I choked, gaping. She was barely recognizable. She was wearing a dress with a gathered waist, short sleeves, and little flowers printed all over it. Topped by a neat pink cardigan sweater. She was wearing nylons and shoes that didn't look like they came from a lumberjack emporium. All that looked strange enough, but the hair was the killer. She had it pulled back in a barrette shaped like a bow. She was laughing at me.

"Like it?" she wanted to know.

"It's really awful," I said. "You look—" I hesitated, searching for the word. Then I had it. "Neutralized. Can you carry it off, I mean walk around like that and look natural?" She smirked at me, enjoying my confusion. "Do you think maybe you went too far? I mean, couldn't you have dug up something more, uh," I hesitated again, thinking of the way Iris had looked at lunch, "fashionable?"

Rosie was shaking her head. "No, no, no, Jake. You're missing the whole point. I don't want to look good. I want to be unimpressive, unremarkable, boring, nonthreatening in every way. Isn't this perfect?"

I had to agree. She was practically invisible. Her plan for the evening was to go the campus and seek out information about joining CORPS. She figured they'd have a notice up somewhere. I wished her luck and told her I'd be back early from dinner and wanted to see her before she went to bed. Just to find out how she'd done.

—25—

Rebecca was waiting for me when I got to Sen Ying's. She looked even thinner than she had the last time I'd seen her, and she was working on a half carafe of wine. I sat down and ordered one for me.

She managed a bent smile. "Looks like the police are moving along nicely on Eddie Cutter." I nodded, noncommittal. "I guess they'll have him on more than arson soon." I shrugged. My wine came. If Cutter had told the police about her, I guessed they hadn't visited her yet. If they had, that would have been her conversational opener. "I guess you and Harley have settled up for your work on the case?"

"No," I said, "we haven't. I'm not finished yet."

Rebecca's smile bent a little more and was slipping badly on one side. "What are you trying to do, get more money out of Harley? He's not a rich man, you know, and the police have the killer." Not a rich man, I thought, but he was due to pick up an extra hundred thousand soon.

"Now look, Rebecca . . ."

"Oh, come on, Jake, be a sport. Admit it. How about a toast? To the conviction of Eddie Cutter. For murder."

"I'm not sure he did it."

"Oh, stop it," she cut in. "Of course he did."

This was beginning to sound like a replay of my last conversation with Harley. I was sick of them both.

"Did you invite me out to bitch at me or to have a little company on a lonely evening?" I asked.

"That's the whole point, Jake." The sharpness was gone. "Lonely evenings. This has got to be settled. Then Harley and I can slowly start seeing each other again and eventually not even worry if we're seen together, and then—"

"And then," I interrupted, "you will get married and live happily ever after."

"Why not?" She asked the question like I'd told her she could never have another glass of wine.

"No reason. I hope you do."

"Thank you," she replied suspiciously. "But I don't think you understand how it's been. Months of secrecy, and now it's even worse. Now I can't see him at all."

"And just because of a little thing like a woman's death." I spoke gently to take some of the sting away.

She drew her breath in sharply. It sounded like a hiss.

Even though I'd had only a salad for lunch, I didn't feel hungry. I felt a little sick. Sizzling rice soup and a couple of egg rolls were all I thought I could handle. Rebecca's appetite had improved since the last time I'd seen her. She ordered ginger beef.

"You know, Rebecca, your relationship with Harley wasn't as much of a secret as you seem to think."

She frowned at me, as if she were considering an argument.

"Cutter knew about it. So did Harley's wife."

She paled, then tossed her head. "Nonsense. It's not possible."

"I'm afraid it's true. Tell me something. How could Cutter have known who you are?"

"I don't understand the question."

"He told me he knew Harley was having an affair with you. He saw the two of you together once. I asked him how he knew who you were, and he told me he'd heard things. Could he have heard things?" She stared at me blankly. "How could he have heard things if you two were so good at keeping your secret?"

She collected herself enough to speak. "Maybe they had Harley's phone tapped."

"They who?"

"CORPS, naturally. Trying to get something on him so they could destroy his reputation."

"But if they meant to do that, why haven't they used it against him politically?"

"Maybe they decided to wait. I don't know. How could I know?" She was no longer pale. She had a spot of color on each cheekbone, like a tuberculosis victim. "Anyway, I don't know Cutter and he doesn't know me. How should I know where he heard my name? Why are you asking me these idiotic questions?"

I ate an egg roll, dipping it into hot mustard.

"I don't know," I told her. "Just a habit. Looking in a lot of different directions. Little bits of information. Some of them matter. Some of them don't."

She settled back, relaxing. "Priorities, Jake. You really should learn to get them straight." I choked back a retort. I was feeling kind and generous.

"I am looking for more evidence against Cutter, Rebecca. If my questions seem strange, it's because I know more about this case than you do, and there are some pretty convoluted interrelationships involved. Incidentally, had you heard that they found Cutter's prints at the scene of the killing?"

Rebecca smiled, actually smiled. She hadn't known. "That's wonderful! Now I know this mess is almost over."

I smiled and patted her hand. Rebecca was in worse shape than I'd thought she was. She'd been so busy spinning happy fantasies of Cutter's immediate indictment that she hadn't taken his knowledge about her all the way to the logical next step. He was in custody. He had no reason to conceal her identity. The police would be visiting her.

—26—

When I pulled up in front of my house about nine-thirty that evening and parked behind Rosie's pickup on the street, I felt a sudden flash of fear.

Oh, God, I thought. Her pickup. That battered truck with the tool chest bolted to the side. Her dress, her stockings, her barrette, and a pickup truck that not only didn't fit the image but could be traced to her.

She was home, dressed in a more familiar fashion, and she greeted me with a big smile. I walked in calmly and sat down.

"Rosie, your truck. You shouldn't be driving your truck. It's probably okay right now, but not again."

She glared at me, hands on hips and one eyebrow quirked sardonically.

"You know, Samson, you're a jerk."

"Huh?"

"I borrowed a car. I will continue borrowing a car while I am a member of CORPS. A very ordinary all-American Japanese car."

The heat of embarrassment crept up my neck and into my face.

"You should blush, Jake," Rosie said self-righteously. I nodded. "I'm going to assume," she continued, "that you would have said the same thing to anyone you thought was inexperienced and maybe a little dumb. Not just a woman. Not just me." I nodded again. Then she dropped the attack and got to the important business. "I found out about a meeting tomorrow night. I'm going. Here's the address." She handed me a scrap of paper. A North Berkeley address.

"Can I keep this?"

"Yes," she said, "I wrote it down for you."

"Any problem finding out about the meeting?"

"None at all. There were notices up all over the place. Looks like they're anxious to recruit members."

I told her about my dinner with Rebecca.

"Poor woman," she said. "I wonder if he really does plan to start seeing her again when this is over. I think she wonders, too."

We talked about Cutter's confession and his fruit-bowl fingerprints. "Maybe," Rosie said, "he'll confess to the murder next. Maybe that blow knocked his conscience loose."

I snorted. "He didn't need to have anything else knocked loose. His brains have been rattling around for a while."

By the time we'd finished catching each other up, we were on friendly terms again. It was still early when I got in my own door, so I put in a call to Debbi.

She sounded strange. I couldn't tell whether she was glad to hear from me or not, but I decided she probably was not. Her throat sounded tight and her words came out a little fast.

"Yes, Jake. How are you? What can I do for you?"

"It's like this, Debbi, I've been talking to some more people and now I've got a few items I need some help with. Maybe you could answer a few more questions?"

She sighed with exasperation or exhaustion.

"I don't know what more I can tell you, Jake."

"Maybe there's something you forgot. If I could come and see you?"

"Tonight? I don't think so. No. Is there some reason why you always want to see me at night?"

Like my father always said, there's no justice. I didn't think it would do much good to argue with her, deny my lust, accuse her of seducing me. I had to stay on her good side. Not under her, not on top of her, but on her good side.

"No, that's not what I meant," I protested. "Not tonight. But soon. It's important. You know Cutter's in jail?"

She sighed again. "Yes. I saw the paper. Why should I care?"

"Can I see you?" I repeated.

"Oh, all right. Tomorrow morning. Before eight. Before I go to work. But I don't know anything I haven't told you already."

"That's great," I said. "I won't take up much of your time, I promise."

She hung up without saying good-bye. You let them use you, and they lose respect for you.

When I awoke early Monday morning, I felt more like my old self. Cuts, bruises, and cracks healing nicely, no unusual fatigue. I even sang in the shower.

Debbi was wearing workclothes. A neat little suit that made her look efficient. Her wounds, too, were healing well. She offered me coffee but avoided my eyes.

"Before you start asking questions," she said, "I should tell you that the police came to see me. I told them you'd been around asking questions. And I told them what I'm telling you. I don't know anything."

"Did you tell them that Cutter was at Bursky's house the day she died?"

"No. And I never told you that either."

"Why not?"

"They'll get him without my help. I don't have to be a witness. If I don't know anything, they can't drag me into it. Right?"

"Sure." Unless the police found out she'd wanted Cutter and Bursky had gotten him.

"Ask your questions."

"Okay. Who is Jared?"

"I don't know."

"Did the people in CORPS know Bursky had left the group some money?"

"I didn't. Was it a lot?"

"No, not really." Thirty-three thousand dollars was a nice sum but no fortune.

"Who's really behind CORPS?"

"I don't know. Nobody."

She was lying transparently, with just the slightest touch of defiance in her near-monotone. She'd have to learn to do better than that if she wanted to succeed in business.

"Debbi, there's something I've never asked you. And if you get brought into this at all, the police may want to know. Where were you that morning?" She just looked at me, tight-lipped. "You told me you were supposed to meet Eddie for an early lunch, but he canceled because he was going to see Margaret. Were you at work? What time did he call?"

"Eddie won't tell them about that. About me." Her torso looked rigid, like her face.

"Then just to set my mind at ease . . . ?" After all, I'm a nice man, remember?

She shrugged stiff shoulders. "We were supposed to meet at eleven-thirty. He didn't know how long he'd be with her, so he broke our date. I guess it was around ten when he called. I worked for a while, then I went out to lunch. Alone. I can't prove where I went."

"What time did you get back to work?"

She thought a minute, struggling between indignation and fear. "A little after noon, I think." I decided to get back to Cutter.

"How did Cutter get Bursky's drawings?"

"I don't know. Is that why he went there?"

"Possibly. In any case, he did have them. And Frank sure didn't want anyone else seeing them. Neither did Jared." I told her about my run-in with Frank, the return of the drawings, and the meeting with Jared. She didn't respond.

"Jared's picture was in there. So was Frank's. Among others."

"Mine? Was my picture in there?" Her lip trembled. I was glad I could tell her it wasn't. She was very relieved, and relief made her more friendly.

"What else do you want to know, Jake?"

"There's something I can't quite figure out, Debbi. It's not particularly important, but it might connect with some other things." I leaned forward, confidentially. "Cutter knew about John Harley's affair with someone. He knew her by sight and he knew her name. Did people in the group know Harley was being unfaithful to his wife?"

"We didn't even know he had a wife. And we certainly didn't know it was Margaret. Not until she died." She was confirming what she'd already told me once before. It was probably true. "I don't remember anyone ever mentioning a wife. Or a mistress. It never came up. He was just a goat anyway."

"What's that?"

"A goat. The group was looking for someone to take on, just any left-wing professor. Someone to make an example of."

"How was Harley chosen?"

She laughed. "Margaret suggested him." She tilted her head at me. "So he was having an affair? I guess she knew about it. I suppose that's why she sicked the group on him." She laughed again. It was not a pleasant laugh.

"I guess so," I said. "Sure you never heard of a man named Jared?"

"I said I didn't know who he was. His real name. He was around. Around CORPS."

"Why? I thought it was a student group."

"I don't want to talk to you anymore. I'm tired of this. I have to go to work. Go talk to someone else." I got up, thanked her for her help, and left. That might be about all that could be squeezed out of her. Ever. She was going to close the whole thing off, pretend it wasn't happening, pretend she didn't know anyone or anything. Maybe it would work.

—*27*—

Bit by bit, the picture was forming. Nasty goings-on. Rivalry. Hate.

Maybe Cutter went to get the drawings, fought with Bursky and killed her. Or Jared killed her because CORPS needed a little money. Or because she had sketched his face. If I were Jared, I certainly wouldn't want anyone to draw my face.

Or a stranger meandered in off the road, shoved her over the railing, and meandered off again, cackling insanely. And apples grow on walnut trees.

The story would all fit together, I knew, if I wasn't missing something. A piece. Two or three pieces. But I was beginning to run out of places to look. Did that mean the pieces were hidden where I'd already looked or that I didn't know where I should be looking next?

Infiltration of CORPS seemed an unlikely way to find the answers. The answers to the murder anyway. Rosie would probably be stuck listening to a lot of raving fanatics for a while, and that would be that.

The answers, I reasoned, would come through individuals, not through groups. But then, maybe that was just my noncollective mentality rebelling against the idea that a group could achieve anything. Even an efficient murder.

I thought I'd head over in the direction of the campus, have some breakfast, harass Billy once more, and check in with Harley. The police hadn't shown a lot of interest in Billy, and I didn't plan to waste much more time on him either, but it wouldn't do any harm to mention Cutter and CORPS and other odds and ends and watch his reactions. He might eliminate himself once and for all, or he might come at me with a paper knife, screaming a confession.

Billy was at his usual stand, behind the counter at the Earthlight Meditation Center. He greeted me in a neutral fashion and inquired softly about what I had come for.

"Nothing much, Billy. Just to say hello. Ask what you think about some of what's happening. Shoot the shit. So, how ya doing?"

The good ol' boy approach pleased him, as I thought it might. It was probably a rare event when Billy got let into the club of masculine shit-shooting. And it probably never happened with heavy masculine types like me, guys who wrote for magazines. Guys who asked questions about murdered women.

He slouched over to the counter, his thumbs hooked in his belt loops. This man, I decided then and there, could never kill anyone. He'd be so busy watching himself do it that he'd never get it done.

"Yeah," he said. "How about that Cutter? Looks like he's the one, right?"

I raised my eyebrows and pursed my lips. "Yeah? What do you think?"

Billy lifted his shoulders in a languid shrug. "Good a guess as any."

"Did you know Margaret Bursky was involved in CORPS?" I

just tossed it to him. None of the newspapers had printed anything, as far as I knew, about Cutter and Bursky's common cause.

"Not until today," he said. "It's all over the place this morning. You know how stuff like that gets passed on."

"No, how?"

"Those CORPS people have got big mouths, that's how. They're making speeches on street corners, picketing her husband, and talking about how even she understood he was a corrupter, and how she joined CORPS to fight against her own husband. All kinds of disgusting stuff like that. Like I said, it's all over the place."

"Has anybody said anything about any other aspects of her private life?"

He was puzzled by the question. Billy, like Eddie Cutter, seemed to "hear things," but he hadn't heard anything about Rebecca. Nor had he heard anything about Bursky leaving the center money in her will. We talked for a while longer. I let him contribute more quotes for my article, and then I let him get back to work. If he'd killed Margaret Bursky in a fit of jealous passion or unrequited love, neither the passion nor the love had been strong enough to last a week after her death. She seemed to be a dead issue with Billy.

Before I went to see Harley I drove past the address Rosie had given me, the place where the CORPS meeting was going to take place that night. Just an apartment building, and a big one at that.

Then I found a parking place, this time in a yellow zone, and walked across the campus to Chandler Hall. Out in front, marching around on the sidewalk, was a clutch of CORPS picketers. I was relieved to see that Rosie was not yet among them. These seemed to be special friends of Eddie Cutter because their signs, this time, were all about his innocence, at least as a killer. One young man was haranguing a bored-looking crowd of about a dozen students. When I came closer, I heard him saying,

"Eddie Cutter didn't kill Margaret Harley. That woman had a political conscience. That woman was Eddie Cutter's friend. She didn't die of friendship. She died of shame, shame that her husband was working to bring this country down in moral ruins. . . ."

They were being premature in defending their friend against a crime he hadn't been charged with. Aside from that, I didn't think this kid would have anything original to say about sin. I'm as much opposed to moral ruins as the next guy, especially when someone's lack of morality gives him leave to beat people up. So I went upstairs to Harley's office. The door was partly open, and I looked inside. He was with a student, a woman. He was leaning across his desk toward her, and she was leaning across the desk, from the other side, toward him. They were talking softly. I had time to see that his office was somewhat more put together than it had been the last time I saw it before he caught sight of me and jumped out of his chair. The student, also startled, saw me and blushed.

Harley was too pleasant. "Oh, hi there, Jake," he said. "I'll be through here in a minute if you want to wait." I grinned back at him, nodded, and lounged against the wall outside the door. The two whispered a few more words to each other, and the young woman came out. Very young. About nineteen or twenty. A lot younger than Rebecca.

I went through the door and sat down in the warm chair she had vacated. Harley was, at this point, less pleasant.

"You should have called before you came here," he said.

"Just stopping by on my way from here to there," I said cheerily. "Wondered if you'd want a little progress report."

"Of course I would," he said grudgingly.

"Okay, but first I think you should tell me something. Why didn't you keep me informed about the will?"

"Because I didn't think it was relevant. You knew about CORPS."

"She left you half of it."

"Of course she did," he said indignantly. "I was her husband."

I decided to leave my thoughts unspoken and told him the good news about Cutter's fingerprints. That made him very happy. I didn't say anything about the peculiar circumstance of the printless coffee cup. That would have just confused him.

"Hah. So that's why the police wanted to know if the bowl was out there when I left that morning. It wasn't, of course. That certainly pinpoints when he was there."

"It certainly does," I agreed. It also had corroborated what Debbi had already told me. That Cutter had been there that morning.

I gave Harley a few more crumbs of information and finished up by telling him I'd found out why CORPS had chosen him as a target. He was very interested. He leaned forward, looking eager, just the way he had with the student. Well, maybe not exactly the same way.

"They just needed someone to go after," I told him. "Anyone. Your wife suggested they go after you." He stiffened right up, the eager look gone. I didn't give him time to react but went right ahead and asked a couple of questions.

"Do you have any idea who's behind CORPS, Harley?"

He shook his head. "Not really. But it seems obvious that a larger group is behind them. What's that got to do with Margaret? Are you sure that's why they picked me?"

"Yes. No indication of what the group is, huh?"

"I don't know. But they don't talk like real Nazis. Nothing about Jews or blacks or any particular ethnic groups. And they tend to get religious—I guess that's what you'd call it—in their preaching. One of those moral righteousness groups. They all sound alike. They all think they're the only ones who know what morality is. They all hide behind patriotism and Christianity—"

I didn't particularly want to listen to Harley's ideas on morality either, so I interrupted him.

"About Cutter and Rebecca, do you have any idea how he might have known who she was?"

He waved a disparaging hand and looked vague, gazing into the middle distance. "I've been thinking about that. He didn't. He couldn't have known her. I don't know where he got her name, but I'll bet that's all he knows."

"What makes you so sure?"

"Because she would have told me. If they knew each other, she would have mentioned it to me. After all, with all that going on . . ." He waved his hand again, this time toward the window and the demonstrators outside. When his eyes refocused, they were fixed on me. "Who told you that's how they chose me?" I was a little slow in catching up. His mind was jumping around like a fraternity boy in a room full of prom queens. He had returned to his arbitrary selection by CORPS as a bad political example.

"An ex-member of CORPS."

"Oh. Well, he probably didn't know." Harley was beginning to look vague again. I stood up. He barely noticed. I said good-bye. On my way to the stairs, I noticed the woman student standing near a water fountain, watching my departure. I wondered if she was planning to go back to Harley's office. I wondered what the hell the man had that fascinated so many women. I sure couldn't see it.

—*28*—

The sky had been blue when I'd stopped in to visit Harley. Now dark clouds were filling the last clear gaps overhead. Not fog. Real rain clouds. The first since June. Autumn was ending, and winter was getting ready to start dumping on Northern California.

That was the only break in routine I could see coming in the next couple of days. I felt stale and dead-ended, in the case and in my life. The prewinter blues, a leftover from a time when the season meant months of cold and ice and snow.

I went home, filled the tub, made a large cheese, salami, bologna, tomato, onion, mayonnaise, and mustard sandwich, poured a glass of cranberry juice, and settled down for a long session with my stomach and my mind, the two of which are very closely related.

Two hours later I'd added hot water a dozen times and gone over the case again from beginning to possible endings from a dozen different angles.

The result? Wrinkled fingers and toes.

Wrapping myself in a warm robe, I made a couple of phone calls.

Hal didn't have much that was new. Cutter had admitted that he'd visited Bursky at home once but said he'd been there days before her death. He kept insisting that Harley was the killer and had, indeed, told the police about Harley's extramarital relationship.

"Has he got an attorney?"

"Public defender."

So CORPS might have been one big family, and maybe the student members were spreading their loyalty to Cutter all over the jaded streets of Berkeley, but the big kids with the money weren't about to stick out their creased necks on his behalf.

I was just about to dial again and try Rebecca when my phone rang. It was Artie. He wanted to let me know that an Oakland detective had visited *Probe* magazine and asked about me. "They wanted to know how long you've been a writer and where you've worked before."

"What did you tell them?"

"That you'd done some stuff back East. I was as unclear as he'd let me be. Said you were a pal and I was giving you your first big break. I don't think he believed me." Artie did not sound worried.

"Okay," I said, "thanks for the tip."

When I got Rebecca on the line, she told me that Hawkins had also paid her a call.

"Are you all right?" I asked. She didn't sound good.

"Yes. Fine."

"Well, what did you tell him?"

"That the Harleys were clients. That Cutter might have seen me paying a friendly follow-up visit, but I couldn't recall when that might have been."

"That sounds okay," I said reassuringly. Unless they got more evidence linking her with Harley.

"Jake?" Her voice was ragged with tension.

"What is it, Rebecca?"

"Maybe it would be best if you didn't call me here again."

I agreed to try to reach her only at home. I was relieved that she hadn't panicked when Hawkins had questioned her and denied that she'd ever met Harley or his wife. It would be easy enough for the cops to find out who had handled the purchase of their house.

Tension was building in me, too. Even the bath hadn't helped. I needed to get out and cut loose a little, get away from the case completely. The date with Iris was still two days away. The hell with her. There were other women, after all. Like Alana. For dinner and wine and whatever else happened.

Alana answered on the second ring. She sounded glad to hear from me, but when I asked her out, she said she was sorry and did I remember Evan?

Sure I remembered Evan. The leader of the meditation group. The slick, cozy type who had given me a little red ball and then let it get away from me. Her escort at Bursky's funeral.

"Oh, yes," I said. "Of course I do."

"Well, we've agreed to have an exclusive relationship, just to see if it works out." She sounded very happy. I thought of Beatrice, the woman who had helped Evan with the group that night, and wondered how she felt about it.

"That's wonderful, Alana," I said with some sincerity. "I hope it does."

"Oh, it may or it may not," she said casually. "If it doesn't, I'll call you." We both laughed and said good-bye.

I wondered briefly if I could whip together a poker game on short notice, move it up from Tuesday to Monday, but dismissed the thought before I dialed the first number. That was not at all what I was in the mood for. Did I want to dash around town with a friend, drinking and carousing, or did I want to slide into a singles bar looking solitary and mysterious and devilishly attractive? First I eliminated the friend. Then I eliminated the singles bar. I would have a drink somewhere quiet, then go out for some entertainment. There was a place on College Avenue, a jazz club, that attracted a lot of the local beautiful people, whatever they are. I don't care much for most jazz. I think there are a lot of mediocre musicians wandering around looking cool and imitating people who were innovative thirty years ago. And I think there are a lot of people pretending to be jazz buffs because it suits the role they've chosen to play. But I love the atmosphere of jazz clubs. Like Alana, they represent the other side of the fifties, and I'm crazy about history.

I took a nap and woke feeling pretty good. Then I cooked and ate a leisurely dinner, spent some time dressing in clean jeans, royal blue shirt, and genuine Norwegian ski sweater, and stuck my head out the door into a fine drizzle. I added a thin waterproof jacket to my ensemble and topped the whole thing with an item I save for very special occasions: my genuine Basque beret. I looked terrific.

My first stop was a place called the Corner, a local bar that attracted an after-work crowd. Very mixed. Everything that lived in the neighborhood coexisting in one small, dim, warmly decorated space. There's a dessert place down the block that's four times as big and attracts the same kind of crowd. Everyone who feels at home in what a painter friend of mine once called the fern-hung, bentwood-chaired, half-the-people-are-wearing-contact-lenses atmosphere. He's a house painter, by the way.

I slid onto a barstool and thought about drinking something. I was getting tired of wine, and that severely limited my choices.

Once, when I was young and thought I was someone I'd read about, I also thought I liked whisky. Sippin' whisky straight up or on the rocks but never mixed with anything. Good solid sour mash. I'm not so young anymore, and I know damned well the stuff makes me gag. Watered down, maybe, or with a lot of soda. But who wants to pay whisky prices for a glass of tinted water? So I ordered a wine spritzer. White wine, soda, and lots of ice. When my drink came, I turned sideways on my stool, looking around, getting my bearings, outlining the cast of characters. It was close to eight o'clock, and the remains of the after-work crowd needed their dinners very badly.

This was not easy to tell with the kind of people who hung out here. Drunk was not what one was supposed to be. So they paced themselves, most of them, or failing that sat quietly in a corner until they pulled themselves together enough to go home or have a Perrier with a twist. Some of them, I guessed, just didn't want to go home. I could understand that. A little apartment some-where, where the only other living thing was a philodendron. The divorced ones. The aging singles of various sexes who didn't think it was all so much fun anymore.

The guy on the barstool next to mine was tall and chubby, with sandy hair and moustache. He was wearing brown cor-duroys, a Levi jacket, and a T-shirt that said he was a great lover. He was watching two women at the end of the bar. To my right, three stools down, a young gay man was leaning on the bar sipping a light beer and talking to the bartender about a bar on Castro Street in San Francisco. In the booth across the aisle from me, a woman was telling her friend she would never again fall in love with a punk type. I got the impression the punk was another woman.

"Yeah, well, listen," her friend said, "pink hair?"

"It was purple."

In the booth next to them a young couple sat holding hands, out on a date, he wearing a suit, she wearing a dress.

Farther away, more stray men and a few more women.

I had no idea what the late crowd was like. This time of eve-ning it was a neighborhood bar and these people represented the neighborhood. Or that part of the neighborhood that went to bars.

The sandy-haired guy turned to me. "Can't seem to catch her

eye," he said, blushing a little. I looked down the bar. The dark-haired woman's light-haired friend was looking our way. She turned her head and pretended she hadn't been.

"Which one?" I asked him.

"The dark-haired one. Of course." I looked again. I didn't understand why it was "of course." The dark-haired one looked gaunt and affected to me. The light-haired one had a nice smile.

"Oh," I said. "The other one was looking this way."

He shrugged. "I like dark-haired women."

"Oh," I said again. He reminded me of a woman I once knew who said she only went out with long-legged men. I didn't have anything to say to her, either. I glanced again at the two women at the end of the bar. Sure enough, the light one was watching chubby T-shirt next to me. The dark one was running her fingers through her own hair. No one was watching me.

I'd no sooner had that thought than I realized it wasn't true. The young guy who'd been talking about Castro Street was trying to make eye contact. A very pretty young woman at the far end of the bar was smiling at me. I killed two birds with one stone by smiling at the woman.

The guy turned to see who I was grinning at, smiled, and shrugged. I also smiled and shrugged at him. He went back to his conversation with the bartender. The young woman turned away. I was supposed to give chase, but I didn't know whether I felt like it. Alienation and objectivity can also be amusing. Besides, I hadn't planned on spending a lot of time in the place, and I hadn't planned on meeting a woman there.

Inflexibility is one thing, though, and absurd obstructionism is another. I finished my wine and caught her eye again. She really was awfully cute. Dark brown hair, sensual mouth, small, rounded, soft-looking body.

My plan: go to the men's room and maybe stop near her on my way back. Not original, not even subtle, but better than marching over to her, all the way down the bar, like it mattered how she responded.

Have people truly always gone through this nonsense?

So I went to the toilet. When I came out, I nodded to her and she said "Hi." She had changed her position just enough to place herself in the path from the men's room to my barstool.

Abandoning my sandy-haired friend and his hopeless passion for the dark-haired woman, I stood next to my new companion, ordered another drink, and asked if she would like anything. She was drinking old-fashioneds. I couldn't remember the last time I saw anyone drinking those.

She was about twenty-six and her name was Kim. After Novak, I assumed. Every generation saddles its girl children with movie star names. If you eat the heart of your enemy you will have his courage. If you bear the name of a movie star you will look perfect and be famous. Or burn out on drugs or alcohol or multiple marriage.

I don't think Kim was famous, but she didn't look burnt-out yet, even though she was drinking her old-fashioned a little fast. She told me she was a commercial artist and that she worked for an ad agency in The City. She didn't say what she did, and I didn't press it, just in case she was doing menial production work and didn't want to admit it. Instead, I babbled on about a woman I had known who had been a fine graphic designer and how she threw it all away to become a sculptor.

"What happened?" Kim wanted to know.

But the story had no end, and I felt a little silly. "I don't know," I admitted. She laughed. She had a nice laugh and a sexy smile, and she touched my arm from time to time when she talked. But ten minutes into our relationship I realized I wasn't remembering anything she said. She'd had one drink too many and was tending toward run-on sentences, leaving me no openings for response. I was fading out on the whole thing.

"Kim," I interjected finally, in desperation, "you are talking too much and too fast. You're not giving me a chance to know you."

She stopped, stared at me, said, "Who says I want you to get to know me?" and burst into tears and left the bar.

I hung around for another half hour and then took off for Carmino's jazz club.

There was a pretty good crowd for a Monday night. A group of musicians was standing on the small stage messing with its instruments, leaning down to catch what the pretty redhead was saying, talking to each other softly with much use of hands. Four guys in various colors and various styles of dress. One of them was wearing a pair of baggy tweeds that looked like something he'd inherited from his father, with a yellow button-down shirt. One was wearing black stovepipe pants and a black turtleneck jersey. One was wearing jeans and a T-shirt that didn't say anything. The fourth, the drummer, hadn't come out from behind his drums long enough to show what he looked like.

The tables were small, and I knew from experience that the chairs were uncomfortable. I never drank enough to make them bearable for more than an hour. I stood at the bar. That gave me mobility and a good view of the population.

Carmino's is not small. There's the bar, farthest from the stage, about twenty of the aforementioned tables, and several large booths for the dinner crowd. One booth was full, and about half the tables.

Sitting at one of the tables near the bar were two young women. They were looking at me and giggling. Too young. They thought my beret was funny. No woman I could ever be interested in would think my beret was funny. The woman lounging a few stools down the bar from me looked more interesting. She was dressed in boots, baggy knickers, a T-shirt, and an embroidered vest. She was rangy and tall, with a strong high-bridged nose and full lips. Her hair was dark. She looked arrogant as hell. Letting my eyes rove the bar and bringing my focus back to her from time to time, I saw that she seemed to be alone. She wasn't talking to anyone. One or two men glanced her way and then looked away again. Maybe they were afraid she had a riding crop hidden in those boots. She turned toward the bar and, en route, caught me looking at her. She raised that beautiful arched nose a little higher and ordered a drink.

The musicians were looking more organized. They stopped fiddling with their instruments, and one of them fiddled with the microphone. He mumbled some introductions, and each player, in turn, nodded, smiled, or raised a drumstick in casual salute. They began to play. I glanced back at the baroness with the beautiful nose. She was looking at me. We gazed coolly into each other's eyes for a moment, then I turned away and listened to the music. It was okay. But her voice sounded better.

"Nice hat," she said.

"Thank you," I replied, and turned to her. She looked amused, the way an Amazon might look if she were challenging a man to combat. I sent the same look back at her, and she didn't flinch.

Her name, she said, was Faye, an oddly old-fashioned name for a woman who looked like she did. She bought me a drink and I bought her one. We listened to the music. We both got bored with it.

She said she was a landscape designer and I said I was a writer.

"I did my own yard," I told her.

"I can imagine," she said.

"Would you like to sit at a table?"

"No, I'd rather stand."

"Would you like to go somewhere else?"

"No, I'm in the mood for this."

"So was I. But I'm not so sure anymore."

Faye gave me a slow smile. "I'm still in the mood for it."

A couple of barstools opened up, and we took them. Our knees touched. She was listening to the music again. I didn't interrupt her. The group finished the set and dropped off the stage to join friends at a nearby booth. Faye turned to me. This was the point at which, by the old rules, she was supposed to ask me about my work or my hobbies. Draw me out. Get to know me. But Faye was a very direct woman.

"You married?" she asked.

I shook my head. "Not lately." I was surprised by the question, one that people don't seem to bother to ask anymore. If you were out alone—well, you were out alone. Surprised and impressed. Then it occurred to me that she might simply be looking for common ground. "You?" I asked.

She smiled. "Not ever." I liked her smile and was about to say so when a familiar figure came in the door, followed by an unfamiliar one. It was Debbi, with a good-looking if nondescript young man in a suit that could have fit him better. They found a table. I watched while the young man ordered drinks, unbuttoning his jacket and leaning back casually and precariously on the small, wobbly chair.

I didn't think Debbi would be glad to see me, but I felt that it behooved me to know as much of Debbi's business as possible.

"Please don't disappear," I said to Faye, "but I have to talk to those people for just a minute."

She looked at them. Debbi and her companion both in prim little office suits. "Whatever for?" Faye asked. Then, "Don't tell me."

"Will you wait?"

She looked around the bar and laughed. "Sure. I don't see anyone else to talk to."

Small comfort, but I strolled off anyway.

Debbi looked up as I approached the table. She stared at me

blankly, as though she were going to deny knowing me. The young man followed her gaze. His eyebrows raised a fraction when he caught sight of my beret. I got the impression he was expecting to see a rhinestone brooch clipped to it.

"Hi, Debbi," I said with a nonthreatening grin, "nice to see you again." That proved I knew her name. She couldn't very well ask her escort to get rid of the fresh stranger. He stood.

"Joe," she said listlessly to her companion, "this is Jake Samson. Jake, this is Joe Sharples," and she added with great clarity and emphasis, "a co-worker of mine. Joe, Jake is a writer." This was, I assumed, by way of explanation for my eccentric dress.

For some reason the explanation seemed to reassure him. He relaxed a little and stuck out his hand. I shook it. Then I grabbed a chair from the next table and sat down. Debbi frowned slightly when I plunked my glass down on the table. Joe looked me over very much like an executive assessing the suitability of a job applicant. I smiled back stupidly.

"So," I said to Debbi, "what have you been doing with yourself?" Then I added, "It's been at least a year since we last ran into each other—at the drugstore, wasn't it?"

"At least," she said, smiling slightly for the first time. "And it was at the supermarket." Joe began to look bored. He had evidently decided I was no threat to his romance, and he probably wanted to settle down for a nice long chat about the money market. Debbi, I decided, was in good hands for the moment. I rose, said it was nice to see her again and nice to meet him and all that sort of thing. Debbi bade me a cordial good-bye. I think in that moment she almost liked me. I walked back to where Faye stood at the bar.

"You didn't stay long," she said.

"With you waiting here?"

She threw me a sardonic glance. The musicians were leaping acrobatically back onto the stage. I was beginning to wish we were sitting down. Close.

"Ready to sit at a table yet?" I asked her.

"All right," she said, and our relationship advanced a notch. From casual just-meeting at the bar to actually sitting down together and admitting, thereby, that we were in some way together.

I didn't want to talk about my exciting work as a writer, so I got her to talk about her work instead. She was happy with it.

"I love drawing up the plans, designing a yard, an environment, really, and then letting someone else do the physical labor."

"Do you have an aversion to physical labor?"

"Yes," she said, and then she surprised me. "I grew up on a farm in the Central Valley. Hot and dusty and always something dirty to do. Where did you grow up?"

"Chicago," I said. "Hot and muggy and always something dirty to do." If Faye had been a lesser woman, the "Where are you from?" game would have deteriorated into a "Where are your moon and Venus?" conversation. Very few people are so gauche as to ask "What's your sign?" anymore. And, bless her, she didn't make some idiotic remark about the "Windy City" either. I glanced over to where Debbi and Joe were sitting. They were holding hands and talking eagerly. And he didn't look anything like a soldier. I pulled my chair closer to Faye's and put my arm around her. She moved against me.

"Jake, I think I should tell you something about myself." I gazed at her lips. They were wonderful.

"You're a lesbian," I said.

She laughed. No, that wasn't it.

"You're bisexual." She pulled my earlobe. I drew back in mock horror. "You're a man in drag." She squeezed my hand and smiled at me. "You eat garlic before sex to ward off pregnancy." She kissed me on the lips. "You're a sex maniac."

"No, no, and no, or however many there were. What I wanted to say was that I'm free Thursday night, and I never go to bed with anyone the first time I meet them."

"That's reasonable," I said. "It's always nice to let the mystery build for a couple of days."

"Unless"—she grinned—"they don't push me to do it. Do you like this music?"

"No."

"Then let's go."

She had a pretty apartment in a fourplex in South Berkeley. She also had good brandy and a fireplace and a waterbed. And she made love like she was at a banquet after a three-day fast, her long, strong legs wrapped around me, her mouth holding mine, her tongue probing, her hands caressing. We fell asleep sweaty, wrapped around each other, and I suspect she was smiling just like I was. Before I dropped off, I thought of Debbi and her husbandly friend. I wished them well, if it wasn't too late for well wishing.

—*29*—

I awoke to mingled smells of coffee, hours-old lovemaking, and, oddly enough, lemon. Not, I hoped, some body-insulting room deodorizer. Following my nose to the night table and the lemon-scented hand lotion, I smiled and yawned.

Faye appeared in the bedroom doorway. She had the slightly wry look some women get when they've had a good night and aren't sure they should admit it.

"Towels in the bathroom for you. When you've showered, the coffee will be waiting."

"Thank you," I said, trying to equal her romantic repartée. She grinned and disappeared again.

I stood under the spray for a good five minutes, humming under my breath, controlling the impulse to sing as loudly as I usually do, and feeling a little angry with myself for playing cool games.

The coffee was waiting. She was wearing a jacket and looking antsy.

"I have to go, Jake. I've got an appointment with a client." The implication was clear. She liked me okay and everything, but she wasn't in the habit of leaving men alone in her apartment on such short acquaintance. I could understand that. Debbi had been more trusting, but she was younger than Faye and I sus-pected that she had, and would probably continue to have, an easier life. This woman knew from experience that a person could wind up buying a lot of stereos and color TVs by trusting the wrong men.

We kissed at the door, promising to get together on Thursday, and went our separate ways.

A note from Rosie had been slipped under my door. Aside from having filthy cat pawprints all over it, it was clear enough. It said, "Fed the cats. Meet me at 3 P.M. I need to wash myself clean in an atmosphere of sanity. Polly's."

I laughed out loud. Polly's was, depending on your vocabulary and your politics, a neighborhood tavern, a women's entertainment center, a lesbian club, or a dyke bar. It was actually a whole complex: bar, combination game room and dance floor, restaurant, and, at the rear, a big performance hall. Polly herself was a likable wise ass who had been known to insult those with thin skins or humorless dispositions. She kept a nice place, and she didn't let anybody hassle anybody else. I'd been in there only a couple of times before, both times with Rosie and her friends as escorts. I behaved myself and was more or less acceptable.

Even though the cats refused to listen, I talked to them for a while and then went back to bed. There might have been other dreams, but the one that lingered after I woke was the one about the steak and the baked potato. I was ravenous and went out for a steak and baked potato. By the time they were tucked away, it was close to three o'clock.

Polly's was quiet. It was dark and foggy outside and not yet happy hour for the nine-to-fivers. There was a small afternoon crowd of night workers, self-employed, and outdoor workers who quit early on wet days if they worked at all. In the lot I had noticed a truck that belonged to Mickey's roofing, a couple of Volkswagens, one with a UC Berkeley sticker, an old red Gremlin holding a tarp full of cuttings, a lawn mower, a rake, and, I assume, other gardening paraphernalia. A couple of vans.

The barroom had red flocked wallpaper, left over from a previous tenant, a gaslit fireplace at the left, a long bar at the right, and red carpeting. There were four women in the bar: one of them sitting alone by the fire reading a book in the dim light; another, at the bar itself, wearing overalls splattered with roofing tar; another wearing muddy jeans; another wearing a business suit, stockings, the whole works. Two women were playing pool in the next room, and one was sitting rapt and intense at an electronic game.

Polly was behind the bar talking to her afternoon bartender. She looked me over when I walked in, either remembered me or made a favorable decision, nodded cordially, and wandered off into the back regions of her empire. She was wearing a Panama hat.

The bartender was a woman named Judy, a friend of Rosie's I'd played poker with once. She was small, with a great body, shoulder-length brown hair, freckles, and a cute smile. She had a tendency to say things like, "You're okay, for a man." The kind of thing you take as a joke because what the hell else can you do with it?

"Jake, right?" she said, flashing that smile. I smiled back and climbed onto a barstool, two down from the woman with the muddy jeans on one side, three down from the business suit on the other.

I skipped the happy hour specials and had a Danish beer. An old guy from the neighborhood ambled in and took the stool nearest the door. He and Judy exchanged greetings, and, without being asked, she brought him a beer. Then she began a flirtation, or probably continued it, with the woman wearing the muddy jeans. The two playing pool sounded like they were having a lot of fun, laughing and screaming and carrying on. I strolled to the door of the game room.

"Mind if I watch?" I asked. The shorter one, a blonde with paint on her pants, shrugged "Why not?" and the taller one, a black woman wearing tweed slacks and a silk shirt, pointed to the chalkboard and told me to sign up if I wanted to play. I'm not a bad pool player, but I prefer to play with people I know if I'm going to make a fool of myself. So I leaned against the door frame to watch and see how good they were and whether I should get into the game.

The blonde was just learning. The black woman was good. I watched her make an astounding bank shot to get around the eight and sink her five ball. She whooped gleefully, and the two women hugged each other. I decided she'd be fun to play with, but I was rescued by a pinch on the butt heralding Rosie's arrival. I almost spilled my beer, recovered nicely, and threatened to complain to the bartender that I was being sexually harassed.

Judy wanted to know if I was making a pun. The roofer chuckled in her beer. The woman with the muddy jeans smiled blindly on Judy. The business suit looked at Rosie blankly, then looked again a bit less blankly, and returned to her small bottle of champagne and her menthol cigarettes. Then, unaccountably, she suddenly got the joke, laughed uproariously, and startled everyone in the room, especially the old guy at the end of the bar, who I suspected hadn't heard anything up until that point.

Rosie and I took a table so we could talk without being overheard.

"Those people," she said without preamble, "are terrifying."

I nodded soberly. "I thought you might not like them."

"No, you don't understand. I knew I'd hate them, but I hadn't imagined them to be quite as nasty as they are." She took a long pull from her beer. "We have to stop them."

"Calm down, Rosie," I told her.

"Hardest thing I've ever done. Ever. Acting friendly and interested in that bunch of—God, I can hardly even talk about it without palpitations."

"Think they'd kill for thirty-three thousand?"

"I think they're capable of anything."

"Right. Now give me the basics."

"Okay," she said. "Okay. There were fourteen people there counting me. My little dress was a big hit with one guy. He really turned on to me. Sat next to me through the whole disgusting thing and impressed me with the importance of the group and the people in it."

"He told you about them?"

"Yes. I wrote it all down later, what I could remember." She pulled a sheaf of notes out of her pocket and handed it to me. "But there are a couple of items in particular that I think will be useful." The glint of triumph was in her eye. "Frank. That Frank character. He was there. And this guy was telling me all about how he's a big real estate man in Oakland, and he really believes in what this group is doing and helps them out and gets support for them." She looked at me over the rim of her glass, smiling. "We should be able to find him. Frank Shane. Real estate. Oakland. Great, huh?"

I smiled my love at her. Shane. I knew the name. I'd heard it back in the days of my brief real estate career, but there was more to it than that. I'd remember. It was right on the edge of my mind.

"And the other thing was this," Rosie went on. "This asshole kept bragging about how big this thing was, with a big organization behind it. One big organization in particular."

"Did he say what it was?"

She shook her head. "He wouldn't. He got all sly and cutesy and said I'd find out if I kept coming to meetings."

"Apparently it's not something they're supposed to blab all over the place, even when they're trying to score," I said. "He didn't mention any other names, did he? Like Jared?"

"No. And I don't think I should ask too many questions yet. I just acted all impressed and wimpy and batted my eyelashes at him."

"Careful, Rosie," I warned her. "He'll ask you out, and then what will you do?"

She stood up. "I'll have another beer. You?" I handed her the money for my beer and glanced through her notes. A few occupations, and just a couple of names. None of them meant anything to me except Frank Shane and Eddie Cutter. Hard to tell whether any of these other people were important to my case or not, but it occurred to me that they might be important to another case that connected arson with political terrorism. I stashed the notes in my hip pocket and glanced over at Rosie at the bar. She was standing with her arm around the woman with the mud on her jeans, and the two of them were laughing at Judy. The roofer was talking to the business suit, and the two pool players, I could hear, were still prancing around the pool table, laughing at their bad shots and hooting victoriously when they did something good. Meanwhile, I kept trying to remember what the name Shane meant to me.

Rosie returned to our table.

"Maybe this lead to Frank will be enough," I said to her. "Maybe you won't have to go to another meeting."

She glared at me. "I'll decide that. I want to find out more about this group."

I couldn't argue with her, but I must have looked skeptical.

"You don't understand," she growled. "You can't understand. How it felt to hear them saying the things they were saying."

"Hey," I objected, "you forget that I've been called names, too, and had to fight off a lot of sons of bigots when I was a kid. I'm Jewish. That ought to count for something."

"You're right," she agreed. "Sorry. But on a scale of five things these bastards can hate you for, you might qualify as a two. I'm a five."

Hoping to get some kind of handle on who was behind the group, I asked, "Who do they seem to hate the most?"

Rosie sighed. "I don't know what they hate besides moral corruption, queers, 'women's libbers,' and un-Americanism. That's mostly what they talked about. They didn't mention anyone by race or culture."

"Nothing about white supremacy?"

She shook her head. "But maybe they don't talk about it all the time." She was right. It would be premature to start crossing off possible affiliations without learning more. But I was afraid for her.

"Rosie," I begged, "you've got to get out of that group as fast as possible, before one of them sees you coming in here or talking to me."

She reached across the table and patted my hand. "I'll be all right, Jake. I'll get out just as soon as I can. Believe me." She shuddered. "I'm scared to death of them."

"Good." It was just about three-thirty, plenty of time to check out Frank. "Be right back." I went to the phone booth and ran a finger down the real estate listings. Sure enough, there was a Shane realty over on Broadway. Then I remembered. Rebecca had been in real estate for years. She'd worked for a lot of agencies. Shane was a name I connected with her. I went back to the table, swallowed the rest of my beer, told Rosie where I was going, waved good-bye to Judy and pushed back out the padded door into the gray, depressing light of the afternoon.

—*30*—

Ten minutes later I found a vacant parking meter half a block down from Shane's office and walked back to the entrance. Looked like a small operation to me. Rosie's admirer had been exaggerating about this important real estate man.

There was only one person in the four-desk office. She was a woman in her fifties, wearing half-glasses and, I thought, a wig. The face she raised to me was friendly, nearly unlined, and rather sweet.

"May I help you?"

"I hope so," I told her. "Is Frank Shane around?" She glanced toward a door at the back of the office as though she were trying to remember whether he was behind it or not.

She remembered. "Oh, no. He isn't in his office."

"When do you expect him back?"

"I don't really know," she admitted.

"Perhaps you could give me some information then?"

She smiled. "I've been here for five years. I might be able to tell you what you want to know."

"Okay," I said, jumping right in, "I'm looking for a friend of mine, someone I kind of lost touch with. I think she used to work here. Or works here now?"

"Sounds romantic," the woman said. I played it her way.

I looked at my shoes, shrugged, looked into her eyes, and said, "Her name is Rebecca Lilly."

The woman's smile drooped. She shook her head. It looked like I'd been wrong.

"Oh, I'm afraid I can't be of much help there, Mr. . . ." I ignored her search for my name. "She hasn't worked here in, oh, a year or more." That was it then. She'd gone to Shane's agency right around the time we were dropping each other out of our lives. The woman brightened a little. "But we may still have her file stored away somewhere. Of course, it would be old information. Perhaps you should talk to Frank after all. He might know where you could reach her."

"Yes," I agreed, "I think I should talk to Frank." I looked thoughtful. There was one more item to clear up. "Say, I know Rebecca had a friend. Someone who might know. Let's see. Maybe you met him. His name was Eddie . . . um . . ." I pretended to think some more. "If I could remember his last name." I screwed my face into a painful caricature of tortured memory.

She was no longer smiling. "I didn't know they were friends," she said. "Poor Eddie. He seemed like such a nice boy. I can't understand what happened. Mr. Shane was terribly shocked."

I managed to look inquiring.

"You know, that fire on the campus? The police think Eddie did it, of all things. Surely, you've seen it in the papers? Eddie Cutter?"

"That's right," I gurgled triumphantly. "Cutter. That was his name." Then I pulled a solemn face. "Rebecca's friend was that Eddie?"

"Well, as I said, I don't know whether they were friends."

"But they did know each other?"

"Oh, certainly. Eddie used to stop by every so often to see Frank. Some kind of family connection, I believe. Of course she knew him." She brightened again. "Perhaps if the police would let you talk to him, he could tell you where Rebecca is."

I nodded eagerly, boyishly, feeling a bit guilty for the lies. She was such a nice woman.

Then I heard the door open behind me. "Oh," she said, "here's Mr. Shane. He can probably help you."

I turned to face him. Sure enough, it was my buddy from the Greek Theater. He didn't look happy to see me either.

"Help him what?" he asked, keeping reasonably cool. But he held up his hand to keep me from speaking. "Let's go into my office and talk about it, okay, friend?"

"Sure, pal," I agreed, and slapped him heartily on the back. Very heartily. He lurched forward, caught himself, chuckled like it was all a big joke, and showed me into his office. He closed the door firmly.

"What's the matter?" I asked. "Doesn't your staff know you spend your free time beating up people?"

"You were special."

"No. The drawings were special. The one of Jared maybe? Not to mention the one of you. Here I am, an innocent reporter, trying to write a little something about the life of an artist, and all of a sudden I find myself in the middle of—what am I in the middle of anyway, Frank?"

"You're not in the middle of anything," he said coldly. "And you don't have to be." It was a threat. A warning that I'd better stay clear.

"Jared thinks I am. Didn't you know he came to see me?"

"Sure. And all you have to do to stay out of the middle is do what he says. Keep it out of your story. The fire, CORPS, just keep it out of the story."

"Look, fucker," I told him, "I made a deal with Jared and I'll stand by it. But you and me, that's a different matter altogether. I owe you. I could go to the police right now and charge you with assault and battery. How would that look?"

He was worried but only for a second. "Pretty damned funny, after all this time. You can't do it without explaining the circumstances," he said smugly. "And if you explain the circumstances, you'll be going back on your deal with Jared."

"I only agreed not to write about it."

He sneered at me. "Public is public. Stop playing stupid games."

I raised my hands. "Okay. You're too smart for me. And I must admit I believe you people deliver what you promise. If Cutter could kill Margaret Bursky, just to get those drawings, I'm sure—"

"Hey, hold it right there. That's just not so. Nobody had to kill her for a thing like that. We're an army embarked on a crusade, but we don't kill our own soldiers." More soldiers, I thought. More crusades. From what I'd heard about the original crusades, they weren't exactly exercises in Christian charity. I knew the police would have to be digging into CORPS in their investigation of Cutter, but I was beginning to worry that maybe they weren't working fast enough, that it would take them too long to catch up with Frank Shane.

"Not even for money?"

"Certainly not."

"And Margaret was loyal?"

"Of course." He smiled tolerantly. "But, you understand, she was a woman."

I kept my face blank, while Rosie in a fit of righteous rage marched across my mind. "I'd heard that, yes," I said.

"And sometimes, you know, women don't understand political issues very well. If she had, she never would have done those drawings in the first place, and"—he chuckled affectionately—"she wasn't anxious to give them up, but Eddie convinced her."

"How'd he do that?" I asked.

"I don't guess that's any of your business. I've got work to do. Why don't you run along?"

I stood up and shot out my left hand, grabbing the front of his shirt and pulling him halfway across his desk. With my right hand I slapped him hard, forehand, backhand, and forehand again. His pale skin turned red. He clutched at my hand, and I dropped his soft belly on the desk.

"Did you help him to convince her, Frank? Like you convinced me?" He was straightening his disarranged clothing, looking death at me. I didn't add anything about what had been done to Debbi.

"It wasn't necessary," he snarled, clenching and unclenching his fists, glancing at the door that connected with his outer office. He wanted no trouble in his place of business.

"Now get out of here while you can still write anything at all." He was coming around the desk, presumably to show me the door. I turned slightly, shifting my leg as though I meant to start walking, brought my foot up fast, and kicked him hard in one of the places where he'd kicked me. I let myself out. The woman in the outer office nodded and smiled when I threw her a kiss.

I found a pay phone and spent a few dimes canceling out on the Tuesday night poker game. I had too much to do. Then I dialed Rebecca's number at work. She was still there.

"I want to see you, Rebecca."

"What about? And didn't I ask you not to call me at work?"

"I'd rather discuss it face to face."

"Oh, all right," she barked at me, "pick me up outside the office and take me for a drink."

"You can pay for your own damned drink."

"Well, what's gotten into you? All right, I'll pay for yours, too, if you want me to." The contempt was heavy-handed, but Rebecca never had been a very subtle woman.

I drove to her office. She was waiting about twenty feet down the street from her office door. She studied my face carefully when she got in my car.

"You look terrible," I told her. I was in no mood for being polite. For some reason, my saying that relaxed her.

"Thanks. So do you. I'm just tired. Having business problems."

"Ever close that sale you were worried about?"

"No. I told you about the contingency, and finding a buyer for the first place so he can get the duplex—"

"Yeah," I stopped her. "You told me."

"I thought sure I had a buyer this time, but it's just not working out. It's driving me up a wall. So if I seem nervous . . ."

"You in trouble for money or something?"

"No. Not yet. It's just getting hard to pull together enough business. Everyone's worried."

"Harley's going to be coming into some money. That ought to help."

She closed her eyes and leaned back against the headrest. "Is he? Yes, I suppose he is."

She wasn't showing much interest in the subject of Harley's money.

"Don't you know why I wanted to see you?"

"All right," she said, "why did you want to see me?"

I found a parking place and led her into the dim interior of the Corner. "Been here before?" I asked her.

"Yes. Harley and I came here once." She said it very softly.

"Still won't see you, huh?"

She just sighed. We took a booth, and as I was turning to head for the bar with our order, she gripped my forearm hard.

"This has got to be over soon, doesn't it?"

I didn't answer. She dropped her hand.

When I was back in the booth with her, sipping a tolerable bloody Mary, I let her have it.

"Why did you lie to me?" I demanded.

She kept her eyes on her drink. "About what?"

"About knowing Cutter. You said you didn't know him, but you did. Not to mention Frank Shane. And they both know you. They could hardly help knowing you, since you worked for Shane, and Cutter's like one of the family over there." It was at that moment that I remembered a mention of *R* in Cutter's diary. Something about *R* pretending not to know him. Rebecca was shaking her head back and forth, staring at me with that peculiar deadness that can mean either stunned surprise or horror. But I wasn't finished. "Why couldn't you tell me the truth?"

Her words were as empty of expression as her face. "I don't have any idea what you're talking about, Jake."

"Frank Shane," I growled. "Eddie Cutter. Your friends."

"My friends?" she repeated. "What does Frank Shane have to do with this anyway?"

I told her.

"You're really something, you know that?" she said, her eyes glittering with anger. "How was I supposed to know Frank Shane was involved with this?"

She had a point, but I persisted. "You worked for the man. You must have known his politics."

"I worked for him for a few months, sure. I had some idea of his politics. But I left because a woman doesn't have a chance in that office. And I certainly didn't remember meeting Eddie Cutter. Why would I, if he was just one of Frank's visitors? I thought he looked familiar." She gestured around the bar. "But so do half the people in the East Bay."

"Looked familiar?" I said. "When did he look familiar?"

"His picture," she shot back. "In the paper." She looked at me, waiting for me to fold under her superior argument. I lied and told her Cutter's photo had never been in the paper. "Wasn't it?" She looked puzzled, as well she might, since it certainly had been published. Then she laughed. "Well, I thought it was. I guess maybe I half-recognized him around the campus or something, and I'm making the connection now."

"When did you half-recognize him?" I felt the whole argument slipping away from me, and I didn't think it should.

She glared at me. "What is this, Samson?" I glared back at her. "Oh, all right," she said, in a resigned voice. "I'll try to remember if I ever saw him on the campus. Or whatever." She sipped and made "Isn't this silly?" faces, but I turned away, watching the other patrons in the bar. That was when I noticed the skittish one from the night before, the one who had burst into tears and walked out. She was talking to some guy. I turned back to Rebecca.

"You know," she began, "that was a good idea, pushing my memory. I think I did see him once, and it rang some vague kind of bell but only partly registered. It was at the fire. He was right up in front watching when I got there."

So what? I was thinking. He'd already confessed to the fire.

"So you didn't know Shane was involved and you didn't quite remember Cutter. Is that what you're saying?" I summarized offhandedly.

She nodded, then reached across the table and laid her hand over mine. "That's exactly right, Jake. And I'm going to be honest with you." I could hardly wait. "Even if I had connected Frank with this thing, even if I had remembered Eddie Cutter, I wouldn't have made the connection and I wouldn't have remembered."

I realized that I was cocking my head to one side like a bemused beagle and straightened up.

"What I mean is this: I don't see much point in Harley knowing I actually knew these people, actually worked among them for several months. You can see that might upset him." I shrugged. Anything might upset Harley. And she wasn't making much sense. She saw my doubtful look and chilled again, leaning back in her seat and looking somewhere over my head. "Besides," she said, "the whole point of hiring you was to find out who did it and keep me and Harley out of it."

I leaned forward. "Are you saying you did know or you didn't? This is all getting a little coy for me, Rebecca."

She sighed. "I suppose it is. I told you I didn't remember Cutter. That's the truth."

"What about Frank?"

"I told you the truth. I want another drink. Why are you harassing me this way? My life is messed up enough without you harassing me. Just buy me another drink."

I went and got her drink and another one for me and brought them back to the table.

She began talking as though there had been no interruption.

"I don't understand you, Jake. I got you this job. Why are you trying to confuse me, attack me? There's nothing in my life that's any good right now. Harley is free and he won't see me. Business has been rough, and if it keeps on going this way, I will need to start worrying about money. And now you, my friend, the man I recommended to Harley, accusing me of God-only-knows-what."

"Of lying," I snapped. "Of hiding something. Not from the police. Not from Harley. From me, your friend, the man you recommended to Harley." She looked at me as though she would have liked to throw her drink in my face. "And the weird part of it is that it doesn't make any difference that I can see, whether you knew these guys before. What difference does it make whether you recognized Cutter?"

"That's exactly right," she said. "What difference would it make anyway? So what would be the point in my lying?"

I was beginning to feel as though one of us was about to burst out in some Lewis Carroll rhyme. " 'The time has come, the walrus said. . . .' " I held up my hands, palms out, in surrender. "Okay, let's just drop it. You're telling the truth and I'm a nasty beast."

"Yes," she said, tossing off the rest of her drink.

I took her home.

— *31* —

I did not have an easy night. Asleep, I dreamed about an army of Franks and Jareds roving the streets burning buildings and killing people. Awake, my thoughts skipped and stumbled, and my conscience babbled accusations.

Late Wednesday morning I went to see Sergeant Hawkins. He was sitting at a desk drinking coffee. He didn't offer me any. And he wanted to play with me before he'd let me tell him why I was there.

"I guess you don't work much, right, Samson?"

"I've got a little money."

"Yeah?" He narrowed his eyes at me. "Nice for you. And of course you write articles."

"Right."

"But not very many. What have you had published lately?"

"Nothing."

"Uh huh. We know that already. Too bad there's no reward for turning in Cutter." He looked at my jeans and flannel shirt. "Looks like you could use a few dollars."

"Sounds like you're pretty sold on Cutter," I probed.

"Does it?"

"Okay, Hawkins, I came to tell you something. You want to hear it or you want to play games?" Dangerous to talk to a cop that way, but I was getting damned tired of acting like a twerp.

"I'm after your ass."

"You can't have it."

He grinned at me. "Why don't you do it legally?"

"Do what?"

He shook his head. "Shit. I hope you came to tell me who beat you up. And why. I know," he added sarcastically, "that you want to protect your sources and all that crap, but I also know you've been withholding information. And this is homicide. And you're going to tell me or you're going to jail. How's that?"

Not bad, I thought. Especially since he knew I was there to tell him something. Good guess.

"Very direct," I said. "That's why I'm here." I started out by telling him I'd heard some vague rumors about some drawings. I didn't tell him I'd broken into Cutter's flat to get them or that I'd ever had them. What I said was that I asked Cutter about them, and his friend Frank had beaten me up for asking. Then I said that Cutter had accidentally dropped Frank's name, and I'd finally found him the day before.

"Why didn't you tell me any of this stuff before?" Hawkins's voice was soft and dangerous.

"I didn't know anything to tell you. Just that I'd heard about the drawings and was trying to find out if they existed and where they were. For my article."

"I suppose it didn't occur to you that they might be important evidence?"

"No," I insisted, "they were just art to me. But I got to thinking about it last night after I saw Frank Shane. That maybe these guys don't just beat people up for asking questions. That maybe they were trying to cover something up. That whoever had the drawings had gotten them from Margaret Bursky, and maybe that person killed her. I just hadn't been thinking along those lines. After all," I added parenthetically, "I'm not a policeman anymore. I'm not used to thinking in those terms. It seemed more like they were trying to cover up something about their organization. The faces in the drawings. A whole separate issue." I hoped my acting was better than I thought it was.

He wasn't buying any of it. "Uh huh. And now you've thought about it and decided to let us in on your little secrets."

"I didn't know what to think, but I figured it was your business not mine."

He laughed shortly; it was more like a bark. "And you weren't withholding evidence because you never had any, right?"

I nodded, trying to look dumb and praying some very intelligent prayers.

"Were you seriously injured?" he asked solicitously.

I thought about it. A cracked rib, a few stitches. He'd had a gun, but I couldn't prove that. The broken bone did make it battery with serious bodily injury. "Well, no . . ."

"And you want to make a complaint so we can slap his hand for picking on you?"

I knew that was about what it would amount to. And before they could slap his hand I'd be spending a lot of time with the city's law-enforcement apparatus.

"No," I said, "I just wanted to tell you what I know."

"I appreciate that." He didn't mean it. "What's the guy's full name and address?"

I gave him Shane's business address.

"Thanks. Now get the hell out of my office."

I got out. I felt better.

There was still a chance that Hawkins could give me some trouble if Shane and Cutter both told him I'd stolen the drawings. But that seemed unlikely. Cutter would have to be more of a fool than I thought he was to admit he'd gotten those sketch pads from Margaret Bursky.

But there was no longer any question that Rosie's right-wing political career was going to have to end. The police would be closing in on CORPS, and Hawkins had, after all, met her when we'd turned Cutter over to him. About all we'd need now would be for Hawkins to identify a member of that group as my friend Rosie. Rosie the ringer. He'd toss us both in jail and regret that there was no local Devil's Island.

—*32*—

I stopped for lunch at a Chinese restaurant near downtown Oakland. The almond chicken wasn't so good, but the fortune cookie was even worse.

The fortune said, "Someone in authority is watching you with an eye to promotion." Yeah, I thought. His.

Loose ends were plaguing me. A dead artist. Radical students. Lunatic fringe groups. A will split four ways. A political science professor. A lot of real estate people.

Real estate.

Houses for sale could mean people coming and going. Maybe someone had seen something on Virgo Street the day Bursky was killed. A far-out chance and a tedious job, but I was getting desperate.

Not a bad afternoon for a drive in the hills. The sun had already dried the previous day's mud, and the air was cleaner than it had been before the rain. Nothing's more depressing than a good view of bad air.

There were two houses for sale on and around Virgo and a couple more not far away. Two of them had SOLD notices plastered across the FOR SALE signs. I wrote down the names and phone numbers of all the realtors. If the agencies themselves came up with nothing, I'd take the next step and talk to the householders.

The next stop was home. Rosie was off working somewhere, so I wrote a note, folded it over, and push-pinned it to her door. It said, "Rosie: Get out of C immediately. Will explain when I see you. Jake." I was afraid we'd miss each other that night.

The cats were dozing in the sun and didn't bother to greet me.

There were some messages on my answering machine. One from Harley and one from Rebecca. Harley wanted me to call him back. I did. He was terse. He was in his office and wanted to see me right away.

Rebecca had left her office number. I guessed that meant she was anxious to talk to me, and she was. She wanted to see me that evening. I told her I was busy. I had a date with Iris.

"Why do you want to see me?" I asked her.

"Can't we just have a friendly meal together, for God's sake?" she replied indignantly. Lunch the next day was out for her, she said. Could I come to her house the next night, she wanted to know. I had a date with Faye that night, but I told Rebecca I'd stop by for a drink about five-thirty, if that was okay. It would have to do, she sniffed. I was beginning to feel like a substitute boyfriend.

When I got to Harley's office he didn't waste any time or cordiality on me.

"You're off the case, Samson. There's no case to be on. I'm paying you off today." He pushed an envelope across the desk. It contained the second five thousand dollars, plus expenses. Payment in full. I didn't ask any questions, just thanked him and left quickly. What the hell. I was beginning to think the investigation would drag on for weeks anyway, and I might as well get paid in front.

Harley was anxious to get rid of me, so anxious he was willing to pay me off. That was no big surprise. He believed the killer was in jail, and he wanted me out of his life. I was happy to be rid of him, too. At least now I could move ahead on the case without having to deal with him. That is, I could move ahead on it if I could be sure where I was going. I was beginning to get a few good ideas, but an idea isn't proof, and it wouldn't be easy to push the matter to a clear climax.

On my way back to my car I passed a group of CORPS people carrying their signs and heading in the direction of the political science department. Their silliness was unending. Didn't they know that the social sciences had no effect on anything, anymore? Didn't I know it? Did I?

Time to go home, shower, shave, clear my mind and make myself irresistible. I was picking Iris up at six-thirty. Ten minutes to get to her house from mine, twenty to get home from campus. That left only a couple of hours to get ready.

The note I'd left on Rosie's door was gone, and she wasn't home. Just like I thought. We would have missed each other. She'd come dashing home, pulled the note off her door, cleaned herself up, changed, and gone dashing out again. But she'd gotten my warning. Everything would be okay.

Still, I wished I'd had a chance to talk to her just to make sure.

Tigris and Euphrates greeted me effusively, standing on my feet and directing me to their empty dishes. I started the water running in the tub, fed the cats, selected my wardrobe for the evening, stripped, set a clock on the windowsill, and settled in. Even though I was about to go out with a woman I'd been thinking about for days, it was the death of Margaret Bursky that kept worming through my thoughts. A picture of how she'd died. The movements and events preceding and following that death. Blank spots, scenes in the film fading to black.

I checked the cottage on my way out. No Rosie. Come to think of it, why, I wondered, hadn't she fed the cats if she was going out? She was probably planning to be back in an hour or so, I told myself. Nothing to worry about.

Five minutes late, as required by social law, I arrived at Iris's house in South Berkeley in one of those neighborhoods-united-against-crime where everybody posts notices in their windows saying they're keeping an eye on each other's homes. Good investments, those neighborhoods. Usually.

The house was a small Victorian, frame, with a little gingerbread around the eaves. It was painted cream with royal blue trim. Six rooms, tops. I wondered if she owned it but decided not to ask.

She was ready and waiting for me. She looked luscious.

Our reservations were for seven-thirty at a place called Sheldon's. It had one of the better bars along the Berkeley-Oakland line, and when the food was good, it was very good indeed. Continental. Served with style and grace. After dinner we were going into San Francisco to a club that showcased talent already well known locally and on its way to greater fame. Like L.A. The night approach to San Francisco across the Bay Bridge is a romantic sight, and I was looking forward to experiencing it with Iris. I tried to imagine how I'd feel about it with Faye but got confused and gave up.

The bar at Sheldon's was crowded, and we couldn't get a table right away. We drank our first drink standing, which was not conducive to conversation but was conducive to leaning on each other. When a table opened up, we took possession of it. Then I ordered our second drinks and excused myself. I knew I was probably being silly, but I felt nervous about Rosie. Maybe the note had blown off her door. Maybe she was right this minute being rounded up by Hawkins at a CORPS meeting. Maybe she'd need a sitter for Alice. I used the pay phone near the door. She wasn't home. I let the maître d' know we were in the bar so that he could let us know when our table was ready in the dining room.

Then I returned to the bar and told Iris how wonderful she looked. She wasn't fooled.

"What's wrong, Jake?"

"Nothing's wrong, Iris. Nothing at all." I smiled at her.

She smiled sweetly back at me. "Bullshit." I flinched. "We're supposed to be out having a good time. You're distracted. You're barely even here. But you don't want me to worry my pretty little head about it, right?"

I didn't tell her everything, simply that I was worried about a friend of mine getting a note that had to do with the case. That it was important. And that she could be in danger. Iris was great. She showed just the merest flicker of "What kind of movie is this anyway?" and then she accepted.

"Should we go to her house then?" she wanted to know, just as my name was called. Our table was ready.

"No," I said decisively. "She's probably out carousing somewhere, and we'd be ruining our evening for nothing. I'll try to call again."

We were seated at a nice table in a corner. Reasonably private in the dim light. We agreed on oysters on the half shell for starters. I ordered duck à l'orange and she ordered stuffed trout. We toasted our marvelous palates and ate the oysters with sensuality and a minimum of self-consciousness. When the waiter took away the ravaged shells, I excused myself again and went to the telephone.

Rosie answered on the third ring.

"Hi," I said, "I'm glad you're there. I've been worried. You got my note, didn't you? On your front door?"

Silence. It dragged on. "Rosie? Didn't you get my note?"

Another pause, then she laughed girlishly. "Why, no, Janie," she said, "I'm sure I've never heard of such a thing."

"I put it on your front door early this afternoon. Later it was gone. You didn't take it?" I was beginning to sweat.

She giggled again. "That's silly, Janie. That's not like me at all. You must be thinking of someone else."

"Who's there with you?" My voice cracked dryly.

"Listen, Janie, I can't stay on the phone gossiping with you. I have company. I just got home, and this charming young man I met the other night was waiting on my doorstep. . . ."

"Okay, okay," I said, trying to calm myself down. How the hell did he know where she lived? Had he read the note? "Maybe it's okay. Maybe he's just so hot for you—Jesus, what are you wearing?" I got an image of her in work boots and flannel shirt. Or worse yet, the Gertrude Stein T-shirt. But she was still all right. He'd let her answer the phone, after all. "Do you think you're bluffing him?"

"Oh, Janie. I really don't think so."

"I'll be right there."

I hung up and dashed back to the table.

"I have to go, Iris." She jumped up, threw some bills on the table, and grabbed her coat.

"Let's go," she said.

It isn't easy to drive down College Avenue fast. It's not a wide street, and it's usually jammed with cars. I cut down Alcatraz, over to a side street, angled onto Claremont, and zigzagged home, narrowly missing two collisions. Iris gasped only once, at the first near-miss.

When I pulled up, I saw a familiar car parked on the other side of the street. Eddie Cutter's old heap. Nice, I thought. Sharing the resources. But wasn't that a bit communal? I slammed out of my car and raced up the driveway, stumbling in the ruts. Iris was right behind me. Alice met us a few yards from the cottage. She looked worried but not distraught, so I figured everything was still relatively peaceful. The three of us—dog, woman, and man—crashed in through the cottage door together. Rosie was standing. So were her two companions. I didn't recognize the one who looked like a weasel, but I knew the other guy. He was Jared's bodyguard, the one who had escorted him to his meeting with me. I skidded to a stop.

Rosie spoke first. "Hi, Jake. This gentleman is Walter." She waved her hand at the muscle. "And this is Arthur." *A* for

Arthur, I thought. And he was holding the note I'd left on Rosie's door.

"The writer, huh?" Walter grunted. "I didn't know you guys used spies."

"Get out of here," I said. "Now."

He laughed at me. I wondered if he had a gun tucked somewhere under his blue down jacket. He walked across to me, cocky as hell, sure of his superiority. Just because he outweighed me by thirty pounds. Meanwhile, Arthur the weasel had grabbed Rosie's arm and was trying to twist it around behind her back. She was wearing her cowboy boots. She brought a heel down hard on his instep, and I tried to push past musclehead to go help her. But Walter caught me, wrapped his arm around my neck, and began to bend me backward. Jesus, I thought, there goes my deteriorated disk. But someone was hitting him from behind. I also heard a growl coming from somewhere around my hip. Alice sprang past me to help Rosie by shouting, dog-fashion, at the weasel. Rosie's strong, and I knew that if Arthur didn't listen to reason, Alice would stop barking and get more physical. So I concentrated on Walter. Besides, I was having trouble seeing.

The guy had a steel arm. I was elbowing him and struggling to get out of his stranglehold. He was holding me with one hand and beating on me with the other. At the same time I could feel him being battered from behind by Iris. He was sagging, but he wasn't letting go. I felt my neck crack in the same spot that had cracked when Frank kicked me on the chin, and took a sharp jab in the kidney that nearly put me out. Then Walter gave one last grunt and fell away from me. My vision cleared. Alice was dragging at the weasel's arm, sixty-five pounds of outraged pacifist, and I could see blood coming through his shirt. He was screaming, still trying to hold on to Rosie. Rosie got him turned around just enough to punch him and he screamed louder. All the noise was making Alice even madder. Before I could cross the room, the two of them had backed him into a corner, and he was crying as if his heart would break. He shoved Rosie out of his way, kicked out at Alice, straight-armed me, and ran sobbing out the door. I turned around to see what was going on with Iris. The muscle was lying on the floor, his arms flung out at his sides, a pile of hard flesh. Iris, her face flushed and a tiny smile on her lips, was standing over him, holding Rosie's power drill, the cord dangling. She held up the drill and spoke to Rosie.

"I'm afraid I cracked the casing," she said. The crack had bloody hairs stuck in it from Walter's head. Alice had not bothered to pursue the weasel. She was now sniffing importantly at Walter's body.

"Oh, that's okay," Rosie said, laughing with relief.

"Iris," I said, "this is Rosie." They grinned at each other. We all told Alice what a good dog she was, and I went to the phone, planning to call the police and ask them to pick up the prostrate Walter. There was a scrambling, rushing sound behind me. I whirled. I didn't know how long Walter had been conscious, playing possum while we were being self-congratulatory, but he was up now. He sent Iris spinning and was out the door and gone before any of us could catch him.

We didn't try very hard. My whole body ached, and I thought I might have a pinched nerve in my neck. Rosie could barely move her left arm, the one the weasel had been trying to break off. Alice had a slight limp, probably from being kicked. Iris was unmarked, but she seemed to be having trouble putting down the drill. I pried it out of her hand and noticed that my elbow had somehow gotten wrenched. She sat down on the floor, still grinning.

Rosie went into the tiny kitchen and came back with a dog biscuit and a bottle of red wine. We joined Iris on the floor and passed the bottle around.

What had happened was this: The creep Arthur had really liked Rosie. So much so, that he'd followed her home the night of the meeting to see where she lived. Unlike Frank Shane and Eddie Cutter, he hadn't known my address, so he'd made no immediate connection. But he'd stopped by again that very day, hoping to catch her at home. He hadn't found her, but he had found the note I'd left. And he had read it. Then he'd called for reinforcements—Walter—and come back and waited for Rosie to show up, pickup truck, cowboy boots, and all. They'd been questioning her when I called. She hadn't told them anything. I didn't really think they'd come back and decided to let well enough alone as far as the police were concerned. Rosie was still out of it from their viewpoint, and she might as well stay that way.

After about half an hour of chat and wine, Iris spoke up. "Jake," she said, "this has been a very exciting date, and I'm delighted to meet you, Rosie, but tonight I knocked a man out for the first time in my life and I feel a little strange. Not bad, just strange." I nodded and winced. My neck hurt like hell. "You're hurt, aren't you?" she asked gently.

"No, no, I'm fine. Just a little stiffness."

She went to the phone and called a cab, ignoring my protests.

"Jake," she said firmly, "I'm going home to bed, and I think you should do the same." I must have shown how I felt about her decision because she added, "When can I see you again so we can finish the date?"

Then I remembered that she'd paid for the dinner we'd never eaten. When I mentioned it, she laughed at me. "You can get the next one. But I haven't gotten an answer yet."

"Friday," I said.

When her cab came, I walked her out to the street. She took my head in her hands and gave me a long sweet kiss that damned near finished me off.

—*33*—

The first item on the next day's agenda was nonphysical: calling the real estate agents who had houses for sale in Harley's neighborhood. I used the same line with all of them. I was interested in the house; could I talk to the agent who was working on it?

The first agency I called was Frank Shane's. I recognized the voice of the nice woman who'd been working in the office the day I'd gone there. She said none of the salespeople were in yet, but she'd leave a message if I'd give her my name and number. I said I'd call back.

Two hours later, when I'd learned everything I could over the telephone, it was time to drag myself out of bed, crawl out of the house and do some legwork. I'd picked up some very interesting information, but it had to be taken a step further.

I was glad to see that the day was clear and very warm and that winter was holding off for a while. I didn't feel too great as it was.

Jake Samson, writer, drove up to Virgo Street and vicinity to talk to the owners of the houses. My approach would have to be oblique. A direct question, even one as basic as "Did you know Margaret Bursky?" could lead to a quick "No" and a quick dead end. I was just looking for background information. We would chat about the violent death of their neighbor and see where that went. What were people in the neighborhood—such a charming neighborhood—thinking about it all? What a beautiful house this is, and are you happy with your agent, because I know someone . . . have you had many offers? I'm looking for something like this myself. I couldn't be sure how I was going to work my way around to questions like "Were you showing the house on the day Margaret Bursky died?" and "Did you notice anyone on the street who looked murderous?" But I had a lot of confidence in my ability to get the most out of a conversation.

Only two of the householders were home, but I was lucky. One of those two gave me a big chunk of information to chew on. I wasn't sure it would take me where I wanted to go, but it gave me a good line of attack.

Then I went home and went back to bed until my cocktail hour with Rebecca.

—*34*—

This time, when Rebecca buzzed me in, I didn't take the stairs. My neck still hurt every time I moved my head, the left shoulder was cramped, and my elbow was not working properly. I used the elevator.

She was standing at the open door to her apartment waiting for me. When I passed apartment 14, the one where the nice old guy lived, I could hear the muted sounds of television from within. I glanced at the name card on his door. It said simply: LINDSTROM. I wondered again why anyone would choose to live all jammed together this way.

Rebecca gave me a big smile of greeting and led me into the living room. I sat down.

"It's nice to see you, Jake." I nodded at her. "What would you like to drink? I've got Scotch and vodka and I can make some margaritas if you want."

I told her the margaritas sounded terrific, and she set to work with her blender. I got up, wandered around the small living room, looked out at the balcony with its view of the Bay Bridge and, beyond, San Francisco. It was a clear afternoon, and The City seemed to glow in the distance as though dirt, crime, and misery did not exist on its streets. The glass doors were slightly open to let in the breeze. I turned toward the kitchen. Rebecca was concentrating pretty hard on carrying our drinks, and I wondered if she'd already had a couple of something.

"I thought we'd sit out on the balcony for a while, since it's so warm." She handed me my salt-rimmed glass, pushed the sliding door farther open, and led the way onto the tiny concession to California living. The whole balcony was about four by eight, with duplicates above, below, and off to either side. She had a couple of plants out there and a small table and two chairs. We sat at the table, sipping.

"Well, Jake, how's life treating you?" I almost expected her to reach over and slap me on the back. She ignored my lack of response. "Any interesting women in the offing? You must not work all the time." She chuckled. It really was a chuckle.

"Of course, I've been working all the time, Rebecca," I retorted. "Your boyfriend's been paying me to work." I regretted my flippancy immediately. Mention of Harley put her on edge, which was not where I wanted her to be.

"I talked to Harley," she said. "Very briefly. He says you're not working for him anymore. Because the case is solved. After all, you turned Cutter in."

"Yeah, for trying to kidnap me."

She shrugged as if kidnaping were pretty trivial stuff. "The police found his fingerprints at Harley's house."

"That doesn't prove he killed her," I said, although I knew that enough circumstantial evidence against the man could convict him.

"My God," she hissed, "he started the fire. He was involved with Margaret. He was at her house. What more do you want?" Then she looked at me wide-eyed. "You're not still working at it, are you? On your own?"

"Look, Rebecca," I said quietly, "maybe he did it, maybe he didn't. There seem to be a lot of ramifications."

She snorted at me and swallowed half her drink. "Want another one?" I agreed and she went inside. I got up and leaned against the railing, looking at the view some more. When she returned with our second drinks, she stood next to me.

"Jake," she said, "if the police are satisfied, why aren't you? You've earned your money. Why don't you drop this intuition kick you're on?" She hesitated, walked a couple of feet away from me, and leaned against the table. "The police are satisfied, aren't they?"

"I don't know. They may be."

Her lips formed an etched line across her face. "Then drop it. He was there. He did it." She was talking to me like I was a little kid. She'd spent a lot of time throughout the case trying to push and maneuver me, as though I were not quite bright enough to get from here to there.

"He was there at some point," I admitted, "because he left his prints. But I don't know when he was there."

"He was there! That day," she rasped. "You know damned well he was."

"If you say so," I answered softly. "You should know."

She stood up straight. "What's that supposed to mean?"

"It means you were on Virgo Street that day." She was very pale, and she didn't say anything. "I talked to the woman down the block, Rebecca. The one whose house you sold. She told me you'd sold a couple of houses recently. You were doing well. Why did you lie to me about that?"

She shrugged. "I guess I just wanted your sympathy."

"Right," I said. "The more the better. So I wouldn't look too closely at you. But I did anyway, finally. The same woman told me about the day Bursky died. She remembered that day well. She remembered the police cars and the wagon that came for the body. You don't see that much action on a street like that one very often. So she remembered. And she remembered that you had stopped by that morning with some papers for her."

"So what? I do a lot of business in that area. You didn't expect me to volunteer the information, did you?"

"You were there. You saw Cutter. You knew who he was, didn't you?"

She was studying her margarita.

"Of course, maybe you were afraid to tell me, afraid I'd tell the police." Remembering Debbi, I added, "I guess you just didn't want to have to deal with the police. Was that it?"

She nodded energetically. "That's right." She was nodding too energetically. She didn't stop. She was gripping the back of a chair as if she needed something to hold her up.

"So you didn't trust me. But why should you? You always thought I was a loser." I watched, fascinated, as her head continued to move up and down.

"Tell me this, Rebecca. If you thought so little of me, why did you tell Harley to hire me? He wanted to hire a professional, and you convinced him to hire me, instead. A jerk." I could feel my own head trying to nod along with hers. I controlled it, telling myself that I was sane. I couldn't look at her face anymore. I half-turned away and set my empty glass on the railing. "Maybe you thought I was still interested in you. Maybe you thought I'd never suspect an old friend. But when I wouldn't let you maneuver me, when I kept on looking for the killer, you tried to get me to drop the case. Harley did, too. Was he beginning to suspect you?"

She whispered, "No, Jake, that's not true."

"You knew Cutter was in CORPS. You saw him at the fire. You gave the police his name, anonymously." That was only a guess, but I knew it was a good one. "You saw him at Harley's. Did you figure that Bursky was involved with him or with the group?" No answer. I kept prodding for answers, my voice low and soothing. "You saw him leave the house, didn't you?"

"I saw him," she said. "He was there. He did it." I could hear her breathing, harsh and fast. I thought she might be crying, but I still couldn't bring myself to look at her. I felt sick.

"Did you go in the house then? Did you challenge her about her husband's enemy, Eddie Cutter? Did you do some verbal pushing, Rebecca? And when she wouldn't push verbally? What did you do then?"

I was just turning to face her when my peripheral vision picked up a rushing movement, and I spun, dropped to the balcony floor, and scrambled out of her way. One of the legs of the chair she'd been holding rammed the railing. My margarita glass went over the edge. The chair flew out of her hands, scraping across my cheek as I rose and lunged for her, catching her around the waist and crashing, still holding her, into the glass doors. She fought, punching and kicking. I clipped her hard across the jaw. She kept on fighting. I hit her again, and again, and she stopped. I stumbled back, nearly going over the railing on my own, and caught sight of movement on the balcony next door. He was standing there, his mouth open, his eyes round.

Staggering a little, I turned toward him. "Good evening, Mr. Lindstrom," I said.

"She tried to push you off," he said, pronouncing each word very carefully, as though he were giving me important information.

"I know," I replied.

—*35*—

Hawkins took his time that evening pumping a few dozen three-quarter truths out of me and giving me enough trouble to make him feel better. The three-quarters that was true was everything I could tell him without telling him the one-quarter that might have put me in jail.

"Quite a job of investigative reporting, Samson," he said with a voice like a straight razor. "If you'd stuck to your typewriter, it would have taken you another few days to get the information out of us."

I'd been staring at my right knee. I looked up.

"That's right," he said. "Cutter looked good, but so did Harley. And Cutter's girl friend. And," he added, "we were on Rebecca Lilly's trail." He glared at me. "We're pretty good at our job, you know."

"I know," I said. I meant it.

"What about the husband?" I asked him, as if I barely knew the man. Hawkins looked at me as if to say, "What the hell business is it of yours?"

Then he shrugged. "She says he didn't know. He says he didn't know. Maybe he didn't. He says he never even thought of it."

I doubted that. He'd thought of it. That was why he'd paid me off. That was probably why he had been refusing to talk to Rebecca, except to tell her I was off the case. She must have been pushing him hard to get rid of me. Even Harley might have found that a little strange, especially after she'd convinced him to hire me in the first place.

Before Hawkins finally turned me loose that night, he told me the FBI would be calling on me soon for whatever I could give them on CORPS, and said he was "looking forward to seeing the article in *Probe* magazine." I told him I hoped it was good enough to print. He curled his lip at me.

By the time I dragged through my gate, I was already late for my date with Faye and knew I wasn't going to make it. In fact, I was pretty sure I wouldn't be up to anything amorous or even affectionate for a day or so, at least. I called and apologized and asked if we could move it up a day to Friday. She said I sounded awful and that the postponement was fine with her. Then I called Iris and gave her an outline of the big finish. After all, she'd gotten involved in it, and she had a right to know. Then we agreed on moving our date up a day from Friday to Saturday, and I promised I'd go over the whole thing in detail then. She said she was looking forward to it.

"I'm also looking forward to seeing you," she said softly. "How are all your sprains, strains, and bruises?"

"You'll never know I have them," I said optimistically.

Several beers later my mind let go, my muscles loosened up a bit, and sleep moved several notches from unlikely possibility to no choice at all.

Morning came too soon, but I was feeling better and began the day by putting together some notes for Artie Perrine. Maybe a real writer could make something of them for *Probe*. A few paragraphs anyway. That would give me something to wave under Hawkins's nose if I ever needed to.

The full story of the killing came to me in pieces over the next few hours, from Hal, from Harley, and even, very incidentally, from newspaper accounts. Rebecca had folded. She wasn't holding anything back, although she was coherent only part of the time.

Late that afternoon the FBI visited me, asked me to identify a photograph of Jared, and poked me with questions about CORPS for an hour.

Rosie just missed them. She showed up at my door grubby from work, carrying two beers and ready to talk. She'd seen the papers, too.

"What made you so sure it was Rebecca?" she wanted to know.

I explained that I hadn't been absolutely sure. But once I found out that Rebecca had been on Virgo Street that morning, the balance shifted. Cutter could have done it, but I'd never really thought so. Debbi could have dashed up there, waited for her chance, killed the woman, and gone back to work by noon, but it wouldn't have been easy. Three people hanging around that house was just too much. Debbi had maybe wanted Cutter, but her career was more important to her than he was. She found another boyfriend pretty fast. One who matched her life-style. And she was less reluctant to tell me about her movements that day than she was to talk about CORPS. Just as scared of the group— and of people finding out she was involved with it—as she was of being connected with the murder. She didn't fit any better than Cutter did.

Harley had no real reason to kill his wife. She would have stuck with him, money and all, no matter what. He wasn't enough in love with Rebecca to leave Margaret, let alone kill her.

But Rebecca? She was up there. She had a good reason to kill Bursky. She'd lied to me. It had been difficult, but I'd finally had to admit she'd recommended me to Harley so he wouldn't hire someone with brains. At least, that way she wouldn't have both the police and a sharp investigator on her trail.

"So you think she planned the whole thing?" Rosie asked.

"I doubt it. Not any more than she'd planned on killing me." I filled Rosie in on the murder picture as I'd reconstructed it.

Rebecca had finished her business on Virgo Street. She had wanted to call Harley, but since it was Monday, a day on which he had no classes, she didn't know whether she could reach him at his office. She checked out his house to see if his car was there. It wasn't, but another car, one that looked vaguely familiar, was parked on the other side of the narrow road.

"That old heap of Cutter's you told me about?" Rosie injected eagerly. I nodded.

"But she didn't place the car until she talked to Harley. She called him from the shopping center down the hill. While they were talking, he mentioned that CORPS was picketing him that day. She remembered then."

She'd remembered that she had seen the car at Frank Shane's agency and that it belonged to Eddie Cutter. She'd driven right back up the hill again, looking for ammunition in her campaign to get Harley away from his wife, and had just parked a short distance down the road when she saw Cutter emerging from

Harley's house with a shopping bag tucked under his arm. Eating an apple. There was a choice to make then, and she made the one that messed up her mind and her life. Instead of just snitching to Harley, she decided to confront his wife. You loosen the reins, she told Bursky, and I won't tell Harley you're involved with his enemies.

Rosie shook her head. "Sad."

"Yeah," I agreed. "For everybody."

Especially since Bursky was already upset. She'd just been forced to give up her drawings, possibly by the same kind of "I'll tell your husband" extortion Rebecca was planning to try.

Rebecca bulled her way in and challenged Bursky on Cutter's visit. Bursky tried to make her leave. When she wouldn't, the distraught woman had walked out on the deck and closed the sliding doors. Rebecca opened them again and went after her. There followed a verbal battle, with Bursky demanding that Rebecca get out and calling her names, and Rebecca refusing to go, threatening her, beating her with questions about Cutter and CORPS, demanding that she give up her husband.

Bursky had then, according to Rebecca, advanced on her threateningly.

"I wonder if she really did," Rosie murmured.

"We'll never know."

Also, according to Rebecca, Bursky had grabbed her shoulders and said that Harley had only been playing with Rebecca, that he didn't love her, that he would never end his marriage. That Rebecca was an idiot if she didn't know that men of Harley's age couldn't help doing that sort of thing.

That was when the fight got physical. Rebecca, blind with rage and in "the heat of passion"—as her lawyers were sure to put it—struggled with Bursky, pushing her against and then over the railing.

"She must have been horrified by what she'd done." Rosie groaned.

"Apparently not. Before her attorney could shut her up, she told the cops she hadn't meant to do it, but she wasn't sorry it happened. She had gone down under the deck to have a look and found Bursky dead. Not breathing. No pulse. And she was glad."

Rebecca had then returned to the deck. She didn't know what to do about the signs of the struggle. She hoped the police would see the death as suicide, but she wasn't entirely rational and was unaware of the small injuries the fight had inflicted on the victim. She saw that the coffee cup had been knocked to the floor of the deck. She picked it up and put it back on the table before she thought about fingerprints. Then she wiped it clean and got out of there, leaving the door on the spring lock as Harley later found it.

Over Rebecca's objections, Harley had insisted on hiring an investigator, someone who would "be on his side." Rebecca had sold him on me. Later, when she spotted Cutter at the fire, she saw her chance to get the police sniffing after him with her anonymous phone tip.

Even now, Harley still wasn't admitting he'd begun to suspect her a few days later. His story was that the poor woman had illusions about a relationship with him, a relationship they never consummated. And it looked like he'd be a hundred thousand dollars richer in a short time.

Rebecca would either wind up in a hospital or serve a few years for voluntary manslaughter.

"What about CORPS?" Rosie wanted to know. "Don't they get some money, too?"

I laughed. "They would if anyone was willing to come forward to claim it in the group's name." When Frank Shane had been faced with the combined force of the police and the FBI—and maybe his ulcer—and the information they already had about CORPS and the campus fire, he'd done some talking. He insisted that he'd had nothing to do with the fire and that he had, in fact, been appalled to learn that Harley's fire was only the first in a series planned for campuses across the country. Part of a plan to make examples of liberal teachers, to develop a new and more powerful campus movement, even more disruptive than the radical left of the sixties, a radical right that would sweep a whole generation up in its cause. The cause of morality. With arson and hatred for all.

Frank had told the police he'd only recently become aware of the plan and had been meaning to get proof and take it to the FBI.

How had he met Jared in the first place? In the course of business, he said, as a party to a land deal. Forty acres in Northern California. And Jared had been his only contact with the larger group that was doing the planning. He gave no other names, not even a name for the group, but when the FBI checked out the acreage, they found a cabin full of guns and some old fool who said he belonged to an organization called AMERICA. Eventually, I guessed, they'd find out whether these people were part of one of the more familiar groups already operating, a splinter group, or a whole new bunch of daisies. I couldn't see that it made a lot of difference.

"Cutter, on the other hand," I finished up the story, "isn't talking about anything."

"So CORPS is defunct?" Rosie wanted to know.

"They seem to have scattered for the time being. They sure as hell aren't claiming any inheritance. Their share of the money will wind up going to the state, by law."

Rosie got up and retrieved two more beers from the refrigerator. When she came back into the living room she had a businesslike look on her face.

"So," she said, "what's my cut?"

I shrugged. "What do you think?"

"Well, I spent two evenings on CORPS, not counting Wednesday, when I risked life and limb and acquitted myself brilliantly, I might add. And I led you to Frank Shane. How does fifteen percent sound?"

Fifteen hundred dollars seemed a little high. But Arthur had twisted her arm pretty badly. She might have some trouble working for a few days. And she had, indeed, led me to Frank Shane. Sure, I said, that seemed about right. I got the money out of my sock drawer and handed it to her. I told her I had to get ready for a date.

"Is it Iris? Listen, Jake, she's some woman."

"No," I said, "that's tomorrow night. Tonight it's Faye. You haven't met Faye." Rosie looked at me quizzically, laughed, and kissed me on the forehead.

"Have a good time. See you tomorrow."

"Yeah. Oh, by the way, I thought I'd set up a big poker game for Sunday night. Interested?"

"Sure," she said. "I'm a rich woman."

I dragged the phone into the bathroom and started running the hot water into the tub. I sat on the stool with the phone in my lap. Starting with the poker regulars, I called Artie Perrine, told him I had some notes for him, and invited him for Sunday. Hal said he could make it, too, so that was four, including Rosie, and she might want to bring a friend. I didn't think I'd ask either Iris or Faye because I like to keep love and poker separate. But I could keep a space open, just in case, for someone.

I undressed and settled in the tub, then called Faye and told her I'd pick her up at seven-thirty.

The second that I hung up, the phone rang. A collect call from Isaac Samson, the operator said. Resisting an urge to speak Chinese and slam the receiver down, I accepted the call.

"Hello, bum?"

"Hello, pa."

"I been dialing for an hour. Busy. For an hour. Like a woman on the phone." I heard a squawk of protest somewhere in the background at his end.

"I had a lot of calls to make, pa. Business."

"Yeah. Sure. Monkey business. Don't tell me. I'm sure it's too complicated for a simple old man to understand."

"Pa . . ."

"Your stepmother wants to know if you've got a date tonight. I, personally, don't care if you've got a date."

"Pa . . ."

"What you need is a job."